THE REPENTING SERPENT

A DCI MICHAEL YORKE THRILLER BY

WES MARKIN

ABOUT THE AUTHOR

Wes Markin is the bestselling author of the DCI Yorke crime novels set in Salisbury. His latest series, The Yorkshire Murders, stars the compassionate and relentless DCI Emma Gardner. He is also the author of the Jake Pettman thrillers set in New England. Wes lives in Harrogate with his wife and two children, close to the crime scenes in The Yorkshire Murders.

You can find out more at:

www.wesmarkinauthor.com

facebook.com/wesmarkinauthor

PRAISE FOR ONE LAST PRAYER

"An explosive and visceral debut with the most terrifying of killers. Wes Markin is a new name to watch out for in crime fiction, and I can't wait to see more of DCI Yorke." – **Stephen Booth, Bestselling Crime Author**

"A pool of blood, an abduction, swirling blizzards, a haunting mystery, yes, Wes Markin's One Last Prayer has all the makings of an absorbing thriller. I recommend that you give it a go." – **Alan Gibbons, Bestselling Author**

BY WES MARKIN

DCI Yorke Thrillers

One Last Prayer

The Repenting Serpent

The Silence of Severance

Rise of the Rays

Dance with the Reaper

Christmas with the Conduit

Better the Devil

A Lesson in Crime

Jake Pettman Thrillers

The Killing Pit

Fire in Bone

Blue Falls

The Rotten Core

Rock and a Hard Place

The Yorkshire Murders

The Viaduct Killings

The Lonely Lake Killings

The Cave Killings

Details of how to claim your **FREE** DCI Michael Yorke quick read, **A lesson in Crime**, can be found at the end of this book.

This story is a work of fiction. All names, characters, organizations, places, events and incidents are products of the author's imagination or are used fictitiously. Any resemblance to any persons, alive or dead, events or locals is entirely coincidental.

Text copyright © 2018 Wes Markin

First published 2019

ISBN: 9798420965382

Imprint: Dark Heart Publishing

Edited by Jenny Cook

Cover design by Cherie Foxley

For H & B

00:30

WITH A TUMBLER of whisky in one hand and a photograph of his dead sister in the other, he stared across the living room at the locked drawer, which contained secrets he hid from the world.

He sighed, leaned back on the sofa and let the spirit burn his throat.

He took another look at the sister he'd so admired as a child, noticing the lines around her eyes which would now never deepen, and the dark hair that would never grey. He remembered his failed promise to her, and then thought of her killer walking free.

After replacing her photograph in the drawer with other memorabilia of his personal failings, including a faded photograph of Charlotte, his first love, he locked it and buried the key behind the clock on his mantelpiece.

Despite ending his furtive ritual, Yorke still flinched when he heard his bedroom door open. He turned to acknowledge Patricia, his girlfriend of nearly three years now, standing there in a white-cotton nightie. They exchanged a smile, and as he opened his mouth to reassure her that he was on his way back to her, the mobile phone in his dressing-gown pocket rang.

As he took the call, and listened to the unthinkable, he stared at Patricia. Even in this darkened hour, metres away, he knew she would see the horror in his eyes. She started across the room, knowing that when the call ended, she would need to be there for him.

As he murmured his farewells, she embraced him.

It was unusual for a man as experienced as DCI Michael Yorke to be so affected by evil, but when evil journeyed so close to home, as it had done tonight, no one was exempt.

He sagged in Patricia's arms.

———

DS JAKE PETTMAN stroked one of the dead pigeon's broken wings. He then replaced the lid on the shoebox, finished his third bottle of *Summer Lightning* beer, and replaced the bird underneath the sink.

It was the third such delivery in three years, and rather than contact the station immediately, as Jake had done on the previous two occasions, he'd decided to keep this one all to himself.

Two days on from the delivery, and he was no closer to explaining his reasons behind doing this. Not that this was a problem. He was the only one who knew about it.

After peering in at his sleeping wife, Sheila, who was currently snuggled up with their two-year-old son, Frank, he returned to the kitchen, and the letter which had accompanied the shoebox lying by the sink.

Jakey ... how does it feel to not be able to fly anymore?
Love Lacey x

His phone rang. Even before he answered it, he sensed he was going to hear something that was going to turn his entire world upside down and make a dead bird in a box the least of his worries.

AFTER TAKING THE PHONE CALL, DI Emma Gardner wanted to cry. Instead, she went right into her daughter Anabelle's room, and held her close. The young girl woke and murmured something. Gardner felt momentarily reassured. She kissed her daughter on her head and laid her back down.

She then took a deep breath, said goodbye to her husband, threw a handful of tic tacs into her mouth, and left, beginning what felt ominously like a journey to hell.

WHEN YORKE ARRIVED at DS Iain Brookes' large cottage, pushed back into the Salisbury Plains, he stepped from the car and was immediately confronted by Gardner.

'Sir, I ...' She stopped and started to cry.

Yorke reached out and held her cheek. He held it for a couple of seconds, made eye contact with her, and then embraced her.

'Pathetic, I'm sorry,' she said from his shoulder.

'That's ridiculous, Emma.'

She stepped out of the embrace, rubbed tears away and said, 'I'll hold it together, sir.'

'I know you will,' Yorke said, reaching out to her cheek again. 'That's why this is yours.'

She widened her swollen eyes.

'There's no one better to manage this one. It's your incident room.'

'Sir?'

'No one better.'

He turned to face the house. Gardner flanked him and Jake came up on the other side. He looked left and right at his two colleagues. Like him, neither was dressed appropriately for freezing weather. They had all left their homes with their minds reeling.

In the November darkness, under stars that looked grey and sick, Yorke surveyed the cottage he'd frequented on several occasions before to enjoy dinner with DS Iain Brookes and his wife, Jessica. Tonight, sheltering death from the cold, it looked far from welcoming. In fact, the two glowing windows on either side of the front door looked like the eyes of a preying animal.

1

AFTER PC SEAN Tyler had scribbled their names into the logbook, Yorke tore open his sealed bag and slipped on his oversuit. From the second bag, he recovered some overshoes to cover his brogues.

While passing some blue-and-yellow crime-scene tape, he heard the crunching of tic tacs from Gardner and felt the huge, reassuring hand of Jake, his closest friend, on the small of his back.

He took a deep breath and checked, as he always did, that the oversuit covered his neck. The heating was clearly turned up high in this cottage, but he regularly felt an inexplicable tingle of cold on his neck at scenes like this.

The walls around him creaked as they fended off the winds racing over the plains. On any other night Jessica Brookes might have felt safe and protected from the world's aggression. But the world is so often underestimated, and tonight that aggression had found its way in.

Metres from the living room, he heard Scientific Support Officer Lance Reynolds' camera snapping away. He looked at his watch. It was quarter-past one.

You have no right to do whatever you've done here tonight, whoever you are. Yorke thought. *No right at all.*

They turned into the living room and the metallic smell of blood overwhelmed them.

Sprawled out on a sheepskin rug that was once cream, Jessica had spread huge wings of blood. She looked like a crimson angel frozen mid-flight. Her breasts had been covered already with a blood-stained plastic sheet, but there could be no dignity in a death like this. Patricia Wileman, the Divisional Surgeon as well as Yorke's lover, clearly disagreed. Patricia had left Yorke's house merely a minute before him, but she was already hard at work. He watched her examine the body, treating it like a piece of priceless artwork. It was surreal to think that merely hours before they'd been making love.

She looked up at him. She had her mask on so she offered him a raised eyebrow – her only way of expressing support.

Reynolds, nicknamed 'the Elf' due to his light feet and dexterity, was also diligently working. He manoeuvred around the clusters of SOCOs he controlled, darting in and out, wielding the camera like a machine sucking answers from its materials rather than just documenting them.

Yorke felt Jake lift his hand from his back, and then start gagging beside him. He glanced up at the big man. 'You need time?'

'No, I'll be fine.'

He then glanced at Gardner to his other side and considered the same question. She stared ahead with unflinching eyes. Driven, after her wobble before outside. Driven, like him. Like he hoped they all would be in the time to come.

They stopped a metre from the body, allowing Reynolds the space to weave.

In a world of exploding camera flashes, you could be forgiven for thinking that Jessica's eyes were opening and closing; that her lips were curling up and down into a huge smile; that she was desperate to throw off death's old clothes and join in the investigative dance. The reality was that her eyes were half closed and her mouth was sloped at an unusual angle. He recognised Jessica behind her twisted expressions, but wished he didn't. The kindly host who had welcomed him into her house for dinner with her family on more than one occasion.

Patricia lifted Jessica's purpling top lip and the flash of Reynold's camera burnt the image of her clenched teeth into Yorke's mind. His eyes fell to her plastic-shrouded chest again.

'What's happened to her?'

Patricia looked at him again with the same raised eyebrow. Warning or reassurance? Yorke wasn't sure this time.

'It is particularly bad,' Patricia said, pulling the plastic sheet off.

'Ah, Jesus,' Jake said. He turned and left at pace.

Jessica had been sliced open and her ribcage jerked apart. Her breasts flopped down against her side.

Yorke sucked in air. He wanted to turn away too. Desperately. He forced himself to stare. He heard Gardner muttering beside him, but her words suddenly seemed incomprehensible.

'Her heart has been taken,' Patricia said.

Rain clattered against the window.

'And flesh has been removed from both of her thighs.'

'*Why?*' Gardner's voice was clear now. An instinctive question, but a futile one.

'I don't know, but the pieces were large, five inches by two.'

Yorke took several steps backwards as Patricia recovered Jessica's chest.

'Emma, go and get some fresh air with Jake,' he said.

Gardner nodded. 'Sir.'

He watched her venture outside the house to the preferable onslaught of rain and wind.

He took several steps back, trying to focus on what he knew.

Someone had called this in anonymously at quarter-past twelve. They had the location of this call, but the telephone box had been outside of any CCTV coverage, so no visual. Some officers would already be picking up CCTV footage in the vicinity to see if they could get a view on the caller arriving and leaving the area.

At least there were no more bodies in this house. DS Iain Brookes and Jessica had been divorced for over a year now and their twelve-year-old son was staying at his place tonight. Family Liaison Officer Bryan Kelly and two other officers had gone to break the news. Yorke rubbed his face with his gloved hands. A whirlwind was about to descend on their lives.

A whirlwind that was familiar to Yorke.

He followed the SOCOs with his eyes as they dusted for prints, sampled fibres, photographed and in some instances, sketched.

Breaking his trance, he headed outside and surveyed the area again. The cottages here were flash and expensive. Jessica had been a partner in a lucrative accountancy firm. There was sufficient land between each one to ensure that an intruder could get to the house unseen if they came on foot. Neighbours were still close enough to be seen though, and some flocked to their gardens and porches. They shivered, not just because it was cold, but because death had invaded their neighbourhood. Door-to-door would start almost immediately and a Police Search Advisor would be joining the investigation. He bypassed Exhibits Officer Andrew Waites, a notoriously unapproachable man, swooping for a cigarette butt in the garden. Then, he stood with Jake and Gardner at the side of the incident van.

'Okay, Emma, head back and get the incident room ready, please. And talk to Price. Ensure the press, who will be here any second no doubt, don't get anything they don't need yet.'

She nodded, wiped away a tear and headed away.

'Sorry, sir. I just lost it in there,' Jake said.

'Shut up. It was a normal reaction.'

'I just, you know, saw Sheila's face.'

Yorke paused.

'Selfish, I know. Poor Iain. Fuck.'

'Not selfish – normal. It could be anyone. That's the point. That's why we will get whoever fucking did this.'

'She's back again. A year to the day,' Jake said.

Yorke considered, and raised an eyebrow. 'Another bird?'

'Another. Number three. Posted inside the UK again. Is it any wonder I saw Sheila's face in there?'

'It's not going to happen. Lacey cannot come back ... won't come back. If she does—'

Yorke's phone rang. He looked at the screen. *Iain. He knows already. The news had been broken.*

'Iain?'

'Sir, my son, Ewan, he's gone. Jesus, I only just found out his mother is dead, and *he's gone too.*'

'Don't move.'

He gestured at his police-issue Lexus. Jake nodded to acknowledge the request. They were gone within twenty seconds.

WHEN DS IAIN BROOKES had needed to get away from it all fifteen months ago, he'd literally opted for nothingness. He'd got himself a motorhome and found himself the quietest caravan site in the Salisbury Plains – one that sat in the shadow of a large forest. A local farmer, suffering in the current climate, had dedicated a chunk of his acreage to some long-term tenants in the hope of restoring some declining funds. Consequently, there were about ten people who had opted for the middle of nowhere over the chaos of life.

Yorke, who didn't possess much experience of relationships, had heard that divorce hit people in peculiar and varied ways, but a semi-recluse in a motorhome was a new one for him.

As they neared the site, the forest thickened and the light faded away, so Yorke fought back with fog lights. He took the speedometer as high as it could go without making a safe corner an impossibility. Usually, the conversation between Jake and Yorke came thick and fast. Not tonight.

When Brookes had first bought the motorhome, Yorke had thought it looked like an impenetrable fortress, solid and immoveable. Now, lodged out here in the woods, it seemed vulnerable, rather like a tin, ready to be opened and emptied into a pan. Yorke and Jake parked alongside it and were banging on the door within seconds.

Ewan opened the door.

Yorke's eyes widened and Jake sighed loudly beside him.

Yorke stepped into the motorhome, put his hand on the back of Ewan's head, and pulled him tightly to his chest. 'I'm so sorry, Ewan.'

Ewan cried against him. From the kitchen area, Yorke saw FLO Bryan Kelly raise a hand in greeting, and then turn back to the sink, where he was attending to a build-up of pots and pans. On the sofa was their next-door neighbour Riley Thompson, a sixty-year-old ex-convict, who Brookes and Ewan thought very highly of. He also raised a hand in greeting, before rubbing his balding head. In the other hand, he clutched a walking stick so tightly that his knuckles sparkled.

'Where's my mum, Uncle Mike?' Ewan said, his voice was muffled by tears and Yorke's chest.

Jake came up alongside Yorke and stroked Ewan's head.

Ewan said, 'It's not true, tell me it's not true?'

Yorke said, 'I'm sorry–'

'He was hiding outside in the woods.' Brookes emerged from the bedroom. 'I'm sorry I worried you.'

Yorke looked up at Brookes. His eyes were swollen from crying, and he had a bottle of *Asahi* in one hand. *How many have you had?* Thought Yorke. He flashed his eyes Kelly's way – *you better be keeping an eye on that.*

'No need to be sorry, Iain,' Yorke said. '*We're* sorry. So very sorry.'

'Yes, Iain,' Jake said. 'Anything you need, you got it.'

Brookes put his bottle down on the side, and came over to put a hand on his son's head. 'Ewan ran, hid in the forest for a while, and came back. I get it. Probably would have done it myself for a while if it wasn't so cold.'

Ewan peeled away from Yorke's embrace and followed his father over to the sofa. Brookes sat down, and hoisted Ewan up onto his knee.

Yorke noticed movement in the forty-gallon tank by the sofa. He took a step forward and observed a blood-red snake easing itself out of a pile of aspen shavings.

'Ewan's corn snake,' Brookes said.

Yorke nodded. 'I'm sorry Iain, we need to get back. But can we talk first? It'll only help matters.'

'And rule me out?' He smirked. 'Never thought I'd be on this side.'

'You are *not* on that side, Iain. We just need a timeline.'

'A timeline?'

He'd always struggled with authority at the best of times. Yorke realised that tonight would be no different. If anything, it'd be worse.

'Let me get my son in bed.'

'Of course.

WITH THE NIGHTLIGHT ON, Brookes sat on the bed and Ewan shuffled up close to him. He kissed his son's head and looked up at the framed picture of them all together at Disneyland. Right now, he couldn't believe he'd ever laughed like that, but the evidence was there, as plain to see as the bear-hug Mickey Mouse was giving Jessica.

He heard Ewan murmuring for his mother as he drifted into sleep.

For a moment, he envied Jessica. He doubted that anyone who was dead actually *felt* dead. Right now, that was exactly how he felt. *Dead*. He prayed to God that his son did not feel that way too.

After easing himself away from Ewan and covering him with his blanket, he heard a clatter. The framed picture had fallen. He took a deep breath and went to retrieve it. Fortunately, it remained upright against the wall and hadn't smashed.

As THEY WAITED in the lounge area for Brookes to return, Yorke's mind journeyed back to the moment he had to break the news to his mother that her only daughter was dead.

And not just dead. Murdered.

'I met some bad people in my time,' Riley said, 'but it still stuns me to know that someone could walk into an innocent woman's house and kill her.'

Yorke nodded in agreement, acknowledging that Riley didn't even know the full extent of what this bastard had done to Jessica.

Riley noticed Jake staring at him. 'I know what you're thinking, but I did my time.'

After the man accused of raping Riley's wife twenty-seven years ago was acquitted, Riley had conducted his own trial and delivered the punishment swiftly. The cost? Half his life in a cell, his marriage and his children. Since his release, he'd spent the last two years living like Brookes. In self-imposed exile.

Jake shrugged. 'I'm not judging, someone else got there and did that before me.'

Yorke looked at Jake. 'DS Pettman? Maybe you could get us a glass of water?'

Jake stood up. 'Just what I was thinking, sir.' He joined Bryan Kelly in the kitchen.

Yorke shrugged. 'It doesn't seem like it, but he means well.'

Riley nodded. 'Aha. Can't blame him really. Most people mean well, but most people also can't handle what I've done – what they think I am. Can't really say I blame them. There's a reason I did what I did, but I guess it didn't have to be done in the way that I did it.'

'So violently?' Yorke said.

'Yes.' Riley heaved himself to his feet and leaned on his cane.

Yorke looked down at Riley's leg.

'Prison, first day, kind of an initiation ceremony.' He paused to smile. 'Shouldn't complain, most of me healed.'

As he limped past Yorke, Riley put a hand on his shoulder. He leaned in so Yorke could hear his gruff voice in his ear. 'They mean the world to me these two.'

Yorke nodded.

'*The world.* Will you get this monster?'

Yorke looked up at Riley. His eyes were fixed on his. The moment lingered and Yorke wondered who would blink first. When it seemed like no one was going to, Yorke said, 'We will.'

Riley nodded and left the motorhome.

Jake returned to him with two glasses of water.

'When are you going to sort out your bedside manner?' Yorke said.

Jake shrugged as Brookes emerged from the bedroom. He held up a cigarette. 'Let's go out. I don't smoke inside when Ewan's here.'

Jake said, 'It's about minus ten—'

'Put your coat back on, Jake,' Yorke interrupted.

THEY SHIVERED as Brookes smoked and swigged from another bottle of *Asahi*. Yorke wondered if it had been refrigerated; if so, it would be pretty uncomfortable to drink in this climate.

'How did she die?' Brookes said after blowing out a lungful of smoke.

Not the best question for him to be asking, thought Yorke. He noticed Jake looking at his feet, clearly not wanting to engage.

Brookes noticed too. 'That bad, eh?'

'We are not too sure of that ourselves yet,' Yorke said, maintaining eye-contact with him.

But Yorke was sure of one thing – she had been murdered *brutally* and with a design. He'd had enough personal experience, most notably with the murderous Ray family, and read enough case files to know that the killer had been purposeful in his action, a goal of some kind had been achieved, and he was most certainly going to act again.

'You are going to keep me firmly in the quiet over this one, aren't you?' Brookes said.

Yorke reached out to put his hand on Brookes' shoulder. 'We know you're devastated, Iain. But if we do this right, it'll end right. You know that ...'

'Did you feel that way with Danielle?'

Yorke flinched and withdrew his hand. It was a low blow, but one he had to accept in the current situation.

Danielle had been Yorke's older sister. *Estranged* older sister. Close as youngsters, enemies as adults. She'd run with the wrong crowd. Got herself mixed up with drugs and prostitution.

'Were you told how she died?' Brookes said.

Yorke gritted his teeth, sucked in a deep breath and didn't take the bait. 'I was and it was too soon.'

In a fit of anger, a fellow drug addict called William Proud, had held Danielle's face against a hot stove until she'd passed out in agony. Her heart had been unable to take it and she'd died moments later.

'Harry Butler told me,' Yorke said, 'and look where he is now. It didn't do either of us any good.'

'And how does it feel to know that Proud is still out there?'

Disgraced Detective Sergeant Harry Butler had framed the wrong man. Proud had run and was still out there somewhere. Yorke turned away.

'This is getting us nowhere,' Jake said.

Brookes threw his empty bottle into the darkness. 'And you, Jake, you at least know how it feels to almost lose everything.'

Before they'd had Frank, Sheila and Jake's marital problems had reached a climax. He'd been consumed by work, and then Lacey Ray, an old flame, who was exploring her sociopathic tendencies, had returned to Salisbury.

'I do,' Jake said. He felt a rush of adrenaline as he considered the dead pigeon he'd received – *was she back?*

'Imagine *if* Lacey had done more than just threaten her, Jake? Imagine if she'd put that knife into your wife's belly and into your unborn—'

'*Enough, Iain.*' Yorke turned back around and held his hand up.

Brookes threw away the butt of his cigarette and thrust his hands into his jacket pockets. He looked down, clearly welling up again.

Yorke stepped forward and took him by the shoulders, 'You *need* us back at the station, Iain. Let's just go and get that statement – you be with your son, and I won't let what happened to William Proud ever happen again.'

Brookes nodded. Yorke embraced his friend.

WHEN THEY GOT BACK INSIDE, Kelly had laid on three cups of tea. A clever distraction, no doubt, from the fridge full of *Asahi*. They spoke quietly. A child, broken up by the night's events, was sleeping only metres away.

'It was just before five when I picked him up,' Brookes said, wrapping his hands around the hot cup. 'I know it was just before, because I looked at my watch and thought that this was the first time I'd be on time to collect him in over a month.'

Jake made the notes while Yorke nodded, reassuring him that this was procedure, and just a way to establish a firm timeline around tonight's tragic events.

'Did you go in?'

'No. Never do. Relationship was at rock bottom, you know that.' He paused for a mouthful of tea.

'That's okay, Iain. Did you talk?'

'Briefly. About homework. Ewan needed to practise some spellings for the morning.'

'Was anyone else with Jessica at this point?'

'Not that I noticed.' He paused and looked away. 'And I always *try* to notice. You know I still love her, sir.' He squeezed his eyes tightly together. '*Loved*.'

Yorke reached over and clasped the top of Brookes' arm.

He opened his eyes. 'Besides, Ewan would have told me if that was the case.'

'And at that point you just left with Ewan?'

'Yes, that's it, couldn't have been more than two

minutes. We then went for pizza in Amesbury. I thought I could get him to practise his spellings while we waited for it but the slippery devil had left them back at the house. *Accident* apparently.' Brookes paused for a smirk. 'So, I phoned Jess, and she read them over the phone. And that was the last time we spoke ...'

'What time was that?'

He pulled his phone out of his pocket and turned it to show Yorke. An outgoing call to Jessica was made at 17:22.

Yorke's phone buzzed. He read a message from Gardner: *Sir?* They were clearly raring to go at the station.

'Jake, just call Emma at the station. Tell her, we need to wrap up here. Just check that everything is okay with Price and the press. I'm worried he hasn't come straight to me as usual; maybe, he thinks he'll get more if he chips away at Emma.'

'He'll be in for a disappointment then!' Jake said, rising to his feet. He reached down and gripped Brookes' hand. 'I'm so sorry, Iain.'

Brookes nodded. 'I know you are, Jake. And I'm sorry for some of the things I said ... before.'

'Don't be,' Jake said. 'I won't sleep till we find out what happened.'

'That makes two of us.'

Jake left the motorhome.

'So, what happened after you got the pizza?' Yorke continued.

'The usual. We came back here and ate it. Riley came by. He put his favourite film on.' Brookes paused to finish his tea.

'Which was?'

'*Watership Down.*'

'About the rabbits?'

'Yep – you'd never have guessed. An emotional man Riley. After that, Ewan went to bed. About half-past eight. He always reads for about half an hour before sleeping. It helps him relax.'

Yorke continued making notes in Jake's book.

'Riley and I then stayed up until about midnight playing chess.' He pointed up at the board game on an overhead shelf. 'Once Riley had beaten me a few times, he headed off to bed. I'd only been in bed less than half an hour before Bryan and Collette showed up with the news.'

As Yorke continued making notes where Jake had left off, he considered whether or not Brookes had opportunity. He wouldn't be doing his job if he didn't. If these times added up, and Riley provided a solid alibi, the only window Brookes had was between 12 and the time the anonymous 999 call was placed around 12:15. Could he really have journeyed the ten minutes to his ex-wife's house, performed that barbaric, but rather meticulous deed on her, and then escaped before PC Sean Tyler arrived at 12:20 to secure the scene? Ten minutes to do what he'd seen in that room? He'd have to have that confirmed by Patricia but he really couldn't see how this would be possible. Plus, wouldn't Riley have seen him leaving his motorhome? And did he not risk his son waking up and realising he wasn't there? If Riley checked out as an alibi, Brookes looked secure. This would have to be done within the hour, preferably while he was leading the first meeting at the station.

Which begged the question, 'Iain, do you know of anyone who had a problem with Jessica?'

'That question has been running through my mind for the last hour. I can only think of one person that she ever mentioned ...' He paused and rubbed his head. 'Fuck... what was his name again?'

A sudden burst of wind hurled rain at the window like pellets from a shotgun and, for a moment, Yorke saw Jessica's body in his mind again, ravaged as if set upon by wild animals. He tasted bile in his mouth. They'd had four murders in Wiltshire last year; she could have died any of those ways, but not this way—

'*Preston!*' Brookes said. 'He was called Robert Preston.'

Yorke raised an eyebrow and flipped open his notebook.

'One of the other parents at Ewan's school. Married, but used to flirt with her relentlessly. Drove her crazy. She caught him holding a phone in the air one night at parents' evening and swore that he'd taken a snap of her on his mobile phone. I reassured her that she'd probably made a mistake. I mean, I'm always holding my phone in the air trying to get reception? Doesn't everyone? Shit, was I wrong?'

'Anything else?' Yorke said.

Brookes took a huge sigh, bit his top lip and shook his head. Then, he looked Yorke in the eyes, 'How did she die, Mike?'

Yorke flinched, not so much because of the question he'd already argued against outside, but rather due to the sudden use of his first name. 'Iain, listen ...'

'Did she suffer? Tell me that at least.'

Yorke leaned over and put his hand on his knee. Firmly. 'I genuinely don't know, but believe me when I say to you, I'm going to find everything out and get them. And when I do, you'll be the first to know.'

COLOURLESS AND EMPTY, the incident room in *Devizes* did not welcome Yorke. Neither did the people within it.

They stared at a table too varnished to warrant a place in so barren a setting.

Even Wendy, the ever-trusted Management Support Assistant, struggled to make eye contact with anyone as she delivered the tea and biscuits.

Gardner had already printed the randomly generated name of the case across the top of the central whiteboard. 'Operation Restore.'

Restore what? Yorke thought. *How do you find a way back after damage like this?*

DI Mark Topham waved the biscuits away, smiled at Wendy and said, 'Too many *Syns* in that.'

Everyone stared at Topham, unable to believe that he had made a reference to his *Slimming World* programme at such a sensitive time.

'Sorry.' He looked down at the table.

When Wendy left, Yorke continued, 'All the windows and doors have now been thoroughly checked; it wasn't forced entry, so she may have known whoever it was.'

DS Jake Pettman cracked his knuckles; Jeremy Dawson from HOLMES flinched and stopped typing up the information for a moment.

'So, Robert Preston, the stalker from Ewan's school, is our most viable option then?' Jake said.

'We will know in a matter of minutes,' Gardner said. 'We're picking him up from the *White Hart hotel*, opposite the cathedral. He's been staying for the last month or so, since his wife threw him out.'

Unable to tolerate being seated any longer, Yorke stood up and wandered over to the line of noticeboards around the central whiteboard. Names, assignments and leads had already started to swell outwards from a collection of shocking images. He looked over at Gardner and nodded his appreciation for her hard work in managing the incident room with such thoroughness. She caught the nod and offered a tentative smile.

'I'm not optimistic about door-to-door. The distance between each cottage is considerable, but you never know. Someone may have seen the vehicle, or even more unlikely, someone on foot. We will know soon. PolSA and SOCOs are also still working the area hard. Again, I'm not optimistic. There's a reason for my pessimism,' he turned and pointed at the crimson angel, Jessica. 'Precision.'

He turned back and surveyed the crowd.

'Whoever it was took her heart.' He paused to take a deep breath. 'And, according to Dr Wileman, they took it with surgical precision. Someone with that much skill ... traces will be hard to come by.'

'Preston is an estate agent, not a surgeon,' Topham said.

Jake said, 'Still ... you can't rule him out based only on that.'

'No, you can't,' Yorke said, 'but it's a strong point. I heard, moments ago, that they've lifted a print. They're running it right now, so that might give us something. There's also something else very peculiar here.'

'The urine on the sofa?' Gardner said.

'Yes. They have a corn snake. They don't urinate, at least not in that way.'

'Jessica?' Jake said, looking down at the table again. 'In fear?'

'Possible,' Yorke walked back over to the table for a mouthful of tea while Dawson continued tapping on the keyboard furiously.

'What about Iain, sir?' Topham said.

It was a subject that had not been broached yet and

needed to be. Yorke finished his coffee and then relayed the events of the previous hour at Brookes' motorhome.

'The alibi checks out,' Yorke said. 'He was with Riley during the estimated time of death.'

'And are you a hundred percent certain, sir?' Topham said.

Yorke flashed him a look; it was important to be challenged, but that didn't mean he had to like it. 'As certain as I can be at this stage. The lack of CCTV footage on the emergency call at quarter-past twelve is particularly frustrating. We are correlating the CCTV footage around the local area.'

Yorke turned and stared at the images again. 'We need to get into Jessica's place of work first thing, speak to her colleagues. DI Gardener and DS Simmonds, I want you to head there. DI Topham and DS Bates, I would like you to talk to her friends and family members apart from her mother. I believe she has an aunt and some cousins locally. I've learned that her mother, Karen, is in the Mary Chapman Living Facility suffering from Alzheimer's so I'll go there.' Yorke tapped the image. 'Who has had a problem with Jessica in the past?'

'And the flesh from her thighs, sir?' Simmonds said, 'Why would anyone do that?'

Yorke shrugged his shoulders. 'I don't know, but we need to make damned sure it doesn't happen again.'

There was a knock at the door. PC Sean Tyler poked his head round.

'The print ... it is Preston's. He was in a few years ago on a drunk and disorderly; we tagged him then.'

Jake was already on his feet. 'So do we have him?'

'Bad news I'm afraid. We went to pick him up from the

White Hart – he's not there. He went out at nine according to the hotel, and he hasn't been back since.'

'Check his house out now,' Yorke said, 'and bring his wife into this station. We need to know as much as we can about this man ... now.'

MINUTES AWAY FROM SUNRISE, DS Iain Brookes nursed his final bottle of *Asahi* on his motorhome doorstep. He looked out over the trees, poking out of the ground like the hands of buried giants who may have once ruled the world, and listened. He heard the occasional rustle but was unable to determine the source. Animals or merely the wind? He thought of Louise Lynn, an elderly lady in an adjacent motorhome. She'd had a house rabbit that had happily hopped around the site until a fox had struck. She had welcomed it back in with its stomach split open, and its insides hanging loose like the udders of a cow.

This wasn't the place for people to be struck down like Jessica had. They did a good job, Iain and his colleagues. Wiltshire had low crime rates. This wasn't America with its colourful carousel of murderous fanatics and self-proclaimed artists! What had happened? Where had *this* come from?

Even if Preston was responsible, he wouldn't get any time with the creep. His role in this whole shitty affair would simply end with him at the back of a courtroom. A spare part. Forced to watch Preston take his chances with the lottery of the legal system.

The sun finally rose. He took no solace from the destruction of darkness by light. He could take solace from only one thing.

He looked down at the cloth-wrapped item that Riley had given him earlier, accompanied with the words, 'Don't open it now. I'm sure you know what it is and every part of you is screaming out that it's not right. But that's the way it is. There's a maniac out there right now, and I'm not having you sitting vulnerable with that boy of yours. I promise I'll answer all of your questions about where and why after they've got this maniac, but until then, that stays here, with you.'

He unwrapped the Glock 26 pistol; a gun that he was familiar with from his firearms training.

So, as the birds began to sing in a cloudless sky, to a sun that gave light but promised warmth that would not come, and the foxes moved amongst the trees, he decided that the hunt was on.

It had to be ... what choice was there?

He turned the gun over in his hand; the polymer frame was light and cold to the touch. He ejected the magazine and emptied it into his palm. The cartridges sparkled in the sunlight.

He was crying now harder than ever before. He could feel the darkness that had consumed her, consuming him too.

Dr Carl Reiner watched Karen Firth bring a sudden end to a long period of catatonia because she didn't like what was on today's menu. She arched her back, lashed out at the nurse, and the feeding bag exploded on the floor at his feet, soaking his shoes.

In his fifteen years as Director of the Mary Chapman Assisted Living Facility for the Elderly, he had seen many displays of aggression from patients in the advanced stages of Alzheimer's, but never anything like this.

Karen thrashed her head from side to side while froth oozed from the corners of her mouth. She succeeded in landing a foot on the chest of Terrence Lock, a nurse who had just brought her back from the hospital. Winded, he stumbled back. Then, she demonstrated that her strike wasn't a one off and buried her bare foot in the stomach of Megan Broadhead, a nurse on the other side of the bed. She collapsed backwards against the wall.

Finally, Reiner observed a *third* nurse, Ryan Marshall, with sufficient upper body strength, overpower Karen and plunge a needle into her thigh. Karen glared at Reiner, but as the sedative cooled her heated brain, her look turned to one of gratitude and her limbs relaxed.

Reiner kicked the mush from his shoes and took a step towards Karen. She gurgled and small bubbles burst at the corner of her mouth.

He looked between the faces of the nurses. 'Please get back to your duties now, thank you.'

The skeletal nurse, whose uniform hung off him like a bin bag, said, 'Are you sure you don't want us to see if she's alright?'

Her synapses are being ravaged by dementia, he thought, *of course she's not alright.*

'That will be all, thank you, Terrence.'

Terrence pushed the empty wheelchair out of the door, closely followed by Ryan and Megan.

From his pocket, Reiner took a handkerchief embroidered with his initials. He leaned forward and dabbed the froth at the corners of Karen's mouth. He could tell that she had been a beautiful woman before the living death had set in. Her eyes and nose were petit, and she wore an endearing set of dimples. Her long-gone husband would certainly have admired her in her youth. Not that he would recognise her now if he were alive; with the living death, not only do you become unfamiliar to yourself but to others too.

He continued to wipe her face with his handkerchief, unveiling her dignity as if he was simply wiping dust away from an old painting, acknowledging all the time that the dust would fall again. Just like it did on so many of his other patients in this place.

He took his phone out of his pocket and searched for Dr Page – he would be eager to hear of this latest event—

Karen's hand darted out and snaked around his wrist. He heard his phone clatter on the floor. He attempted to untangle her hand, but her fingers bit too deep into his wrist.

Far too deep for someone in the advanced stages of Alzheimer's and someone sedated up to the eyeballs.

'Jessica?' Karen said with her eyes locked shut.

Reiner knew that Jessica was her daughter. 'No,' he said. 'Sorry.'

'Iain?' Karen said.

Her son-in-law.

Reiner paused before replying in the negative again. Maybe, he should find out what was wrong? 'Yes,' he said.

Her eyes burst open. Reiner would have jumped back if she wasn't gripping him so tightly. 'You are in danger.'

She spoke so clearly, without a pause. He wished someone else was still in the room with him to observe this phenomenon; no one was going to believe him. 'Why?'

'The jaguar waits in the trees.' Her voice was becoming louder and clearer.

'Why?'

'I don't know, but it's disgusting, Iain. Its skin is all covered in blood and flesh hangs from its teeth.'

The grip was starting to hurt so Reiner shouted for the nurse. *'Terrence!'*

He wrenched back again, but her hand gripped even harder.

'Terrence!'

'*His* mirror can see inside all of us.'

Karen released his arm and he jumped back.

The door burst open and Terrence Lock burst in. He injected her with more sedative, but it was unnecessary, because Karen's head had already slumped to one side.

2

W ITH THE BLOOD-RED snake curled around his
wrist, his father sitting to one side of him on the
sofa, Riley on the other, and Bryan Kelly continually
cleaning the kitchen, it should have been impossible to feel
lonely.

But he did. And it was the loneliest he'd ever felt. He
couldn't remember ever feeling such a desperate urge to hug
his mother. His father ended a phone call next to him.

'Who was it?'

'Dr Reiner at Grandma's home. She's ill and he wants
me to visit.'

'Can I come?'

His father turned away. 'It doesn't sound good, Ewan.
Plus, you're going away. Grandad's coming.'

'Dad ...'

'We've talked about this, and we're not talking about it
again. I need to figure it all out and make sure everything's
alright.'

'Safe?'

'Yes, of course. Safe.'

Ewan sighed. He didn't have a great urge to see his grandma anyway. Not because he didn't love her, but because he'd never really known her. She'd been sick for as long as he could remember and now all he could really think about was how unfair it was that she'd outlived his mother.

And he did get on well with his grandad, who was his dad's father.

'Please don't make this harder than it has to be.'

Ewan sighed. He touched his dad's buttoned shirt. 'Have you changed?'

He looked away. 'I will. Before I leave.'

YORKE ENDED a phone call with Brookes regarding the fact that he was heading in to see Jessica's mother, Karen, at Mary Chapman this morning. Yorke had asked to meet him there as part of a series of interviews with Jessica's relatives. Brookes had warned him that getting any information out of her about Jessica at this stage of her dementia would be impossible, but Yorke decided it was worth pursuing anyway.

It was eight-thirty in the morning and he looked around the incident room at those assembled for morning briefing. It was busier than it had been in the early hours of the morning, and all the core and non-core team members were now present. He could tell from their worn faces that very few, if any, had managed some sleep.

With the return of Yorke, Gardner continued where she'd left off with the report on the interview with Robert Preston's wife, Yvonne.

'She knew *years* before she finally chucked him out that

he had a problem. Several women had already complained about him staring, and following, them in public places. But it's when she first got into his office drawers and found the photos of all the women that she fully accepted it. He'd taken photos of women without them realising, probably on his phone, before printing them out.'

'Upskirting?' Jake said.

'No,' Gardner continued. 'Just photos of ordinary women doing ordinary things.'

'Iain said that Jessica was certain that Preston had taken a photograph of her at parents' evening on his mobile phone.'

'Weirdo,' Topham said.

Gardner said, 'It gets weirder when you consider how many photographs of different women there were. Yvonne said she found *hundreds*.'

There was a moment of silence while Dawson from HOLMES typed loudly.

'Was there a photograph of Jessica in there?' Jake said.

'She wasn't sure. She knew who Jessica was, but she didn't recall her photograph. She also burned all the photos when she threw him out two months ago.'

Yorke jumped in. 'The accumulated CCTV footage around the area near where the emergency call was made has flagged up Preston's blue Ford. We can conclude, reasonably, that he made the emergency call. It doesn't sound like Jessica would have had him over for his dinner, so his print places him as an intruder. The APW is out but CCTV lost him when he ventured back out to the Salisbury Plains. So, we don't know where he is yet. We will continue chasing up all his associates and family members – someone will have some idea where he will be hiding.'

There was a knock at the door.

'Come in,' Gardner said.

Patricia walked in; she had a laptop tucked under the arm. She had a slide show ready. He'd already seen it over an hour ago. He shuddered over the memory.

Yorke said, 'In our last meeting, I suggested that the mutilation was done with precision. Dr Wileman has kindly agreed to talk us through her findings regarding the cause of death.'

She set up the laptop in the corner of the room and a projector in the centre of the ceiling hummed. Yorke pulled down a screen at the side of the room. It remained blue for a moment, while Patricia's laptop sprang into life, and a surreal ocean-blue calmness descended over the room; even Dawson stopped typing for a moment. A couple of flickers later and the screen was filled with a graphical image of a chemical of some kind.

'Tetrodotoxin.' Patricia turned to face her audience. 'It was in Jessica's blood.'

She looked from face-to-face, waiting for some recognition that didn't seem to be coming. Until, eventually, Gardner said, 'Pufferfish?'

'Yes!' Patricia said, sounding a little too excited for the situation. 'It's in other sea creatures too. However, she had not ingested any sea creature or any source of tetrodotoxin for that matter; yet, there was enough in her bloodstream to kill her. We've checked the body over for needle marks, but we haven't found one yet.'

'Does that mean she died before ... you know?' Topham said.

'We can't confirm that Detective Inspector. Tetrodotoxin is a neurotoxin, it paralyses the victim, leaving them in a state of near death, but often conscious.'

'And aware?' Yorke said, struggling to make eye-contact with his lover while she discussed something so abhorrent.

'Possibly. The respiratory muscles start failing within minutes of the toxin kicking in. Whoever did this could have waited until after respiratory failure, which could have taken up to ten minutes,' Patricia said.

'So, why didn't the bastard use a different kind of anaesthetic?' Jake's face reddened. 'Did they take pleasure from this?'

'I don't know,' Patricia continued. 'Apologies for the next slide.' She pressed a button on a remote and displayed a close-up of Jessica's opened chest. She flicked the laser pointer on the remote at the centre of the atrocity. 'We've had it looked at by several surgeons. This is almost professional. It is called a *median sternotomy.*' She ran the laser pointer over the cavity. 'It began with a vertical incision with a scalpel down the centre of the chest. A *sternal saw,* which is a battery-operated bone cutter was then used to slice through the breastbone.'

She hit the clicker again and took them to a picture of a sternal saw. It resembled a power drill. 'It works by moving a tooth-covered blade back and forth at lighting speed—'

'I'm sorry ...' Jake rose to his feet and left the room.

Patricia scanned the faces in the crowd and then looked at Yorke. 'Shall I continue?'

Yorke nodded, and wanted to say something, but he found himself completely lost for words.

She moved back to the previous slide of Jessica's chest.

'After the saw was used, Jessica's sternum was cracked open and wedged apart by a steel retractor; finally, the pericardium, a double-walled sack, was sliced open to expose her heart.'

'Jesus,' Gardner said, 'I can't hear any more.'

Several officers at the end of the table were looking away from the screen.

'Can you summarise please Dr Wileman? We appreciate your efforts, but the level of detail is proving difficult for some people,' Yorke said.

'I'll try,' she said, clicking through to a sketched diagram of a heart. She used her laser pointer again. 'The heart has been removed carefully by cutting through the great vessels here, and the left atrium here.' She mimicked a slicing movement with the laser. 'In fact, the method was almost identical to the one used for heart transplants, except ... here, the killer cut through the pulmonary veins in the left atrium, which would be left in place for the donor heart to be sewn to. My conclusion on this is that the killer has operated with some skill. He could be a surgeon or at least someone very practised.'

'Could he have practised this by using animals?' DS Simmonds asked.

'Potentially. I don't see why not ... on animals with similar biology.' Patricia said.

'How about training himself with the internet?' Topham said.

'Like I said, it's skilful, but I guess anything can be learned with time and effort.'

Yorke wondered what had gone so wrong in life that he was now discussing the forced removal of his friend, and colleague, DS Iain Brookes' ex-wife's heart. He looked at his watch. He would be meeting him in less than an hour. How could he keep what he *knew* about Jessica's fate off his face? There was something here that nobody should know regarding the death of a loved one.

'Then, there is the flesh from her thighs.'

'Fuck,' Topham said under his breath.

'The pieces were one-inch wide and five-inches long. *Exactly*. Again, the killer avoided all arteries. He was skilled again.'

'So, we're dealing with Jack the Ripper,' Topham said. 'In Salisbury?'

Yorke flashed him a look; he lowered his eyes.

'Nothing under her nails and no other sign of struggling or fighting. She may have been drugged by the tetrodotoxin before she had chance. We turned up some black hair on her body.'

'DNA?' Yorke said.

'No follicular bulb I'm afraid.'

Yorke reminded himself that hair does not contain *nuclear DNA*, which is only present in the follicular bulb when it is torn out of the attacker's head. Even then, it would only contain *mitochondrial DNA* which could only be used to link the killer to the crime after capture.

Gardner, whose face was a creased mask of hours of tears and sleeplessness, looked up at Patricia. 'Was she sexually assaulted?'

'No evidence of that. We have surmised that her blouse and bra were removed to mop up during the procedure.'

Gardner sighed. Yorke detected some relief in there.

'Anything about the urine yet?' Yorke said.

'There were no traces of any substance abuse or alcohol in the urine. We were discussing the lack of trace evidence and someone suggested that the perpetrator may have worn surgeon's scrubs? This would link to the idea of him being medically trained?'

'Thank you, Dr Wileman.'

'Anything else?'

'That'll be all for now.'

As she left, she smiled at Yorke, but he struggled to

smile back. He knew it wasn't her fault that she'd just brought so much darkness into the room, but still, hearing that horrendous tale, unfolding from the lips of someone he was growing ever more intimate with, had made his whole being sink.

As he wrapped up the meeting and issued assignments, a memory kept plaguing him. Something that had started at the back of his mind and had burrowed its way forward, like a tumour, over the last few minutes.

The memory was of a biology teacher at secondary school telling his class that the heart has its own group of cells which generate electric current, so the heart can beat independently of the brain.

As he left to meet Jake, he couldn't help but consider the question that the twisted events had thrown up: could Jessica have looked up at her killer while he held her still-beating heart in his hands?

OUTSIDE KAREN FIRTH'S ROOM, Yorke looked at Brookes, desperately hoping his eyes would not betray the sickening details he knew about Jessica's demise.

'What was it all for?' Brookes said.

'What?' Yorke said.

'Our lives. All that we've done.'

'We've helped people. We, *you*, made a difference.'

'The only thing that is different is my life. I've ruined it. She left me because I was spending more hours with you than her.'

Yorke looked down, suddenly feeling ashamed. Beside him, a nurse pushed an elderly man past him in a wheelchair. Regression was in full swing; the man was now the size of a young boy and almost curled into the foetal position. The man's eyes flicked open as he passed Yorke. They were glazed over but they still acknowledged him; Yorke could sense his plea for freedom.

The door opened, and Dr Reiner presented himself. His pinstripe suit shone through the white cotton of his gown. He was heavily suntanned, and Yorke's mind wandered to DI Mark Topham - another man whose appearance meant everything.

Brookes had warned Yorke that he was unlikely to get much from Karen Firth regarding her daughter. He hadn't been wrong. In fact, he wouldn't be getting anything.

White and still, she could have been a sculpture carved from ice. He watched Brookes take her hand, probably to confirm it was warm and she was still alive. He kissed her hand. 'Hello Karen.'

There was no movement from her, but Yorke could hear her shallow breathing. It was a familiar clicking, rather like a dripping tap. He thought back to his own mother's death, when her body, ravaged by years of drug abuse, had finally succumbed in a hospital bed. He'd held her hand for two days. Two whole days. He'd been the only one left. Her other sons had long since abandoned her, and her daughter had been murdered several years before.

Yorke reached out to put his hand on Brookes' shoulder. 'You don't need me here.'

Brookes glanced back. 'No, stay ... please?'

Yorke nodded. He could see in Brookes' eyes that he had no intention of sharing the news of Jessica's death with her mother. What would be the point anyway? If Karen did regain consciousness, why would you subject her to such a tale? Despite this, Brookes would feel guilty at holding back; in much the same way, Yorke currently felt guilty about holding back on him regarding the nature of Jessica's death.

'Hello, Detective Sergeant Brookes.'

They both turned to see another white-suited doctor. This one cared far less for his appearance than Dr Reiner. He had long, limp black hair and a monobrow which stood firm and strong. He stepped forward and shook Brookes' hand, then he turned and shook Yorke's. He introduced himself.

'My name is Dr Raymond Page. I'm from the hospital DCI Yorke. Iain and I are already acquainted. I am conducting a trial on a new drug combination for Alzheimer's. Consequently, today's occurrences have been particularly intriguing.'

Other than Brookes and Yorke, no one in the room would know anything about Jessica's death yet. The press had simply announced the death of a middle-aged woman. Yorke had a good relationship with the press, and they had agreed to wait until early evening to name Jessica to the world. It seemed the facility did not even know that Brookes was divorced; maybe, Jessica had never got around to informing them.

'I don't know a great deal about it, yet. All I know is that she became rather active?' Brookes said.

'Active is an understatement.' Dr Reiner came up alongside them, stinging Yorke's nostrils with his excessive aftershave. 'The reason we contacted you, and not your wife Jessica, is due to the sensitive nature of what was said.'

'I can be quite sensitive too, you know,' Brookes said.

Yorke forced back a smile.

'Yes, I'm sure,' Reiner said, 'but I just felt it would be more devastating for her daughter rather than her son-in-law.'

Yorke took a step back, considering the ridiculous nature of the conversation.

Dr Page walked around the group of men to the side of the bed and looked down on Karen. He was a tall man.

'Yesterday, we took her to the hospital to review her medicine and give her a PET scan. You know, or at least your wife knows, that we have been very successful in slowing the deterioration down. However, there is no doubt that she is in the advanced stages of the affliction now and what happened earlier, shouldn't have happened.'

'Okay,' Brookes said, 'so what exactly did happen?'

'She asked for you by name,' Reiner said. 'She had a warning for you.'

'A warning?' Brookes said, widening his eyes. 'A little late for warnings, don't you think?'

The doctors looked confused; Yorke put his hand on Brookes' shoulder to gently remind him not to reveal too much.

Reiner said, 'I don't understand—'

'What was the warning?' Brookes said.

Reiner slipped his hand into his white coat pocket, withdrew a small notebook and read from it. 'She said that you were in danger, and that a jaguar waits in the trees. That it was disgusting, covered in blood with flesh hanging from its teeth.'

Yorke watched Brookes' expression morph into one of incredulity as Reiner blushed some more over his ridiculous words.

'Finally, she said that *his* mirror sees inside all of us.'

Brookes grunted and showed Yorke his bewildered expression. 'And that's why *I'm* here because of the ramblings of this sick lady?'

'No,' Page said, stepping forward and laying a hand on

Brookes' arm. 'It was what happened before too, DS Brookes. She was awake and active, throwing a tantrum, gripping Dr Reiner's arm so tightly he couldn't get it free. And this was *after* she was sedated. Her pressure ulcer is worsening, and she only has days left to live. Her behaviour was completely out of the ordinary. Almost unnatural.'

Yorke looked down at Karen. An IV tube snaked out of her arm, keeping her hydrated in her final hours.

'She always was a tough one,' Brookes said.

'She hasn't spoken in months,' Page continued, 'yet, today, she held a conversation. I can only conclude that the drug trials have had a significant impact and we wish to continue them.'

'Well, you have permission, don't you?'

'Well, sort of … she gave her permission years ago to conduct trials while she was alive …'

It took a moment for it to dawn on Brookes what was being asked here.

'We would like to ask permission to study the body after she passes. She will be treated with dignity and the body returned as soon as the study is complete—'

'Now I see why you wanted the son-in-law and not the daughter!' Brookes said. He looked at Yorke. 'They want my mother-in-law's body for medical research – it's not every day you get a request like that!'

Yorke nodded and looked down. This wasn't his business.

'It could help so many more people in the future,' Page said.

Brookes sighed. 'Well, what can I say to that?'

'She will be treated with the utmost dignity. Can you please talk to your wife this evening and, if she consents, return tomorrow to complete the appropriate documentation?'

Brookes nodded.

Later today, Yorke realised, when the name of the victim hit the news, these doctors would be dumbstruck. He wondered if they would still contact Brookes to press him for the forms in the morning.

On the way out, Yorke said to Brookes, 'You handled that well.'

'Really? I just nodded and accepted it. All I care about right now is getting Ewan out of town.' He looked at his watch. 'Which should be happening right about now.'

Outside, in the corridor, Yorke noticed the withered elderly man in the wheelchair from earlier. He was pushed against the wall and staring intently at Yorke. He looked like he was trying to say something, so Yorke moved closer, but the man was simply murmuring.

A nurse approached and took the handles of the wheelchair. *Ryan Marshall* was written across the badge. 'It's inhumane,' Marshall said.

Yorke looked up at him. 'Sorry, I don't understand.'

'He should have passed a long time ago.'

Yorke looked down at the old man, feeling dreadful about the nurse's words.

'He can't hear. He's one of Dr Page's patients.'

'The drug trials?' Yorke said.

'Yes,' Marshall turned the wheelchair. 'They just go on and on.'

Yorke's phone rang. 'Jake?'

'Sir, Robert Preston's parents own a holiday home in Avebury.'

'Text me the address.'

'If I leave now, we can rendezvous there? It's just under an hour.'

'Yep, see you there.'

He put his hand on Brookes' shoulder. 'I've got to dash.'

'The pervert that photographed Jessica?'

'I'll phone you later; check your son got off okay.'

WITH FREDDY still curled around one arm, Ewan looked out of the motorhome window. His eyes were sore from crying and rather foggy, but a quick rub cleared his vision. He looked over at the patch of beech trees, which were twisted and frozen into white skeletal shapes.

He continued to stroke Freddy's bronze skin which was patterned with red diamonds. Its one and a half metre body adjusted itself so its head was resting on the back of his hand; its forked tongue flicked in and out with approval. Ewan considered for a moment that the cold feel of a reptile confirmed that it was alive and well; while the opposite remained true of humans.

He felt tears prick the corner of his eyes again.

It was a clear, cloudless day so he could see into the woodland. Despite it being only a small patch of trees, it looked large at this short distance. As he stared, he noticed movement. Directly opposite the motorhome, about ten metres away, he was certain he saw something flicker behind the trees. Maybe it was a fox or some other kind of animal?

Behind him, he heard the bread burst free from the toaster; its charred smell filling the air. Riley always burnt it. He smiled though. He was so glad he was here, and the

FLO, Bryan, too. Especially when he felt so lonely and nervous.

He stroked Freddy again. He remembered how his mother had rustled around in her handbag for her car keys one morning, only for her hand to settle on this cold reptilian back. It had been a loud scream.

Sunday night, Dad's night, had immediately become Dad and Freddy's night.

And that posed an interesting question. What now? Dad and Freddy's night forever?

He guessed so. I mean, what else was there for him?

He saw the flicker of movement again and then turned from the window.

3

ROBERT PRESTON WAS grateful for an end to the trembling in his hands so that he could put a glass to his lips without spilling its contents down his front.

He was also grateful that he was now able to hold the photographs that so calmed him.

He looked down on the other photographs scattered out on the table; all of them were young and beautiful. There was Sandra Evans, a waitress in an Avebury café, who he had snapped preparing a cappuccino; Becky Fullerton, stretching several rows in front of him at a Yoga class; Marie Pemberton, the fishmonger in Salisbury, who was descaling a seabass with such skill.

He stroked their faces, pressed the photographs against his cheek, moved them around into different collages. It all helped.

But it didn't solve the problem. Because every time he blinked, he saw the twisted butcher with his hands in Jessica's chest.

Jessica Brookes had been the most beautiful woman he'd ever seen, but he couldn't bear to have her photograph out on the table right now. Couldn't bear to see her smiling at parents' evening, knowing that she would never smile again. He'd left it in his hotel room and, when the police finally found him, which he knew they would, then they were welcome to it as evidence.

He stood up and stretched out, listening to his back cracking. His spine was s-shaped. It was part of a catalogue of evidence that he was physically unattractive. Premature balding, halitosis, body odour, boils on his fucking back; he felt he could be forgiven for thinking life rarely gave him a break.

But he had been given one break, hadn't he? Yvonne? She'd loved him, given him children, accepted his faults (all but one), and he'd blown it. Completely.

The office drawer. Why had he left the photographs in the office fucking drawer?

And now his life was ruined, because the police would find him, and they would think that he'd killed her.

The kitchen door blew open and a blast of cold air raced in. The photographs, dozens of them, rose into the air and showered down like confetti. He scurried to the door to close it and slammed on a deadbolt. He then darted over to the pile of photographs on the floor, dropped to his knees and began gathering. So many photographs. So many moments. A cascade of memories that he never wished to lose ...

He felt something on the back of his neck. His hand flew there as if to swat a fly.

Nothing.

He stood up, clutching the printed memories and turned around.

Nothing. He took a deep breath.

On edge, he thought. But who wouldn't be after last

night? He forced the photographs into his pocket and went through into the living room; there, more photographs awaited him on the coffee table. He had so many moments to pore over, to cherish and remember. They would offer him sanctuary as he sat on the sofa and the afternoon slipped away.

However, the photographs were no longer on the coffee table.

The gust of wind through the kitchen? Had it somehow found its way in, blown his collection to the floor? He rounded the coffee table, knelt and thrust his hand underneath the television cabinet. He felt around in the dust, but only managed to drag out some old coins.

Then he felt something on the back of his neck again; and, this time, he could hear breathing too. He rose to his feet and saw the reflection of a man in the TV screen.

As he turned, slowly, to see who was behind him on the other side of the coffee table, Preston clutched his nose against a sudden horrendous stench.

The man was tall and wore a long black coat that drowned his feet, and his dark hair glistened like seaweed washed up on the shore.

The man stooped, and Preston thought of a snake hidden in reeds, poised to attack. His tiny eyeballs were cold and unmoving.

'Who are you?'

The serpent reeled up. Fast. Too fast to see. The pain in Preston's head was the only evidence that it had come at all.

IT HAD BEEN only moments since Ewan had seen movement amongst the beech trees, so when there was a hard knock at the motorhome door, he flinched. He took a step back while Freddy retreated partway up his arm. Riley and Bryan assembled in front of the door.

'Yes,' Kelly called.

'It's Greg Brookes.'

'Grandad,' Ewan said, bursting between his two bodyguards and yanking open the motorhome door. Greg stood there in a grey trilby and a fading black suit. They embraced.

'I'm sorry, Ewan,' Greg said. 'I'm so, so sorry.'

Minutes later, Greg was on the sofa, drinking tea provided by Kelly. He was cupping the back of Ewan's head and looking him in the eyes. 'Have I ever let you down?'

'No, but—'

'When you were having trouble with those boys at school, what did I tell you to do?'

'Tell the teacher.'

'And what happened to the problem?'

'It went away,' Ewan said.

'And the running?'

'I kept trying, like you said, and I won ... but—'

'So do you trust me?'

'You know I do, but I think Dad needs me.'

'Your dad needs to know you're safe. At least until everything is cleared up. He wants you far from here. With me. Now go and get your stuff together and we'll stop for ice cream on the way.'

'It's the middle of winter, Grandad!'

'So, it's in season then! Go and get your bags.'

ROBERT PRESTON COULD SEE Jessica's killer hovering less than a metre over him, cocking his head slowly from side to side, examining him. Preston gagged at the stench of sulphur, and almost swallowed the material which the man had stuffed into his mouth.

The intruder's face was paler than a dead man's and only an occasional flicker in his stony eyes betrayed the fact that they were organic. His long hair was unwashed, and some flecks of dandruff broke loose, swirled in the shaft of light that speared through the living room window, and sprinkled on Preston's face.

'Shouting offends me, Robert. I will take the cloth out if you promise not to shout.'

Preston nodded. He entertained a fleeting idea of putting his hands around the creature's throat as he pulled the rag free, but then realized that his hands and legs were tied. The bastard must have done it while the world was spinning.

'I have a wife and daughter.' Tears filled Preston's eyes.

'I know, they are very beautiful,' the killer said, drying Preston's tears with the rag. 'Do your wife and daughter know you were standing outside Jessica Brookes' house last night?'

Preston closed his eyes and willed the scene before him to be a hallucination that would evaporate as quickly as it had come into being, but when he opened them, the monster was still there.

'And the night before that, I saw you inside her house, Robert,' the killer continued.

'Because I loved her.'

'I see, so you went into her house while she was out. It does not seem much like love to me, Robert, not in the traditional sense of the word.'

'Let me go. I didn't say anything, I won't say anything. They'll think it's me for Christ's sake! Why would I turn myself in?'

'What about hate, Robert?'

'Hate?'

'Your hatred for me?'

'There's no hatred. I don't want revenge.'

'But you saw what I did to her.'

Preston saw him again through the window, in the dimmed lights, leaning over Jessica, with his hands inside her chest. The image merged with the sunken eyes that were looking at him right now. The killer had seen him looking in.

'I didn't, it was too dark.'

'Now, you lie Robert. Are you not supposed to be her knight in shining armour?'

Preston strained against the ropes.

'Please relax, Robert, I don't come here to cause you pain. On the contrary, I come here to offer you something I think you will want.'

'All I want is for you to let me go.' Preston felt breathless now.

The man didn't reply. He cocked his head to the side again as he looked into Preston's eyes, he then switched sides. Preston thought of *Nosferatu*, the rat-like vampire with the long fingers, but, unfortunately, unlike that particular monster, the shaft of light coming through the gap in the curtains did no harm to this monster.

'Who are you?' Tears ran into his mouth. '*What* are you?'

'A Tlenamacac.'

'I don't understand.'

'Are you happy?'

'Yes, of course ...'

The killer paused. 'But you look at them, Robert, and they don't look back.'

'I don't know what you're talking about.'

'I will ask you one last time: are you happy, Robert?'

'No then ... no I'm not fucking happy!'

'You are a slave to need, and now I come here offering you the chance to do something good. Would you like that?'

'Yes, of course.'

'Good.'

'Just let me go after.'

The man seized hold of Preston's bound legs and started dragging. When they reached the hallway, he slid easily over the polished tiles. They were heading to the front door. *This is good*, Preston thought, *outside, someone might see, someone might help.*

Then he remembered that he too had seen yet not helped.

But I couldn't have done, could I? He thought. *It had been too late - the fucker had already started to pull out her heart.*

Preston wondered if all of this would be happening to him, if he'd been born one of the beautiful people. As he was dragged to the front lawn, he noticed that his photographs were falling from his pocket and marking the trail like breadcrumbs. Then he saw a big wicker basket and a large tin of lighter fluid.

YORKE FIRED up the flashing blue lights on the front grille and contaminated the quiet country roads with his two-toned siren. Ahead was a tractor which was desperately trying to clear some room on the road for him – and failing. Yorke streaked around it and held his hand up to thank the driver for his attempt.

He was grateful for the high-speed pursuit course from several years back; however, this made him remember that Jake had not taken this course yet. He phoned his colleague on the hands-free to see if he was alright.

'You okay?'

'Well, sir, I'm not in my comfort zone, which I guess is why you phoned?'

'Don't push yourself too hard. I've organised back-up local to Avebury, so they might even get there before me now. You don't want to be picking up any dead pedestrians along the way.'

Ahead of Yorke, brake lights on a black van glowed. *Make way*, thought Yorke. It did. He sped on.

'I'm sorry again, sir.'

'About what?'

'Leaving the incident room.'

'I'm surprised you were the only one who left the room. Maybe you are the only one with a soul ... Wait a second ...'

The driver of a BMW ahead of him was clearly pumping his music too loud to notice Yorke's approach; he shot around him, agonisingly close, with his speedometer dancing around 90. This time, Yorke offered the driver his best pissed-off expression.

'Back again. Look, you've got Lacey on your mind. That would be enough to put most people off work, and into hiding. Which reminds me, call into Emma now, get her to contact Southampton HQ, and find out if there have been any updates on her whereabouts.'

'Do you not think we'd have had an update if there was one?'

'Probably, but no harm in double checking. She's left bodies in Southampton, here and in France; I think we have the right to nag.'

The phone went silent for a moment, and Yorke acknowledged that it was now Jake's turn to negotiate some tricky driving.

'I think my driving is improving,' Jake said.

'It couldn't get any worse. Listen, Jake, there's one thing I want you to keep in your mind. Lacey had the chance to hurt Sheila, didn't she? But she walked away. I don't know why, but let's assume she has some kind of code. Her victims have never been squeaky clean and usually seem to have some history of violence towards women. Take reassurance from this, until we catch her.'

'She is sending me dead birds, sir?'

'I know, Jake.'

'An ex-girlfriend, a malignant narcissist, wanted for murder, and she's sending me dead birds? She despises me for rejecting her advances and the last thing she said to me was that she would decide when our paths divide. I am really struggling for reassurances.'

'Jake, if you need some time, I would totally ...'

'That would make it worse.'

Yorke sighed, took a corner at a phenomenal speed and overtook a row of three cars. 'Jake, contact Gardner, get that update. Let's get Preston, and we'll get Lacey on our radar too. I promise. See you in twenty.'

'Okay, sir.'

PRESTON WASN'T sure if he was asleep or awake, but hoped for the former, knowing that a nightmare, even one as bad as this one, wasn't fatal.

It seemed to take an eternity to roll his head from one side to the other, so with time working in such a laborious way, it did seem reasonable to assume it was a dream. At the very least, it proved he was still alive.

'Stop the head rolling, I have to be up first thing, you're a mean dickhead, you know that?' he heard Yvonne say.

So he stopped the head rolling and moaned instead, which still affirmed his existence. But then he remembered the man who butchered Jessica. He tried to see him, but he had become a black blur, and he realised he was still rolling his head and had probably never stopped.

'Stop it!' Yvonne's voice again.

'Okay, sorry, it's been a long day. I saw something last night.'

'What?'

'Something I shouldn't tell you about.'

'Sounds familiar.'

'Yvonne, I feel heavy, heavy enough to sink into the ground.'

'For pity's sake! Are you not listening to me? I'm trying to sleep.'

'I think I'm seasick. If I lie in your lap can you stroke my hair while the boat is going nuts? I like it when you push the hair out of my eyes and tell me it's going to be alright.'

'It's going to be alright my darling.'

Preston took a quick dose of reality. *Quick, sharp and clear.* Yvonne had gone. Left him. He couldn't quite remember why.

'Because you care more about all the others than you do me,' she told him.

'That's not true.'

'Yes, it is.'

'I can't feel my arms!'

He wondered why. Unless, no ... it couldn't be? Something to do with the man who had put his hands in Jessica's chest. *Cracking, toiling, removing*. Jessica was so beautiful; he had loved her.

'I loved you too Yvonne.'

'I know.'

'I think this man has cut off my arms.'

'No, my darling, they're still there.'

'Good.'

'My legs?'

'Still there.'

'But I can't feel them.'

'Sometimes we just stop feeling.'

'I saw something beautiful today bobbing up and down in a plastic bag. How nice it looked! How interesting was this little yellow creature with its dark brown rings. Oh and I got to touch it! Or did it touch me? I can't remember but I liked the way its rings suddenly glowed blue like a peacock.'

'Like a peacock?'

'Yes.'

'And now how do you feel my dear?'

'It's hard to breathe and things are getting more confusing.'

'As confusing as that pathetic need to take photographs?'

'Yvonne ...'

'Confusing like those fantasies that destroyed our life together?'

'Not now, please. Not now.'

His mouth was dry and he couldn't swallow any more.

It must be hot. Maybe, he was back in the Caribbean? Hopefully, he had flown there. He didn't handle boats too well. Sunshine was nice. The sunshine, Yvonne, his daughter, in no particular order. Salisbury was cold this time of year and life was good when they were all away together.

'It's really hard to breathe now ... *Jesus, who are you?*'

The man in black leaned close, his breath smelled rotten, and he chanted in an unfamiliar language and held a picture of a cartoon man, wearing many different colours and dancing, holding a bow in one hand and a basket in the other.

'I feel strange, like I'm locked in or something.'

'Just relax.'

'It feels like I'm drowning.'

'It will be over soon.'

'What are you putting me in? I know you're doing it. Why can't I *feel* anything?'

'Just relax.'

'It's dark now, ah Jesus, Yvonne, please talk to me some more, I'm sorry for everything, I'm afraid now, I don't want to die, I don't want to be in darkness forever.'

WHILE GREG BROOKES waited for his grandson to pack, he took a seat beside Riley. Bryan Kelly had retired to Brookes' room for some much needed rest after being awake most of the night.

'So, one old man to another,' Riley said, 'why did you leave Wiltshire for the North?'

Greg sighed. 'I worked my entire life in this area. Police, same as my son. After a while you need a change.'

Riley took a sip of his tea. 'I take it you saw some stuff you don't need reminding of?'

'Saw some stuff, heard some stuff, knew about stuff. You remember the Rays?'

'Everybody remembers the Rays. Pig-farmers. It began with Reginald Ray at the end of the nineteenth century. Killed six local kids.'

'Yes, my own grandfather had the pleasure of investigating that one. There was no need to catch him though – neighbours hung him from a tree.'

'Deserved it from what I heard. He used to eat the children by boiling their bones and liquefying their flesh because he had no teeth left to chew with.'

Greg took off his Trilby and held it in his lap. 'Didn't get too much better. Years later, my own father, bless him, had to investigate the murder of Beatrix Ray by her brother. Point is they've always been a bad lot. I spent years of my own career dealing with the madness of Thomas Ray until I retired and then my son had to pick up the pieces when he did what he did to that poor young lady.'

'I know the story, everybody knows the story. But it's over now.'

'Well, you asked why I left, and that's why I left. There's only so long you can put up with the disease in this place. After Fran died, I couldn't stand to be here any longer. And sure enough, look what's happening again. Jessica? The place is bad. Rotten.'

'Well, I kind of like it, but I do take your point,' Riley said.

Greg laughed. 'Good.'

'There are things you miss though?'

'Beer … they just can't get it right up there. So, one old man to another, how did you get the limp?'

'Well, I take it you know my history?'

'Of course, I wouldn't be letting you sit in the motorhome with my family if I didn't. If my son trusts you, I trust you, so don't think you have to waste your time justifying anything to me.'

'Well, the story is not as entertaining as yours, so I'll keep it brief,' Riley said, leaning forward and rolling up one leg of his jeans. His calf was crisscrossed with white and pink welts.

'Shit,' Greg said.

'You should see the other guy!' Riley smiled.

'Really?'

'Nah,' Riley said. 'It was the first day in prison and a couple of lifers gave me a grand welcoming in the canteen. They gave this young newbie a blade and pointed me out – kind of an initiation ceremony for him. I still feel sorry for him.'

'*Why?*' Greg said. 'Look what he did to you?'

'He wasn't doing it to me. He had a lot of anger in his eyes – I watched it as he cut me up. But he wasn't angry towards me. Why would he be? He didn't even know me. He was just so bloated with hate. Angry at himself, mainly, for doing what he was doing. The lifers knew that. They were playing with him and never let him in to their group afterwards. So, he may have ruined my leg, but he ruined himself completely. Six months later, he killed himself in solitary confinement. Poor kid.'

'You're very forgiving,' Greg said.

Riley smiled, rolling the leg of his jeans back down. 'No. Just philosophical. That kid wasn't bad. He was just fighting – the wrong way. Same as me with what I did. I just fought the wrong way.'

Greg put his hat back on and reached over for his cup of tea.

'That's what I don't get about Jessica,' Riley said. 'I see no logic in it. I know why I did what I did, I kind of know why that kid did this to me, but how could anyone kill an innocent mother in her own home?'

Greg nodded. 'Thought this many a time over the years about the Rays and the stuff they did.'

'Maybe this is what evil is,' Riley said.

'Jesus, you are getting philosophical.'

'Look after Ewan,' Riley said. 'He's a good boy.'

'I know, he's my grandson.'

'Yes, but just really look after him, you've got something special there.'

'And do you have anyone Riley—'

'Grandad, I'm ready,' Ewan said.

Greg and Riley both stood up and turned to face Ewan who was now wearing his backpack. Ewan stepped forward and hugged Riley.

'Please look after Dad,' Ewan said.

'You have my word.'

As they drove away from the caravan park, Brookes senior looked out over the trees. He couldn't help but think of Reginald Ray, the child killer.

He remembered Riley's words: *it's over now.*

Sorry Riley, but it feels anything but over.

A WHITE FORD Transit van came out of nowhere and Yorke swerved. After steadying his Lexus, he beat his horn while the ancient box-on-wheels grew smaller in his rear-view mirror. He fought back the urge to chase the bastard and instead phoned Jake.

'Yes?'

'A white Ford Transit van just almost ran me off the road.'

'*Shit* ...'

'Jake?'

Yorke could hear the screeching of wheels and more of Jake's obscenities down the phone. '*Jake?*'

'I'm here. Shit ... a white Ford Transit van you say? Yes, just seen it.'

'Bollocks! I was going to ask you to clock its reg, catch up with the nutjob later. I can't believe how close you are!'

'I told you I was improving behind the wheel, sir. Do you want me to give chase?'

'No, I want you with me. I'll call it in.'

He hung up and called in the van. Some local officers would try to flag it down.

He drove through the three stone circles that surrounded the village of Avebury. He'd visited this Neolithic henge monument three weeks earlier with Patricia. While not as famous as Stonehenge, Avebury Henge could claim the credit for being the largest stone circle in the world. Patricia and Yorke had spent the day listening to a guide talking about both its history, and its religious importance to contemporary pagans. They'd followed it up with a night in a local bed and breakfast that was probably even more memorable.

His eyes widened when, ahead, to his left, he saw a dense patch of smoke hovering above the centre of town. He followed his Sat Nav to the postcode Jake had texted him, realising that he was getting ever closer to the black cloud. As he turned onto the street with the Preston holiday home, he was forced to acknowledge that the source of the smoke was definitely here and was probably unlikely to be a coincidence.

A small crowd was already gathering around a picket fence where the charcoal black plumes were billowing into the air. A quick glance at the Sat Nav identified the fact that it was indeed the Preston holiday home.

He punched the brake, jumped from the car and plunged into the mass of residents. He was immediately assaulted by a smell like roasted pork.

'Police, let me through.' The crowd obliged and started to fan away so Yorke could get through to the fence to see.

A large, flaming wicker basket sat in the centre of the garden with the air shimmering around it. Yorke gulped. A burst of wind caused the side of the box to glow red like a fiery eye.

He vaulted the fence as he heard Jake calling from behind him. 'Sir?'

At first, Yorke moved slowly, uncertain of what was inside or even behind the box. He looked over at the cottage door which was banging open and closed in the wind.

'Bloody hell, wait!' Jake came alongside him, out of breath. 'Can you not smell it?'

'Yes.' Yorke gestured towards the open back door. 'We need water, quick.'

'Someone could be in there though.'

'Remember that white Ford Transit van?'

'Shit, do you think it was Preston?'

'No,' Yorke said, 'I don't. But I hope I'm wrong.'

Jake turned to the gathering crowd. 'Police, we need water.'

'Here,' a woman said, holding a small fire extinguisher in the air at the fence.

Jake moved for it, but the fiery eye would wait no longer. The side of the box split like a bloated cocoon and its twisted stillborn spilt out onto the grass. A gasp rose from the gathering crowd.

Jake sprayed the box with the fire extinguisher before Yorke stepped forward, shielding his eyes from the smoke rising from the charred remains. Having been folded inside the box, the unfortunate victim had assumed the position of a foetus. Their lips had melted away, exposing clenched teeth; fluid dribbled from burst eyes and glistened on the cheeks.

Jake joined him, holding his hand to his mouth. '*Fuck.*'

'My God, is this Robert Preston?' Yorke said, holding his hand over his mouth.

Parts of the body still glowed, and small flames still danced on the jeans that had melted to their legs.

It only took two minutes to check the small cottage; as predicted, it was empty. Back outside, his phone started ringing. He answered it with his eyes on the half-cremated remains, 'Iain?'

'Unbelievable, sir, I was back two minutes and I got the phone call.'

'Phone call?'

'Jessica's mum, Karen – she died.'

'I'm sorry.'

'I'm not, you saw the state she was in.'

'Look – I can't talk right now, Iain. Give me twenty minutes.'

'Did you find him? Preston?'

Yorke looked at the body. 'I don't know ... not really. Twenty minutes, I promise Iain.'

'Okay.'

He walked forward and climbed the fence, noticing the woman who had given Jake the extinguisher vomiting.

He looked up at the black cloud that hung like a tar-filled balloon over the crowd. Over in the distance, he could see the B&B where, only weeks before, he'd been making love with Patricia.

4

LACEY RAY STARED down at the body of the young girl and chewed her bottom lip. The fact that her head had been caved in with a jade ashtray didn't bother her too much, but the fact that she was dead, did bother her. It bothered her very much.

'Billy, Billy, Billy ...' she said. 'What have you done, Billy?'

But Billy Shine was not there to answer. He was long gone. Lacey chewed her bottom lip again and tasted blood.

You can run, Billy, but you can't hide.

———

LACEY LOOKED out of the bedroom window at Brighton pier, burning under 67,000 bulbs. A cascade of light and a mix of colours and emotion; all of it blended together in one tiny space. Her eyes rose to the moon. The crowning light, ruling all. She smiled and turned back to look at the body.

How many times did you hit her, Billy?

She could barely recognise the girl she had spent the

last three months with. Seventeen-year-old Loretta Marks. A girl from a bad family – just like her. A sensitive girl who cared too much – unlike her. A stupid girl who cracked a joke about Billy's impotence and lost her young life.

Lacey walked over to the bed and took her small hand.

'Why did you not listen to me? Keep quiet?'

I had a plan. You didn't know what that plan was, granted, but you seemed to trust me. But now, sensitive and stupid Loretta Marks from a bad family, you're gone.

The bedroom door opened, and Claire Murray walked into the room. Claire's hand flew to her mouth.

'Don't scream,' Lacey said, 'not if you want to be gone before the police get here.'

Claire started to cry. 'Is she ...?'

'Yes. Billy went too far as we knew he would.'

Lacey came around the bed to put her arm around Claire.

'You said you were going to stop him.' Claire said, letting her head settle on Lacey's shoulder.

'I will.'

'But it's too late.'

'Better late than never.'

WITH CLAIRE SITTING beside Loretta's body sobbing, Lacey wandered around the room, examining Billy's belongings: necklaces, earrings and other jewellery made of shell, turquoise, jade and gold.

You are a funny bunny, Billy.

She opened a drawer and pulled out a feathered head-dress and a reddish mask.

The funniest.

She held it up for Claire to see.

'I remember when we first got here, and he was wearing it,' Claire said. 'I thought it was funny then, but not later. Not when ... you know ... we were doing it while he was wearing it.'

'Tell you what Claire, if it makes you feel any better, I'll make the freak wear it while I kill him.'

———

LACEY SENT Claire to pack her belongings and was clear in her instructions that she should clean all traces of herself from the place. Claire could start again. It would be more difficult for Lacey; the police had her DNA and fingerprints on record. Yes, Claire could run easily. Lacey couldn't.

But when have I ever opted for easy?

She sat on the bed beside Loretta's body and phoned Simon Young.

Instead of *hello*, Simon answered with: 'Is this a burner?'

'Of course. It's Sarah May. One of the three girls you have working for Billy Shine.'

'I know who you are.'

Of course he knows who I am, thought Lacey, *this is one of the biggest contracts this pimp has ever had. One whole year, paid in four instalments. Time for some bad news, Simon.*

'I'm resigning.'

He snorted. 'You can't fucking resign.'

She snorted back. 'Funny that, because I just did.'

'Who the fuck do you think you're talking to, Sarah?'

'That's not my name. Never was. You are not entitled to my real name, Simon. In fact, you are not entitled to much.'

'Do you not realise how well you've been paid?'

She looked down at her expensive watch and shoes. 'The job's over now, Simon. Billy has gone, and he's left you a little treat.'

'What's happened?'

'Let's just say, you won't have to worry about Loretta resigning. Although, you may want to think about funeral costs.'

'I don't get it ...'

'Let the police worry about—'

'Wait, hang on, no police.'

'Too late,' she reached down to stroke Loretta's face. 'This pretty young girl is not ending up in a vat of your acid, Simon, she's going home. Her grandmother was good to her. The only person who was ever good to her. Her grandmother will see her again.'

'For fuck's sake, you do as you're damn well told!'

'I understand you're emotional. Nine more months of Billy's money would have been a big pay day, add that to the fact Loretta could be traced back to you. I get it. But, if you shout at me again, Simon, I may be forced to change my agenda.'

'Your agenda?'

'Yes, there's only one person on it at the moment.' She stroked Loretta's face again. 'And if you want to keep it that way, I'd appreciate a *thank you for your service, Sarah, good luck with all future endeavours.*'

'You're fucking deluded.'

'It's been said before, but I never really believed it. In fact, why waste my time? I could just leave this burner by her body ...'

'What?'

'*Thank ... you ... for ... your ... service ... Sarah,*' Lacey said, emphasising each word.

There was a long pause.

'Three seconds,' Lacey said. 'One ... two—'

He interrupted with the words she requested.

'Good boy, I doubt very much that our paths will cross again. So, just remember, to always treat your employees how you would like to be treated yourself.'

'The burner?'

'I'll think about it.' She hung up.

LACEY LOOKED AT THE TIME. Not that she needed to. *There was always time for the Blue Room.*

She assumed the lotus position beside Loretta's body and, with some rhythmic breathing, took herself there.

She'd truly mastered the descent over the years and the depth to which she ventured today astounded her even more. Even though it froze everything around her, it wasn't cold in the traditional sense; and even though it was hollow there, it certainly wasn't empty.

It was the essence of everything she was.

Loretta was gone, replaced with the sleeping Billy Shine, wearing his headdress, his mask and a cape, and nothing else.

In her hand she held a surgical scalpel. She stroked it down over his bare chest and then, his torso. He stirred but didn't wake. She caressed his genitals with the tip of the blade and smiled.

His eyes opened.

The scalpel sliced through Billy's femoral artery so

easily and so quickly that there was no trace of blood on it for Lacey to clean off.

He sat up and threw his arm out at Lacey who darted backwards, evading him. He then looked down at the blood gushing from his thigh and pooling around him.

'It'll be quick,' Lacey said, 'but there should be just enough time to consider what you did to Loretta.'

Billy reached down and plunged a hand into the rising puddle. 'No...'

'Lie back, Billy, now relax.'

He looked up at her. She was unable to watch him grow paler, because the blue masked that, but she could see his facial muscles beginning to sag.

He was also struggling to talk now. He lay back on the pillow and his breathing started to grow shallower.

'You don't have forever, Billy. Nobody does. Except in this place. My place. But you are a mere visitor and it's time to go—'

She was pulled from the Blue Room sharply.

Too sharply.

She opened her eyes to full colour, and to the fact that she was straddling Claire with her hands around her throat. Claire's face was greying, her tongue was poking out and her eyes were fading. Lacey snapped back her hands. *Too late?*

Claire took a huge gulp of air.

This was the first time that Lacey had ever been pulled so dramatically from the Blue Room, and she made a mental note to ensure that she never let it happen again.

LACEY FOUND Billy's mother's address in his bedside drawer. That's where he kept his letters from her; all of them came complete with the sender's address on the back of the envelopes. Lacey didn't bother reading the letters. Why? An irrelevance. Billy was not long for this world.

What was most interesting was where she lived.

Tidworth in Wiltshire. Not far from Salisbury.

Lacey was going home.

———

AVEBURY WAS HAVING a day off from being a major tourist attraction and, instead, was now a major crime scene. The spectators had been cleared, and a blue-and-white taped line ran around the picket fence and the entrance to the cottage. Instead of PC Sean Tyler, who was working closely with the local station to try and determine the whereabouts of the fleeing white Ford Transit, DC Collette Willows was diligently logging names.

The thick smoke from the charred corpse continued to hang heavy in the air, and some light had been set up to illuminate the remains. Yorke watched Patricia handle the body, while feeling incredibly guilty for feeling uncomfortable around her earlier in the incident room. She may not show that she cared – but she did. Deeply. She separated the science from the emotion. It was her job. And he'd been wrong to feel resentment over it.

Gardner stood alongside him. 'What's going on?'

'We are dealing with someone very bad,' Yorke said.

'I didn't sleep last night, just lay in bed with Annabelle until briefing.'

'How is she?'

'Fine, could do with a visit from her godfather more regularly.'

'Invite accepted.' He paused. 'Keep her close, Emma. And keep it separate. Don't, *ever*, take this home with you.'

'Easier said than done.'

Topham approached from the hulking black major incident van. 'Used to love it here as a kid.'

Yorke almost told him that he'd only been here on holiday a few weeks ago, but held back. It wasn't relevant right now.

'Have you spoken to Dr Wileman yet, boss?' Topham said.

'She's waiting for dental records to be pinged over. It's Preston though. No question. His stuff is all over the house, including his photographs. I don't know what he was doing at Jessica's, but he *saw* the killer. *Whoever* that was must have realised, found him and then did this.'

Jake came over. 'A right mess this bastard's made of him.'

'If you need some time, Jake, I'd understand.'

'No, I'm fine. It's disgusting, no question, but I don't feel like I did earlier.'

Probably because it doesn't remind you of your own wife, in the same way that Jessica did earlier, thought Yorke, but he didn't bring it up.

Lance Reynolds emerged from the house and wandered over to the cluster of detectives; his camera was bumping against his chest.

'There was a struggle in the living room. A trail of photographs, marks on the carpet, the pattern in the frost on the grass out here suggests the victim was dragged before being placed in the basket.'

'Any traces of blood in the house?' Yorke asked.

'None. He was dragged out here and executed.'

'Footprints?'

'We're trying, but the ground is rock solid this time of year. We've gathered fingerprints and fibres, and we'll get onto it asap; let's hope we have more luck than we did at the last scene.'

Yorke turned to Jake. 'Take a team of officers, DS Pettman, and grill everyone. There were enough spectators about and residents are knitted far closer together than they were at Jessica's – I'm confident you'll get something.'

Andrew Waites, the exhibits officer, came over holding up a plastic bag with a photograph inside it. 'Thought you might be interested in this.'

Yorke looked at what actually turned out to be a colourful drawing of a cartoon man, rather than a photograph. It looked like a cave painting or something you might see stitched into tapestry. A dancing man dressed in many colours. Yorke squinted. In one hand, the man held a bow; and in the other hand, a basket.

'It was mixed in with the photographs strewn all over the house,' Waites said.

'Preston's?' Gardner said.

Yorke stared for a moment. He revisited the nature of Jessica's death. 'No,' he finally said. 'He's made his first mistake.'

'He dropped it?' Topham said.

'Yes. We need an expert. We need to know what this picture is all about.'

Blood and chopped flesh had never really bothered Tezcacoatl; after all, it was only nourishment for the earth.

The screaming, on the other hand, was taking a lot more getting used to.

Consequently, a minute or two of escapism following last night's, and now today's screaming was welcome; and time spent with Matlalihuitl, his precious blue-green feather, was the most welcome escapism of all.

Behind him, the large fire began to dance higher in its stone-lined hearth, as if to flaunt its honoured position dead centre in the house. The fire had many purposes; it warmed Tezcacoatl, lit the hallway now it was dark, cooked his dinner and provided him with a visual trick - the reflection of the flames on the glass fish tank made the interior look like a city on fire rather than the intended ocean bed.

In the tank, Matlalihuitl had curled its eight arms over a large rock while its bulbous head was slumped back on a smaller rock; an easy position to recline into without the burden of a skeleton. Although it was difficult to tell in the flickering amber glow given to the tank by the flame, his beloved octopus was yellow with dark brown rings. In camouflage mode.

An observer could be forgiven for thinking the motionless sea-creature was dead, burning as the flames licked at its boneless body. Only in its stubbornness to be turned to dust, would the observer eventually realise that they had been deceived and that the creature was actually sleeping.

Tezcacoatl tapped the glass and his creature stirred.

He had not felt excitement in a long time, but Matlalihuitl's coming display of power, the fierceness and the efficiency with which it would strike, interested him.

He opened his right hand and looked down at a plastic tube. Within the tube, sat a clump of brown hair, Preston's will and determination, taken away at precisely at the right moment to make what needed to be done all the easier.

In his other hand, he felt the crabs struggling in the leather bag. There were more than usual; Matlalihuitl had done well these past days and deserved its reward.

It uncurled its suction-cup covered arms one at a time; each stretch intensifying the yellow colour of its skin. With its rubbery head bouncing off the sandy bottom, it scurried forward, raising clouds of sand behind it before swooping upwards.

Tezcacoatl lifted a small panel on top of the tank and shook out the crabs, noticing his hands were paler than usual. As the amber offering sank to the floor, Tezcacoatl watched the reflected flames dance and his thoughts turned to *Teyolia,* the divine fire. The very force within the heart that animates, shapes, and invigorates. Three separate hearts beat within his beloved octopus. Two serving the gills, and the other its beautiful body. *Three hearts, my precious blue-green feather,* he thought, *how you shine!*

The brown rings covering Matlalihuitl exploded into a brilliant blue. It darted forward, and the crabs scattered, but the octopus had already pulled its eight spidery arms forward into a claw to snatch up its first victim. A sand storm rose as crabs fled everywhere but to freedom and Matlalihuitl enveloped its prey. Each spasm and flash of its oily body was a sign that its beak was delving deeper.

Tezcacoatl smelled burning. He leaned over, pulled on the oven glove by his feet and swung to pull the grill from the hearth. Immediately, he felt the heat through the glove, so he dropped it quickly onto the heat-proof tray beside the hearth.

He looked at the blackened meat. His attention

elsewhere, he had not realized that the flames had lifted far too high and burnt Jessica's flesh.

THE COUPLE'S argument next door penetrated the paper-thin walls. It was distracting to say the least. Reminded of Jessica's and Preston's screaming, Tezcacoatl pushed his half-full plate away.

While chewing on the chunk of burnt meat still in his mouth, and trying to ignore the shouting and cursing, he examined his pallid hand. Alabaster skin wasn't surprising after twenty-four hours of fasting; he should have taken more of his supplements. He swallowed, knowing that the iron in the meat would go to work on his pale skin soon.

The argument next door continued. Over the last few weeks, the relationship had been worsening. They'd regularly argued but had always made up and enjoyed each other's company again. Tezcacoatl had heard some of those more intimate moments too. To hear both sides was a good thing. Pleasure and pain were inextricably linked, and Tezcacoatl had the right to experience both. Recently though, the arguments had taken over and raged, sometimes for hours, sometimes days.

He leaned back in the *Ipcalli*, resting his tired head on the high back, and admired his kitchen. There was so much colour. Dark colours. Blue walls, black surfaces, purple kitchen utensils and red plates. He felt at ease; whiteness sometimes made him feel empty.

On his black dinner table, beside a red plate topped with blackened flesh, sat a portable television. The screen showed tragedy. Blown-up bellies and washed-out faces. Starving African children melting away to nothing.

Increasing the volume, seemed to intensify the stench of decay and the crushing heat, rather than just the sound of desperation. A reporter described the great drought that had plagued this village, before the image changed to show the rains pouring on the village. Tezcacoatl leaned forward in his Ipcalli. Against all predictions, rain had come. Villagers, who had the energy, stood admiring the rainfalls. A few even danced.

After turning the television off, he noticed that the argument had stopped.

He slid the picture of a young woman, which sat by his plate, closer to him. Gillian Arnold had been at the cemetery visiting her father's grave when he took this photo. With his finger he traced the sadness that creased the corners of her eyes.

As THEY JOURNEYED up the M1 to Leeds, Ewan stared out of the window at the traffic in the other lane, wondering if any of these people had experienced the senselessness he was currently experiencing. And, if they had done, how had they coped with the sudden hollowness inside? Had they run away, as he was currently doing, or had they stood tall?

'I wish you'd put Freddy away,' his grandad said, 'just while I'm driving, you know?'

Ewan stroked its back. 'Why? He won't do anything.'

'Still ... a snake, a motorway? Not a great combination.'

Ewan sighed and slipped the snake into the backpack. 'See you for dinner, Freds.'

'Anyway, how you holding up buddy? Still in the mood for that ice cream?'

'Not really,' Ewan said. 'Do you think they'll catch whoever did this to Mum?'

'Of course. But you don't need to worry about that. Not right now.'

'Well, what am I supposed to worry about?'

His grandad paused for an answer. 'Well ... you need to be thinking about how you are going to keep an old man company for the next couple of days.'

'Have you got an Xbox?'

'Can't help you there?'

'We could go running?'

'You know my arthritis is bad.'

'We're going to struggle then!'

'You haven't seen my DVD collection in over a year, Ewan. We'll be fine.'

His grandad's phone started ringing and he answered with a button on the dash. His dad's voice came over the speaker. 'Everything good?'

'Fine,' his grandad said.

'Great,' Ewan said.

'Shit ... how to say this?'

'Say what?' Ewan said. 'And don't swear.'

'I'm sorry, Ewan, to give you more news like this, but your grandmother died this morning.'

His grandad indicated to come off at the next junction.

'I'm sorry, Ewan ... for everything.'

'It's not your fault.' But Ewan knew that his dad wouldn't believe this. 'Maybe, I should just come back?'

'I'm sorry about that too Ewan, but you need to trust me. As soon as you get to Grandad's, call me. I've got to head into the nursing home.'

'Love you, Dad.'

'You too, Ewan. And you, Dad.'

'Love you, son.'

Ewan looked out of the window at the passing cars again.

Running away, he thought.

That's all this is.

AFTER SOME WORK on the internet, they'd identified the peculiar colourful picture from the crime scene as being an image of an Aztec deity. So, opposite Yorke, Topham and Gardner, sat Gary Utter, a graduate in Mesoamerican studies. Despite a studious appearance with a perfect side parting, expensive glasses and a buttoned shirt, he brought an edge to his look with an ear lined completely with piercings. Yorke worried that Topham, ever the enemy of subtlety, would come straight out and ask how it was possible to squeeze so many rings in so small a space.

'I apologise that we cannot be any more detailed than that,' Yorke continued. 'We believe that the person we're looking for accidently dropped this picture, and we really need to know what it is.'

He pushed the picture found at Preston's parent's holiday cottage across the table and then flipped open his notebook to start taking notes.

It didn't take Utter long. 'That is an image of Tezcatlipoca, the Lord of the Smoking Mirror.'

Yorke looked at Topham, predicting, and guessing correctly, that his eyebrows would be raised.

Utter continued, 'He is an Aztec deity. One of the most important in fact; He is the god of fate.'

'Okay, so what does it mean to you that the person we're looking for had this particular picture?' Yorke said.

Utter looked confused. 'It doesn't really mean anything. I've seen the image thousands of times, as will many of the other students on the same course. He's a popular Aztec deity.'

'Okay,' Yorke said, 'Tell me more about Him.'

'He has a jaguar for a companion spirit. He is also associated with leadership and often features in coronation speeches and prayers. Does that help?'

Not a great deal, thought Yorke.

'Do people still worship this deity?' Topham said.

'Yes – and other gods too, of course.'

'Do you?' Topham said.

Utter looked taken aback by the question. 'Is that relevant right now? I thought you were asking for my help?'

'Of course,' Yorke said, glaring at Topham. 'Ignore that question. Being in England, far from Mexico, we are all a bit rusty on Aztec history. As you can see? Maybe you can fill us in on some more of the background.'

Utter nodded and continued.

5

T EZCACOATL'S EYES FLICKED open when the
first ray of light touched his bedroom window. He sat
upright on the mat, turned his head and looked at the
rising sun.

He never missed it.

Not only did it reassure Tezcacoatl that the gods were
still happy, but it also reminded him of his mother, who
used to hold him close on a bench outside, with a blanket
wrapped around him to fend off the cold. He remembered
tracing the scars and bruises on her face with his finger as
she told him that this first light signalled a new day, and a
new day was indicative of hope.

He lay back down on his mat, and for the next hour,
vowed to keep working to keep hope alive.

Then, naked, Tezcacoatl rose from the mat.
Goosebumps covered his body. He walked through to his
adjacent room for morning-prayer, reaching out to adjust
the metre-long wooden sword on the wall. He touched one
of the eight cold obsidian blades glued into the grooves
along the edges. He gazed at the thong protruding from the

bottom; here, the warrior would secure his hand. The Spanish had been in awe of the *Maquahuitl* which could take a horse's head from its body with one stroke.

He couldn't see, so he flicked on the lights and a red glow settled over the room. The windows were covered with black shrouds which afforded him immediate separation from the outside world. It took him a few minutes to build a small wooden fire in the stone basin by his altar and once he had stirred up a natural light, he switched the artificial one off. He ensured the grille was in place over the basin to stop any stray sparks setting fire to the tapestries he had pinned up on the walls. Then, he heated the charcoal tablet to burn the incense.

His eyes were drawn to a large picture of the island city of Tenochtitlan, the capital of the Aztec Empire, on the wall. Rich in colour and detail, Tezcacoatl was not in the least surprised that the Spanish conquistadors had been stunned when they arrived in 1519. Not in a million years had they ever expected to find such an exercise in architecture on such a bleak side of the world. It was so often compared to Venice, but Tezcacoatl felt that did not give enough credit to this grand expression of Aztec beliefs.

The artist provided a bird's eye view of Tenochtitlan. Long causeways ran from the Great Pyramid in the centre and connected the city to the mainland; it resembled a giant cross that divided the city into symmetrical quarters. Tezcacoatl traced the southern causeway with his finger. It was the route by which the Spanish first entered Tenochtitlan. He then traced the western causeway; here, four of the eight bridges had been missing, so the Spanish had used a portable bridge to escape the Aztecs after a fierce battle. Thousands of warriors had come alongside them in canoes and slaughtered them with arrows, darts and stones.

It was a site of great carnage, but the Aztecs had allowed them to escape. *A mistake*. When the Spanish returned, the Aztec Empire had fallen.

Tezcacoatl ran his eyes over the crisscrossing canals that allowed the people to travel around by boat and gave the warriors access to Lake Tetzcoco to fight nearby enemies. His attention lingered on the carefully drawn houses; the small, rectangular houses with adobe walls and thatched roofs for the *macehualtin*, the lower classes, and the raised, colorful homes of the *pipiltin*, the upper classes - which often consisted of several buildings surrounding a courtyard.

He reached out to touch the sacred precinct at the heart of the city, where the mountainous dual pyramid, the Great Temple, stood tall. Two shrines gleamed in the sunlight; to the south, Huitzilopochtli's red-painted shrine; and to the north, Tlaloc's blue-painted shrine.

Underneath the picture was a poem from *Cantares Mexicanos,* a 16th century collection of Nahuatl poems. Tezcacoatl read the poem out loud.

> Keep this in mind, oh princes,
> do not forget it.
> Who could possibly conquer Tenochtitlan?
> Who could possibly shake the foundations
>   of heaven?

He turned to his altar and approached the statue of Lord Tezcatlipoca, the deity he served above all others, he spoke His many titles in Nahuatl, 'Ruler of the North ... the Realm of Darkness ... Lord of the Smoking Mirror ...'

The statue was carved from obsidian and showed Lord Tezcatlipoca in profile. He had two spears readied in one hand and a spear-thrower in the other. A head dress of raised eagle feathers connected Him to the sun and showed He was primed for hunting and war. 'Lord of the Near and Night ...'

The smell of Copal was strong enough for him to begin. He sucked in a deep breath through his nostrils. From a tepetlacalli on the altar – a stone box depicting a fire serpent - he took hold of a maguey thorn. He held the end of his penis and speared the point of the thorn through an old scab on his foreskin, and with the tips of his fingers he forced out some droplets of blood into a jade bowel.

MORNING BRIEFING. The atmosphere in the room was so thick that it felt as if you were moving through tar. Door-to-door around Preston's parents' cottage had thrown up nothing. Yes, the white van was seen, and there were even a couple of flashes of it on CCTV around various locales as it had journeyed away (almost ending Jake and Yorke's existences in the process). However, the bastard had left the REG plates to fester in the winter mizzle, and identifying it was proving impossible. Granted, Preston's body had been identified from dental records, but DNA of the killer and evidence of him ever being there – assuming it was a *he* – were practically non-existent. Just that one picture. The picture of an Aztec deity called Tezcatlipoca.

At least the whiteboard covering the entire right side of the room was developing at an incredible rate – it helped mask how slow 'Operation Restore' was really progressing. Gardener had done a fantastic job, but when the bodies were piling up faster than clues, you knew you were in trouble. Permanent ink had been used to scar the board with information because this room got busy and shoulders could easily take out an important fact.

Gardner had placed a picture of Jessica, looking young and happy, at the top. It gave everyone a focal point when they got sick to the stomach of looking at the photo of her remains just beneath it. Around her were names and pictures of friends, family members, work colleagues; all accompanied with little titbits of information. Nothing negative. Jessica had been a kind, humorous and popular individual and leads down that path were running dry.

And Preston? Well, responses to his existence had been anything but positive. His own family didn't even like him. The wealth of names spreading out from the photo of his corpse, were taking up far too much police time. Numerous women were aware of his predatory nature and that he 'snapped' them when he thought they were 'unawares.' There were definitely many people with motive.

To make matters worse, Yorke was not fit to work. Several bottles of *Summer Lightning*, hours of Google research, and a brief, fitful sleep dreaming of Aztec sacrifice on a grand scale were not the recipe for a productive day. He was also conscious of the strangeness of his next task – to brief the team on Mesoamerican beliefs. He looked down at his notes.

But why not? They had very little else to go on.

He began by handing out a photocopy of the picture of Tezcatlipoca left by the killer and then taking them through his discussion with Utter yesterday. He kept this brief. Utter had been thorough with them, discussing the history of the great Aztec city of Tenochtitlan and how it had evolved into the place now known as Mexico City. To win his audience, Yorke knew, he would have to link everything he said to concrete facts in the case.

'So, Aztecs sacrificed humans, we all know that,' Yorke said. 'I'm not concluding that Jessica was sacrificed, but there are some striking similarities with the methods that have been used.'

He threw out another image that he had found online the evening before. He didn't look at it again. He didn't really need to because he'd been dreaming about it all night.

'This kind of sacrifice is called *Tlacamictilztli*. Excuse the mispronunciation. I've written it beneath the image too.'

In this image, a small man was face up on a stone, while a tall and goggle-eyed man, almost twice his size, split his chest open with a knife that was almost the same size as the doomed man's leg. Blood gushed like a geyser from the opening. The priest, depicted as a kind of cartoon character, had no emotion on his face, his teeth were bared, and he had a quiff that looked like three raised snakes.

Yorke noticed everyone exchanging glances. Even Jake and Gardner, which was disappointing. He continued regardless. '*Tlacamictilztli* means heart extraction. This is what happened to Jessica, albeit by more modern methods, and is the first link I want to make.'

DC Collette Willow's hand went up and Yorke nodded.

'I obviously know about human sacrifice, but not really why they did it?'

Yorke was grateful for the curiosity, even if it was laced with scepticism.

'Well, the Aztecs believed that the gods had sacrificed themselves in order that they could live, and that they need to continue to sacrifice in order to honour them.'

He waited for Willows to nod in understanding before continuing, 'The other link I want to highlight is the missing flesh from Jessica's thighs. After sacrificing, Aztec nobles would consume flesh from the sacrifices.'

Before the looks could begin again, Yorke jumped to his feet and strode over to the board to put his finger on the photograph of Jessica's body.

'So, we have a picture, possibly left by the killer, of an Aztec deity. We have a murder than resembles a traditional Aztec sacrifice *and* we have the possibility of cannibalism - another Aztec ritual. It is an angle we will pursue. I am bringing Utter in again, later today, to assist with the investigation. His knowledge is limited on the investigation; however, his knowledge of the Aztecs is anything but. If I'm right, which I think I am, we can use him to profile the killer. He will, of course, be granted access to the specifics of the case but will sign a non-disclosure agreement. Assignments are typed up on the board. We will continue with existing investigations, including Preston's web of disgruntled folk; but, in addition, I have assigned some officers to investigate forums online. Many people still practise this religion, usually within the confines of the law. But, we will contact all these forums to determine if there are any indications of their clientele taking it further. I have also assigned team members to trawl through cold cases in the UK which may carry a hint of Aztec sacrifices. There were alternative methods of sacrifice, so these are clearly listed in today's briefing notes.'

He excused himself to go to the bathroom. He splashed cold water on his face and looked at his tired eyes. Eyes that had spent the night bathing in shocking images. Jessica had died in a dreadful way, no doubt about that, but when he considered the sheer number of people who had died in that same way, albeit a long time ago, he felt his blood run cold.

80,400 humans were sacrificed over a four-day period during the reconsecration of the Great Pyramid in 1487. Fourteen sacrifices a minute.

Outside, the toilet, Patricia grabbed him and pulled him into an embrace. 'Not here,' he said, but it felt so good, and he was unable to unlock himself.

'Don't worry, there's no one coming. I checked.'

Yorke kissed her and took a step back.

'I want to see you tonight,' she said.

'You can, but I won't be good for much. I've barely slept in two nights.'

'I *still* want to see you.'

'And I want to see you too.'

'Eight o'clock. Let me know if your plans change.'

'I will.' Yorke moved in for one last quick embrace.

AFTER ANOTHER COUPLE of hours talking to Utter, developing his knowledge of the Aztec empire and hoping that it would all prove relevant, he stared out of his office window. The days went quick at this time of the year, and the sky was darkening already. The grounds were frozen, but not snowy, although snow was forecast for that evening. He shivered when he thought back to the last time the snow had been fierce and he'd made that journey to a pig farm where all manner of atrocities had taken place ...

His phone rang. It was Brookes. He knew it was him before even looking at the screen.

How he longed for a run right now. An anxiety-quenching, dread-numbing, run.

'Hello, Iain.'

'You know what I'm about to ask, sir.'

'I know, Iain, because you've asked it three times already. And the answer is still the same. We've got something, you know that much, and as I said before, I can't be specific about what it is. I know it's important, but I can't give you what you want. And before you ask, there is no time scale.'

'There's always your promise.'

'And that promise still stands.'

Although I could do with some sleep first, Yorke thought.

'How's Bryan keeping?' Yorke said.

'He's okay, but you can take him away now. I don't need babysitting.'

'I know that. We're just looking after our own, that's all, Iain.'

'Well, no more *looking after* needed. You know, last night, he started telling me about how he lost his own wife to cancer.'

'Does talking not help?'

'A change of subject would be preferable.'

'And Ewan? Heard from him again?'

'He's okay. In Leeds now. Far from here. Prefer it even further if I could. Australia?'

Yorke laughed. 'It'll be over soon, and then he can come home.'

'You know what I caught that dickhead, Dr Reiner, doing yesterday when I went back to Mary Chapman to sign the forms for Dr Page?'

'No, you never said.'

'I caught him eating a fucking sandwich right by my dead mother-in-law. I lost it with him.'

'You didn't hit him?'

'No, just raised my voice. No violence. I'm still holding it together, don't worry. Some people, eh?'

'I know, Iain.'

'I'll check in later if that's okay?'

'You can check in as many times as you want, you know

that, but the answer might always be the same.'

'If you weren't working, and I didn't *want* you working, I'd probably expect you to buy me a drink.'

'Sounds good. Let's keep it on the table.'

'Thanks, sir.'

'Bye, Ian.'

He stared back out of the window and noticed the first flakes of snow. The white reminded him of ghosts.

And suddenly his head was full of them.

He turned his phone off. *Just for five minutes.*

He locked his office door, sat in his chair, and cried.

He then fell asleep with his head on the desk.

GARDNER OPENED her office drawer and pulled out an empty packet of tic tacs. She sighed and started rustling around for one that might have come loose. The phone rang.

'Hi, is that Detective Inspector Gardner?'

'Yes, who is this please?'

'Detective Inspector Jackson from Brighton. I need five minutes if that's possible.'

'Of course.'

'A case we're investigating has flagged up a connection to yourselves in Wiltshire via an old APW. In fact, I was really looking to talk with DCI Michael Yorke, but I tried a couple of times and I've just got voicemail. Your reception suggested yourself? It links to an older case you investigated called 'Operation Haystack.'

Gardner bolted upright in her chair. 'Yes, what about it?'

'A suspect you had an APW out on ... a Lacey Ray?'

'That's right.' Gardner could feel her heart beat quicken.

'Well, history seems to be repeating itself, DI Gardner, we've just put out an APW on her again.'

Gardner was now on her feet.

The door opened, and Jake stood there. She pointed at the phone and tried to maintain a calm expression; she didn't want to betray the nature of the call and panic him. At least not until she had the details. Jake held his hand up to apologise and closed the door.

'DI Gardner?'

'Sorry, I was just closing the office door. Lacey Ray disappeared a long time ago after she terrorised half the people in the area.'

'I know, we have all the files here. She's wanted for murder in Southampton and Wiltshire. She also went under the alias of Lucy Evans in Nice, France, for eighteen months and is wanted in connection with murder there too. It seems her DNA is doing the rounds, which is why we have an APW out again. Her DNA showed up at a crime scene yesterday.'

Gardner had a vile taste in her mouth; she longed for relief in the form of mint. 'What happened?'

'Are you okay, DI Gardner?'

'Yes ... I'm fine. You just took me aback. We'd almost lost hope of getting her.'

'Well, we haven't got her yet unfortunately. The body of a prostitute called Loretta Marks was found yesterday at a rented house in Brighton. She'd been bludgeoned to death, and she was only 19 years old. The murder weapon is missing too.'

That doesn't sound like Lacey, Gardner thought, *vulnerable females are not her MO.*

'The house was rented to a man called Billy Shine. Heard of him?'

'No,' Gardner said.

'Well, he comes from up near your way – Tidworth? He's 28 and has been renting the house down here for the previous three months. No occupation and he does have a record for minor misdemeanours. Not sure where he was getting his money from because rent is pretty high round here at the moment. Local residents have pointed out that they've seen three different females coming and going from the property. There's a lot of DNA and fingerprints from these three females and Billy Shine. The only match we have, apart from Billy, is Lacey Ray.'

Each time Gardner heard the name, it was like a bolt of electricity running down her spine. 'What do you think is going on?'

'We are working on the angle that Shine was trafficking these females. Something went wrong between Loretta and either Shine, a customer, or potentially Lacey. The sooner we can catch up with someone involved in this messy situation the better. As soon as Lacey Ray was flagged up, your office was all over our computer screens.'

'I bet it was.'

'I'm sure DS Jake Pettman is going to be concerned about this - that file made me cringe.' Jackson said. 'I'm the SIO on this case, so I've made the decision to send all the information over now, so you can assist us.'

'Of course.'

'If Billy Shine has run back up there, we need you to arrest him.'

'In a heartbeat,' Gardner said.

'Have you got a pen? Here's his mother's address in Tidworth.'

LACEY HAD MET many monsters in her time, but she didn't remember ever meeting one of their mothers. So, she sat and considered Hillary Shine, the mother of the monster she wanted to find, and bleed to death.

What interested Lacey the most was how far the den had come to mirror the dweller. The ceiling was yellow like Hillary's skin, and the wallpaper, drowning in damp, sagged like her eyes. Old radiators clunked in rhythm with her wheezing, while the stench of regurgitated alcohol hung over the living room with the cloud she was chain-smoking into existence.

Beside her on the old sofa, Lacey took her hand, and held it in her lap.

'When was the last time you saw Billy, before today?'

'Today?' Hillary said. 'I never said I saw him today.'

Lacey smiled and stroked her hand. 'I just went to the toilet, remember? It wasn't you that left the toilet seat up now, was it?'

Hillary cackled and exposed her teeth. Lacey wondered if a photograph of her at this moment could very well find itself onto a packet of cigarettes as a health warning. 'You're a bright cookie.'

'Thank you, Hillary. I won't pretend it hasn't been said before.'

Hillary laughed again. 'You know you remind me of myself when I was your age.'

Lacey held the smile, thinking, *please don't say that Hillary.* 'So, did Billy tell you why he'd come back so quickly?'

'Of course he did! I'm his mother – he tells me everything.'

'Did he now? Everything?'

'Everything. He was having women troubles with a young girl called Sarah!'

'Was he?' Lacey smiled again.

'Yes! And he needed a few days to get away from it all.'

'With his mother, of course,' Lacey stroked her hand again. 'So where's he gone?'

'To meet Paul, his friend, at his place.'

'Which is where?'

Hillary tugged her hand away. '*Who* are you exactly?'

'Hillary,' Lacey shook her head slowly. 'Isn't it obvious? I'm Sarah. I'm the woman that your young man is having trouble with.'

Hillary looked confused. 'And you've followed him up here?'

'Come on now, Hillary, you've heard that expression – hell hath no fury?'

Hillary smiled. 'Like a woman scorned. Used to say that to John a lot while he was still here.'

'So,' Lacey continued, 'can I get Paul's address? Surprise him?'

Hillary creased her brow. 'Surprise him? Maybe I should phone him first?'

'But that would spoil the surprise, wouldn't it?'

'Yes ... I see ... but what if he doesn't want to see you?'

'Let me show you something Hillary.' Lacey pulled a necklace out from under her blouse. A silver ring hung on the necklace. 'He gave it to me.'

Hillary took it between her crinkled hands. 'He gave this to you?'

'He did,' Lacey said, 'when he asked me to marry him.'

Hillary threw her arms around Lacey. 'That's incredible news ... why didn't he tell me? Why is it not on your finger?'

'I like to keep it here.' Lacey tapped her chest.

There were tears in Hillary's eyes.

'So, Hillary, can I get Paul's address now, so I can go and see my fiancé?'

Yorke bolted up when he heard the knock at his office door.

'Shit!' *How long had he been out?*

He looked at his phone and realised he had switched it off earlier. *Fuck!* After switching it back on, he looked at his watch. *Three hours!*

He rubbed his face, adjusted his hair and opened the door. Gardner and Jake stood there. Both looked pale. At this point, he remembered his tears earlier, and so he took a couple of steps back in case they saw it in his face.

'What's wrong?' he said.

'She's back.' Jake's voice trembled as he spoke.

'We don't know that for sure,' Gardner said.

'She's back. *Lacey's* back. I'm telling you.'

Gardner quickly ran through her conversation with DI Jackson from Brighton. Yorke, too, was pale by the end of the briefing.

'Jake, you have to go home.'

Jake nodded. 'I literally sent Collette and Sean there moments ago.'

'Does Sheila know they're coming?'

'No,' Jake said. 'They'll be discreet and wait outside.'

'Go home and talk to her now.'

Jake nodded.

'Emma, we'll head to Hillary Shine's house, see if she knows where her son is.'

6

ACCORDING TO HER dead father, Gillian Arnold had one hell of a left hook. And he should know. He'd spent over twenty years of his life boxing semi-pro. Rather than the traditional hi-five between father and offspring, Ronald Arnold, also appreciated that left hook into the palm of his hand, even if it stung somewhat afterwards.

So, when a dishevelled man darted out of the dark, it was hardly surprising that she sent him spiralling into the air. After he cracked his head off a street sign, he lay sprawled on his back.

The snow was spiralling down, harder and faster now, soaking Gillian, but she felt no cold; maybe a sudden rise in blood pressure had helped with that?

A white Ford Transit van pulled up alongside the curb. The would-be mugger was rising to his feet. She saw blood smeared across his forehead where his head had bounced from the street sign.

The van door opened, and a tall man emerged. The mugger, realising that the game was up, broke into a sprint down Harnham Road towards the Rose and Crown – her place of work, from which he'd probably followed her.

'Are you okay?' The man said.

She'd still not seen him properly yet. The glare from his headlights was reducing him to a looming shadow.

'No ... I think someone tried to mug me.'

He emerged from the shadows at pace. 'What happened?'

She noticed he was well dressed; a contrast to the shabby appearance of his van. His shoes were polished.

'Not sure really ... was just on my way back from work and someone came up behind me ... quickly. I hit him.'

'That's awful. You did well! Put him flat on his back. Watched it happening on my approach.'

She leaned against a brick wall behind her and took a few deep breaths.

'We need to get you to the police station,' the man said. He took a couple of steps towards her.

'No,' Gillian said. 'Don't let me interrupt your night.'

'Well, to be honest,' he said, taking another step towards her, 'my night is over. Went on a date and the date didn't turn up!'

He was alongside her now. He wasn't what she expected. His tired eyes sank too far back into his aquiline face; his skin was pale, and this lack of colour was emphasised by the long, black hair blown straight and hanging to his shoulders. Despite this, she felt an overwhelming sense of gratitude towards him.

'The perils of *Tinder*, I guess,' the man continued.

She smiled. It was forced. Her body was still trembling slightly.

'Joe Shaw.' He thrust out his hand.

She shook it. 'Gillian Arnold.' His hand was ice-cold to the touch.

'Well, I'll give you several reasons Gillian, why you have to come with me to the station. One, I'm not leaving you here for that man to come back; two, you need to make a report, so it doesn't happen again; three, it's cold out here and despite the look of the van, it churns out some heat.'

Then why is your hand so cold? She thought.

'Well, a taxi may be best ...'

'Of course,' Joe said. 'Am I okay to wait with you?'

Using his mobile, he conducted a conversation with a taxi rank. 'Twenty minutes on a Tuesday night? Really?'

He hung up and looked at Gillian. 'Short staffed.'

She nodded. The adrenaline was starting to subside now, and her wet jacket was starting to feel heavy and very cold.

He tried another. 'Engaged ... I'll try another.'

'Wait, it's okay,' Gillian said. 'It's only a five-minute drive. I'll take your offer.'

He looked relieved and held the van door open for her. The seats were high, so she took a huge step and settled into the seat. He closed the door, came around the other side and climbed in. She glanced behind her and saw that the back of the van was closed off with plywood.

As Joe started the van, she said, 'What do you keep in there?'

'I work for a kennels, nearby. This is the van for transporting dogs to and from their owners. Don't worry though, Gillian, there aren't any in there at the moment.'

'Wouldn't bars be better?'

'I had a problem with bars before.'

Gillian nodded. She expected him to elaborate; when he didn't, she had to make do with an imagined scene of an

Alsatian's paw settling on Joe's shoulder as he turned onto a motorway.

She looked up at the rear-view mirror that he clearly couldn't use. A green pine deodorizer hung from it.

She smiled. 'Thank you.'

'No need to thank me. Have some sugar, it may help with the shaking.'

He plucked a can of lemonade from the cup-holder and handed it to her. It was already open, and a straw bobbed up and down in the liquid.

As Joe turned off the main road onto the street the mugger had run down only moments ago, Gillian put the straw to her lips.

———

THE SNOW CAME DOWN THICKER NOW as they drove to Tidworth. The build-up alongside the country roads wasn't yet such that a sudden miscalculation could send you spiralling, but Yorke was mindful of not pushing his speeds too high.

He looked over at Gardner who was tapping a message out – probably another apology to her husband for an impending late finish. Yorke sighed, and then realised he had his own apologies to make.

'I have to make a call,' Yorke said.

'Fine, I won't listen.'

Yorke smiled. 'You better not.'

He called Patricia on the speaker phone and her voice boomed out. 'Hello.'

'I'm sorry Patricia, rain check on tonight.'

'Predicted that. That's why I'm still on my way to yours so you don't come home to an empty bed.'

'Before you go any further relaying your plans, you're on the speaker phone, and I have Emma with me.'

Yorke glanced at Gardner, who smiled.

'How far did you think my plans were going?'

'Not answering that.'

'Look, Mike, while you're on the phone, did you check through that list I sent you?'

Yorke remembered switching his phone off. 'Not yet, what did I miss?'

'Shit, well, I think you should check it. We are leaning towards a blue-ringed octopus as the source of the toxin which paralysed Jessica. The bite is practically microscopic, but we did find some slight discolouring on the back of her hand, which could be from the bite, or from a tiny injection.'

'What the hell is a blue-ringed octopus?' Gardner said.

'A vicious little bastard that will attack without much provocation. It's one of the most venomous creatures in the world, and it's only the size of a golf ball! It got its name because its rings glow bright blue when it attacks.'

'How long does its poison take to kill?' Yorke said.

'Usually up to ten minutes, but sometimes longer. Unless you get on a ventilator quickly, you die because your respiratory system shuts down; and even when the victim gets help, it's still touch and go because there is no antivenom.'

'And how would you get one?' Gardner said.

'There are three confirmed species of blue-ringed octopus; one from the Southern coast of Australia; another from the Eastern coast; and one from the Western Pacific Ocean. Australians are rounding them up to produce an antivenom, and they wouldn't be hard to smuggle in, which is how we got the list together.'

'List?' Yorke said.

'We contacted a range of tropical fish dealers within a 50-mile radius. Told them it was in their best interests to supply the names of any people they supplied these creatures to during last year. Most were compliant. Some will need chasing up. The list I sent has the names of these possible recipients. It'll give you a starting point until you can get more officers out to the dealerships ...'

'I'll get back to you soon, Patricia.'

Shit, why did I switch off my fucking phone earlier and fall asleep?

He threw his phone over to Gardner, gave her the pin to open it and she went through to his emails.

'Read through the list,' Yorke said. 'Any name jump out?'

Within thirty seconds, she was staring at him with wide eyes.

'What?' Yorke said.

'Billy Shine is on here.'

GILLIAN ARNOLD PUT the straw protruding from the can of lemonade to her lips a few times but didn't drink any. She couldn't. The stuff repulsed her. Pure sugar, preservatives, all in a syrupy liquid. Sent from the devil. Not the tipple of a triathlete like herself.

She glanced at Joe Shaw a few times, but fortunately, his attention seemed to be on the road; she didn't want him to notice the fact that she wasn't drinking. She didn't wish to offend the man who had come to her aid.

They were crossing over the River Avon; in the distance, she could see Salisbury Cathedral wielding Britain's tallest spire. Her mind wandered, briefly, to happier times, long ago, and wedding photos at the front of that cathedral on a summer's day.

'Don't drink it if you don't want it,' Joe said.

So, he had noticed.

'Just feeling a little bit sick; I've never really experienced being confronted like that before.'

'Well, hopefully you won't again. And by going to the police, we'll make sure he doesn't do it to anyone else either.'

They turned off a roundabout onto New Bridge Road. Traffic thickened around them. Joe increased the speed of the windscreen wipers to fend off the building snowfall.

'Are you from around here?'

'Yes,' Joe said, 'Salisbury, born and bred.'

At the next roundabout, he indicated right.

'Sorry, Joe, the police station is up ahead.'

'Shit ... sorry, Gillian, you're right. It's on Bourne Hill—'

The van jerked as Joe was forced to evade a car racing around them on the roundabout. Gillian took a deep breath. She looked at him. He was still staring dead ahead.

'Idiot thinks he owns the road,' she said.

He didn't reply; maybe, he was angry, but his facial expression certainly didn't suggest so.

'I'll turn at the next roundabout, get us back on track,' Joe said. 'Sorry.'

As they made their way down Southampton road, she thought back through the last ten minutes, considered everything he said, and acknowledged that he had sounded *too sincere* since the first moment. Maybe she should just give a thank you and get dropped off at Tesco up ahead?

She turned to glance at the plywood that separated her from what was in the back and imagined the dogs locked in there during the day, scratching at the corners, hunting for light and air. She then glanced into the wing mirror and took note of the blank side of the van. Joe said he worked for a kennels, so shouldn't the name of the company be written on the side?

With her heart racing, she reached out for the handle on the door, to prepare for an escape if necessary.

She gulped. The handle had been removed.

He cleared the roundabout and headed back down the other side of Southampton road.

Joe glanced at her, smiling. 'Are you okay?' He gestured down at the can in her hands. 'Are you not drinking?'

'The truth is - I don't like fizzy drinks.'

'It'll make you feel better.'

She pretended to drink it. He smiled; his smile looked as if it was painted on, like a clown's.

'Only two minutes until we get there,' he said.

There was a thumping sound from the back of the van. Her hand jumped to her mouth, but it was too late to hide her gasp. He stared at her when he should have been looking at the road. 'Something must have fallen over.'

'What?'

He didn't answer and a few moments later she heard the thumping sound again. '*What is that?*'

Again, he didn't reply. Her father had always told her that she was the master of every situation she found herself in. Empty words when she considered her last two years battling severe depression after Geoff's death. Her eyes darted around the van for a solution; eventually, they stopped on the handle for the window. She started to wind it but the window didn't move.

'*Let me out—*'

He swerved left onto a narrow path off the main road, forcing her whole body down and further towards him; the tires screeched, and she was sure she smelled burning. She was then flung left when the van straightened, and her head bounced off the window.

'Stop the car, or so help me, I'll—'

He punched the accelerator and she was forced back in the seat. Feeling disorientated, she shook her head and then noticed the thumping sound from the back starting up again. It sounded like a giant walking towards her.

She glanced at the sign for Churchill Gardens pushed back into the shadows, desperate not to be found. He veered left to enter a small darkened car park. She clenched her left fist, preparing to introduce this wanker to the left hook her father had always been so proud of.

Joe stopped the van sharply just after the entrance to the park, forcing her to reach out and brace herself against the dashboard.

She turned to strike, but then froze. He had tucked his long black hair behind his left ear, revealing an earlobe hanging free by a thread of flesh no wider than a toothpick; the upper part of his ear was a twisted mess of welts and scars. He held a strange knife in one hand.

'Drink the lemonade,' he said.

YORKE AND GARDNER discussed the possibility of Billy Shine being Jessica's murderer on the way to his mother's, but how could he be? It sounded like he'd been down in Brighton, murdering a young prostitute? Unless, he'd come back early, and Lacey was, in fact, the murderer of the prostitute. Yet, it really didn't sound like her MO.

They knew their best course of action was to find Billy, and find him fast.

At the centre of a huge council estate, Yorke found

himself on familiar territory. As he approached via a rubble-strewn path, he passed a discarded porcelain bathtub broken clean in two. His own childhood had been a long and winding ordeal. Granted, it had been punctuated by occasional moments of happiness, which had been necessary because they had served to remind Yorke that life was, in fact, worth living. This had become the inspiration he needed to break out and find a richer and fuller life away from it all.

It was just a shame that no one else in his family had found this same inspiration.

Hillary Shine answered the door so quickly, it was as if she'd been standing just behind it, waiting for someone.

'Ah,' she said. 'Thought it'd be someone else.'

'Billy?' Gardner said.

'What makes you say that?' She said and flashed a row of neglected teeth.

Yorke showed his badge. 'Detective Chief Inspector Yorke, Mrs Shine. Can we come in for a moment please?'

'I would prefer it if you didn't.'

'And why is that?' Gardner said.

'And who are you?'

'Detective Inspector Gardner, miss.'

Hillary smiled again. 'It's been a long time since I had any of you lot round here.'

'We just need to ask you a few questions, Mrs Shine ... we won't take up too much of your time.' Yorke said.

'Back when Bernard was alive, you lot used to come around here and beat the shit out of him. *Regularly*.'

'I know nothing about that,' Yorke said, 'and I'm sorry if that's true. You can be assured that neither I, nor my colleague, do things that way.'

She led them through into the living room which was,

ironically, not a place fit for the living. The room was bare and strewn with rubbish. Unbelievably, a brand new 50-inch television hummed in the corner. Yorke and Gardner sat on a sagging sofa and declined Hillary's offer of tea.

'Can you tell us when you last saw your son, Billy?' Yorke flipped open his notebook.

'He visited at Christmas, of course. Brought me that.' She gestured at the television. 'Before you ask me if I stole it!'

Yorke wondered if Billy himself had stolen it.

'And do you know where he has been staying and what he's been doing?'

'He's been in Brighton, working for a building company down there. Labouring. Made something of himself my boy,' she said. 'Got some money ... and now he's got himself a fiancé.'

'Fiancé?' Gardner said.

A guilty look spread out over Hillary's face; clearly this had been a slip of the tongue. 'Yeah, he told me over Christmas – said he was in love.' She was obviously lying now; she was no longer looking at them.

'And have you met her?' Yorke said.

'No, not yet. Are you sure you don't want a cup of tea? I do.'

'Mrs Shine, your son is involved with a situation in Brighton, and we believe that he may have come back up here to Tidworth?'

She shook her head. 'No, I don't know anything about that.'

She plucked a cigarette from a packet on the arm of her sofa. Using a lighter, she lit it and took a huge inhalation.

Yorke looked at Gardner; then, back at Hillary, who blew out a huge cloud of smoke.

'Is your son interested in sea creatures?' Yorke said.

Hillary stared with wide eyes. 'Is that a question?'

'Yes.'

'Not that I know of – why?'

Yorke sensed she was telling the truth this time.

'Mrs Shine,' Yorke said, 'I think your son, Billy, is in danger. I don't really know why yet, I'll be honest with you, but I do know that he is. Believe me when I tell you that if you know where he is, it is in your best interests to tell us.'

Hillary smiled and pointed at her lips. 'Read these. *I don't know*. He's still in Brighton as far as I'm concerned.'

Gardner pulled a photo of Lacey Ray out of her pocket and handed it to Hillary. 'Do you recognise this woman?'

No response.

'Well, if you do, I'd start talking now because this woman is dangerous. Very dangerous. And I believe she wants to hurt your son.'

Hillary Shine's eyes widened and then she began to talk.

———

WITHOUT TAKING his eyes off her, Joe clicked open the door behind him, and the van lights burst into life.

He transferred his hand to the tip of the blade to hold it up and show her the handle. It was a long wooden shaft which had been carved into the shape of a man, wearing a headdress, kneeling over and gripping the dark-grey blade. The blade itself bore a menacing face in profile; a huge eye on each side with two rows of white teeth. He quickly transferred his hand back to the handle. 'Drink the lemonade.'

She looked around her, but the car park was empty, and

the light from the adjacent road struggled to find its way through the large bushes lining the gardens.

'*No.*' Gillian had once seen a film in which a killer drugged his victim and then buried her alive; she'd rather die right now than face that possibility.

'You're strong willed,' Joe said. With his free hand, he tucked his hair behind his mutilated ear again and she winced.

'What happened to your ear?'

No reply.

She felt a lump in her throat but didn't want to succumb to fear. 'What do you want from me?'

Joe didn't reply again. He just kept his eyes fixed on her, holding the strange weapon. She considered lunging, but if he was quick, she would fail, and the outcome didn't bear thinking about.

'Are you going to hurt me?'

'That is how you and others will view it, but in time, viewpoints can, and will, change.'

Since he'd stopped the car, the snow had intensified, and now the windscreen was completely obscured. She prayed to God that someone would come into the car park, but wouldn't they just think the van was abandoned if they weren't able to see into it? She felt tears prodding the corners of her eyes.

If only there was a handle on this fucking door; if only it was possible to reach behind and open it—

As if the bastard had heard her thoughts, he edged through his open door, showcasing the peculiar knife to warn her against making any sudden movements.

The deaths of all those she'd loved had been very sudden and she'd not seen them coming. But there was no problem seeing hers coming. She could hear it too, working its way around the front of the van …

Slithering towards her.

She wrenched off her seat belt and dived for the open driver's door. Belly first, she scurried over the seats. She heard the door crack open behind her, felt a sudden rush of wind, and shouted when she felt the grip on her ankle. 'No!'

She was dragged backwards and the seats beneath her seem to disappear; then, the world around her blurred and the air was smacked from her body—

'Stand up.'

She'd only just realised she'd hit the floor. She wanted to plead for a moment but there was not enough air inside her body.

'Stand up now, Gillian, or I'll slide this blade into the back of your neck.'

After finally managing to suck in some air, she said, 'Why are you doing this?'

'There isn't time for discussion, stand up and go around to the back of the van.'

'I won't until you tell me *why*.'

'I promise you, Gillian, if you do not get up before I count to three, I will cut you up into pieces. Please know that I am serious.'

'Fuck you.'

'One … two …'

'Okay!' And, as she rose to her feet, something occurred to her. Something that made her want to collapse to the floor again in despair. 'Was it you? Did you kill Jessica Brookes?'

'To the back of the van,' Joe said.

She was now shaking all over, and she now needed to

take her chances with the knife and use the skills her father had taught her. If he was Jessica's killer, and soon to be her killer, she had to act now. The snow fell like shards of glass, slicing the air, and stinging her face. She almost slipped twice.

Then an idea came to her. She stopped dead, and the tip of the blade bit into her back. 'My husband. He will know I'm not home. He's bound to have called the police by now. He's—'

'He's dead, Gillian, has been for years.'

She swallowed hard. *The psycho knew her. This was planned.*

'That's why I'm here. You are a slave to your sadness, Gillian, and I offer you release from the pills and despair.'

Pills? 'How much do you know about me?'

'I know very little. I'm merely a Tlenamacac. And you Gillian, you are simply a slave.'

'You are insane, Joe. This is the 21st century. How am I a slave?'

'To Him whose slaves we are, we are all slaves. Here, now, is the opportunity to be part of something good. If you knew everything, you would not be hesitant. Now, continue.'

She remained still, remembering the thumping sound from before. She definitely did not want to know what was in the back of the van.

'Continue or I will sever your spine, and you will never run again.'

Not only was it more confirmation that he *knew* her, but it was a warning with impact. *Great impact.* Paralysis was her greatest fear. Death was a preferable option.

Not that she was about to let that happen.

She rounded the side of the van and finished up facing the back door. Clenching her fists, she prepared herself despite the blade pressed against the bottom of her spine.

'Open it.'

Her nails sank into the palms of her hands. He worked the tip of the blade against her; it was starting to really hurt. She wondered if he'd already drawn blood.

After reaching for the handle, she forced back a desperate need to vomit.

'*Now!*' He pushed harder. She winced.

She closed her eyes, opened the door and thought of her father's flawed advice that she could control any situation. *She wasn't in control of any situation. Hadn't been for years.* A mixture of tears and melted snow ran down her cheeks.

When she opened her eyes, she saw it was dark inside the van. It also smelled strongly of seawater. She could make out the silhouette of someone with long hair hunched over in a chair against the far-left corner where the plywood board had been erected; the person was still stamping their foot. *Continuously.*

'Who is that?' Gillian said, squinting. She could still feel the knife digging into her spine as the sound became almost deafening. *Thump-thump.*

'There's an icebox in front of you. Take off the lid.'

A box sat on the van floor to the right; he had looped a rope through its handle and secured it to a rail running along the walls. With trembling hands, she snapped back the clasps on the box and reached over to take the lid off the icebox, but then drew back. *Thump-thump.*

'There is no need to be afraid.'

She lifted the lid and put it to one side; the stench of seawater strengthened, but she couldn't see anything, because in the dark, the water was as black as this monster's soul. *Thump-thump.*

'Put your hand in the water.'

Fuck, was there no end to this madness?

'*Why?*' she said, wishing he would relax the knife chewing into her spine.

'Do as I say, Gillian, there's no need to be afraid.'

What the hell was in the box? A piranha? Acid?

'No!' she yanked her hand away. Joe grabbed her wrist from behind and forced it back over the box. She tried to wrench it free but he had the better of her and he plunged her hand into the lukewarm water. The water splashed up and around the box as she tried to tear her hand free, but he shoved himself hard into her back, squashing the top of her knees against the floor of the van.

The thumping was loud and continuous like a marching army. She struggled against his weight, but she was pinned firmly—

Something moved against her hand. *Thump-thump.*

She screamed until he released her. *Thump-thump-thump-thump. . .*

He backed away from her so quickly that she almost fell. Stumbling back, she examined her hand, almost surprised that it was still there.

'It's done. And now I offer you the flowery death—'

'Fuck off!' She turned and slammed her left hook into the psycho's nose. She'd never hit anyone so hard and the cracking sound was surprising, but it didn't deter her from drawing her fist back for a second strike. It wasn't necessary. Joe had already started his slide backwards on the snow, and he plunged, leaving Gillian to do what she did best of all.

Run.

Lacey Ray rang the doorbell and the stupid boy opened it without even checking who it was.

'Surprise,' she said.

And he looked genuinely surprised – the silly little man.

'You've shaved,' she said. 'A shame, I liked the goatee. Are you in hiding by any chance?'

'What do you want?'

'An invite in would be nice. I mean, we must have had sex like sixty times, it's the least you could do.'

'You always were the gobby one.' Billy ran a hand over his freshly shaved head. 'How did you find me?'

'You left your mother's address, you imbecile. Then, I told your mother that we were engaged. Foolish woman. Stupidity runs in the family I guess?'

'You can't talk to me like this!'

'Of course I can. You're only alive because you paid well.'

'So, why have you come to find me?'

'Because you're not paying me anymore.'

Billy snorted. 'You've got to be fucking joking.'

She lifted her backpack off, unzipped it and threw his feathered headdress on the floor. 'You left this.'

The colour drained from his face.

'And this.' She threw a reddish mask on the floor.

She pulled out a handful of jewellery and threw that down too. 'And all of this.'

He looked like he was going to throw up. 'You're fucking crazy.'

He dropped to his knees and started to scoop up his belongings.

'You're a fucking murderer, Billy Shine.' She pulled out the jade ashtray that he had killed Loretta Marks with. 'And, unfortunately for you, so am I.'

She broke the jade ashtray over the back of his head.

IN HER LAST race this year, Gillian ran her heart out, grabbed a good time and even came third in the woman's category.

And there was no better time to break her record than right now.

With a psychopath behind her, the adrenaline was such, it would take a landmine to slow her.

For some reason the nutter had released her hand and backed away. Maybe he thought that whatever was in the water had bitten her? Maybe some kind of poison was working its way through her system as she ran. But right now, she didn't feel poisoned. Anything but.

She gritted her teeth. The bastard had told her she might never run again. She looked back over her shoulder as she burst onto the road they'd turned off. 'Now look at me run, you fucking arsehole!'

She saw the lights of the white van flare into life and then heard the ominous growl of its engine.

That was quick.

She tried to increase her speed, but realised she was at her max. She glanced behind again and saw him driving over the gardens towards her. Ahead, was a small children's playground. The ground sloped downwards which gave her a short burst of acceleration and allowed her to zip past a slide and a group of swings. Behind her, she could still hear her pursuer flogging his engine.

She neared a pedestrian tunnel that led under the road alongside the other side of the gardens. If she could make it there, she knew she stood a better chance of escape. A vehicle, especially a white van, couldn't get through it.

It was twenty seconds away at the most. She flicked a look back as the maniac hit the slope she'd just run down. It came pounding towards her like a rabid dog, swerving around the park. It clipped the side of the swings and the whole structure came crashing down.

And then he was almost upon her; his bumper was metres behind her and she could see into his eyes—

She burst into the tunnel.

She heard the van screeching to a halt and the entire tunnel suddenly burned under the glare of his headlights. She heard the van door opening. Was he going to follow her on foot?

Her calves and shins burned now. She couldn't remember ever pushing herself this hard. She emerged from the tunnel and turned sharply right. Then, she ran up a hill until she was at the main road.

She didn't need to look back, she could sense him behind her, reaching out to her like the hand of a corpse through the soil of a shallow grave.

Unconcerned about the traffic coming off the roundabout, she charged onto Churchill way, waving her hands in the air. Dazzled by headlights bearing down on her, she stood in the middle of the road. Cars swerved and drivers bashed their horns, but no one stopped. She continued to wave for help. She could see Joe at the side of the road, deciding whether to join her on the busy road. She charged onwards towards the roundabout.

Someone stop!

Another two cars skidded around her; she could see the faces of the drivers going crazy at the wheel.

Just fucking stop!

And then one of the vehicles seemed to come straight for her. It didn't turn. The headlights grew and grew until they seemed to swallow her whole, and for a moment, she thought the driver had hit her.

But she didn't care. Anything was preferable to being dragged back to that van by him.

WHEN BILLY SHINE woke in the chair that Lacey had tied him too, she held a mirror up in front of him, so he could see how ludicrous he looked wearing a feathered headdress, a red mask, a cape and some gothic jewellery.

'My friend will be back any minute,' Billy said.

'Paul?' Lacey said. 'I saw him leaving on a date with a very attractive young lady. I doubt he will be in a rush to get back to this flamboyant transvestite tied to a chair. I love the cape by the way; such pretty patterns and colours.'

'What is it you want?'

'The simple things in life really. Justice, knowledge and harmony.'

He looked confused.

'Justice will come quickly when you admit what you've done. Knowledge will come when you explain the reasons why you are doing all these peculiar things. And finally,' she paused, for a smile and a wink, 'harmony will come when I kill you.'

'You're fucking insane!'

'Yes, you said something quite similar outside, Billy; yet, here we still are.'

She took her mobile phone out and laid it on the floor between them. 'I'd like to record this, a little memento of our time together. Are you okay with that?'

'I'm not saying anything to you.'

'Yes, I thought you might say that, which is why I brought these.'

She leaned down and took her secateurs from her bag. His eyes widened, and his bottom lip quivered.

'They've served me well before. I never really leave home without them. Can I hit record yet?'

'Fuck you!' Spittle hit her in the face.

She cut off the little finger on his left hand.

She let him writhe in the chair for a few minutes and then when he'd finally calmed, she said, 'Can I hit record now?'

He started to cry. 'Yes ... *fuck you* ... yes.'

'Good boy.'

She hit record. 'So, first, you admit what you've done. Now, I'm assuming you got angry because you're impotent?'

He writhed in the chair again, desperately trying to get himself loose.

When he'd finished, she said, 'So the impotency?'

'*Yes!*' Billy said with tears streaming down his face. 'The bitch laughed at me!'

'Fancy that, eh?'

———

A BROKEN MAN, sitting alone, drunk on whisky, with Riley's loaded gun in his hand, Brookes couldn't help but acknowledge that he was a contender for cliché of the year.

Not that he really gave a fuck.

He'd finally sent FLO Bryan Kelly packing and, Riley, god bless him, was great, but he just wasn't in the mood for his words of wisdom right now. He missed his son already, and he missed Jessica. In fact, he'd missed Jessica for a long time now, even before she died.

He turned the gun on himself.

He then raised his eyes to heaven and laid the weapon back down on the table. 'Don't worry, Jess, I won't be leaving Ewan alone anytime soon.'

So why is the gun out of the cloth it was wrapped in then? He imagined her asking. She was always good with the questions.

He kept reassuring himself it was for when he clapped eyes on whoever did this. But what was the likelihood of that happening? Every time he spoke to Yorke, it sounded like they were still rustling around in a haystack and, even if they did find him, then what? Was he going to take him out on the way to the courthouse? That would be another contender for cliché of the year.

He phoned Ewan. 'You asleep yet, son?'

'Well, not anymore.'

Brookes smiled. 'Just wanted to say goodnight.'

'You sound drunk, Dad, are you?'

'Nah. It's cold in here tonight; I'm just warming myself up a little. How's Freddy?'

'You *never* ask about Freddy; you hate Freddy.'

'Hate is a strong word, Ewan. He's been living here for a few months now, I've grown fond of him.'

Brookes poured himself another whisky.

'They haven't got Mum's killer yet,' Ewan said. 'Grandad told me.'

'No, but they will. We'll get justice – don't you worry about that.'

'Won't bring her back though.'

'No, it won't. I'm so sorry Ewan.'

'It's not your fault.'

But it is, Brookes thought, *I should have been there, in that house. All of us together.*

'How's Grandad?' Brookes asked.

'Sad,' Ewan said. 'It's a club growing in membership ...'

Brookes smiled again. 'Where do you pick up these expressions?'

'I don't know. Grandad keeps staring at photos of Gran.'

'Why not? He misses her.'

And what happened recently has just reopened those old wounds. It may have been cancer that took his mother, rather than some maniac, but nature can be a serial killer too, laughing as it dishes out disease.

'Dad, I know you don't want to discuss it now, but I still want to join the police.'

Brookes sighed. 'You're right, I don't want to discuss this now.'

'I want to help people.'

'There are other ways of helping people. Being an officer changes you. I like you the way that you are.'

'When they've got him, can I come home?'

'In a heartbeat.'

He looked down at the notepad that was opened beside his bottle of whisky and was reminded of his mother-in-law's warning about a jaguar. 'Did your mother ever discuss a jaguar with you?'

There was a moment of silence. 'Not that I can remember, why do you ask?'

'No reason, what about your grandmother?'

'I hadn't really spoken to her properly in years. She was too ill, you know that. Why are you asking?'

'Nothing. Just something on my mind. 'I love you son. Now, get some sleep.'

'I love you too, Dad.'

YORKE AND GARDNER waited outside the house that Hillary Shine had directed them too. The lights in the house were all on, but the curtains were drawn, and no one was in a hurry to answer the door.

Yorke knocked again, while Gardner negotiated the rubble-strewn garden and attempted to see something through the window, past the curtains.

'Any luck?' Yorke said.

'No,' Gardner said.

Yorke knelt down, pushed opened the letter box and shouted in, 'Police. Could somebody open the door please?'

Another twenty seconds brought them no closer to getting in and finding out what was happening.

But Yorke already suspected he knew what was going on, and he suspected that they were too late. He looked at Gardner while trying the door handle. She wore an expression of disapproval.

'Now Lacey is involved, we can't delay,' Yorke said. 'If Billy is Jessica's killer, we need him alive, to find out why he did it. And, if he isn't the killer, he needs to explain his connection to that octopus.'

Not that it mattered, because the handle didn't work. The door was locked.

'Back-up?' Yorke said.

'Less than five minutes away, sir.'

'Okay, stay here, I'm going around the back, and then I'm getting in one way or another.'

'Is that wise, sir?'

'Someone's life could be in danger; it's justified.'

'No, I didn't mean that, I meant is it wise putting your own life in danger?'

Yorke shrugged and slipped around to the back of the house.

The back garden was worse than the front. He recalled Hillary's garden with the broken bath tub; this one came equipped with a cracked sink and a smashed-up toilet.

The back door was wide open and led into the kitchen. Dirty plates were piled high on every surface and there were at least five full bin bags littered on the floor. There was a gut-wrenching stench of rotting food and cigarettes. The stink was unbelievable. The kitchen was a kitchen in name only; it would be dangerous to cook here.

He looked at his watch. Three minutes until back-up? He knew he should wait, but then he remembered the state of Lacey Ray's last victim and pressed on.

An inch at a time, he opened the door and looked out into the hallway. It was brightly lit, but he could hear nothing and was forced to concede that there was unlikely to be life in this house.

He reached up to check the top buttons on his shirt were fastened. He sensed death.

As he made his way down the hallway, his heart beat hard and fast. Not through anxiety over the danger to his own life, but rather anxiety over the sight which was about to confront him.

In the hallway, he brushed past old pizza boxes; a mountain of unopened letters; some unwashed laundry and ... he tasted bile in his mouth ... blood oozing out beneath the living room door.

He opened the door. A young man, presumably Billy Shine, slumped forward in a chair with his hands cuffed behind his back. He was completely naked. Blood pooled on the wooden floor beneath him. More than enough to suggest that he was dead.

Yorke took a step back and pinned his mobile phone to his ear to call it in as he headed for the front door.

Three crime scenes in just under three fucking days.

He needed to start doing his job, and he needed to start doing it fast.

When he got back outside to Gardner, his phone rang again; it was Topham.

'Make it good news, Mark ...'

'Well, I guess it's good news of a sort.'

'Go on.'

'The killer came back.'

Yorke put his hand against the wall to steady himself. Feeling light-headed, he tried to control his breathing. 'And how is that good news?'

'Because this time, the victim got away.'

JAKE TOLD SHEILA EVERYTHING. About the birds, the notes and about the murder of the prostitute in Brighton. What choice did he have? Lacey could be back, and if she was back, Sheila needed to be on her guard.

'And what did you do with the birds?' Sheila said.

'Well I chucked them all away.'

'Evidence?'

'I know, stupid, don't worry, Mike's already had me over the coals on that one. I kept the last bird. It's in the freezer.'

'Great.' Sheila lit another menthol cigarette. 'Let's hope Frank doesn't stumble across it.'

'I thought you'd stopped smoking while we ... you know?'

Sheila laughed. 'You want to talk about trying to

conceive after you've just told me there's a sociopath in town?'

'We don't know that for sure.'

'And what does she mean by *how does it feel not to be able to fly anymore*? Is she referring to me and Frank holding you back?'

'How the hell should I know?' Jake said, opening his palms out in frustration. 'She's crazy.'

'Is that how you feel? Not enjoying the ball and chain around your leg?'

'Now, you're being ridiculous—' He broke off. He needed to be more sensitive. She had only just found this stuff out, so she was bound to be reeling.

'Well, maybe you should ask her?'

'I don't intend to ask her anything.'

'Well, don't hold back on my account!'

'For what it's worth, Sheila, I don't think she would harm us. I mean, she had her chance, and she didn't take it?'

'So, she's sending you dead birds because she likes you?'

Jake shrugged. 'Possibly? Is it so hard to believe?'

'Yes, *it is*.'

She looked over to the side of the room where PC Sean Tyler and DC Collette Willows were standing. They looked embarrassed. 'Goodnight everyone,' she said and left the room.

Jake looked at his colleagues apologetically.

EWAN WAS WOKEN by a strange noise coming from outside the motorhome. This was disorientating; he was certain that he'd gone to bed in his grandfather's house in Leeds.

At first, he wondered if it was a fox making the noise,

but if so, this was like no fox he'd ever heard before. It sounded like someone gasping for air.

He looked into his father's room, but when he saw that he wasn't there, he went back into his room and threw on some warm clothing.

Ewan's hand hovered over the door handle while he listened to the sharp wheezing sounds. He saw on his watch that it was past three in the morning, but this didn't deter him from opening the door and stepping out into the night. It wasn't raining, but it was bitterly cold and he was glad he'd stopped to get dressed. The noise was coming from about ten metres ahead in the trees.

He thought of Riley and wondered why he had not emerged from his neighbouring caravan. It didn't seem possible that anyone could sleep through this incessant sound. He headed over to his caravan and pounded on the door. No answer. He tried several more times before eventually stealing a look through his window, gasping when he saw his father's reflection in the glass. He touched his face and, in the reflection, his bigger, darker-haired father touched his face too.

He backed away, staring at his father's face, turned and ran for the beech trees. Why he did this he had no idea. He just felt *drawn* to them. A brilliant bright light forced him to stop and shield his eyes. He identified the source of the light: a lamp swinging from the branch of the peculiar central beech tree. Beneath the lamp was a jaguar.

Ewan recalled seeing the jaguar - third largest feline after the lion and the tiger - hunting on a nature documentary. It pierced a deer's skull between the ears and bit deep into its brain. The killing method is unique to cats.

The jaguar flexed the muscles beneath its tawny yellow

coat and the black rosettes that spotted its body seemed to shimmer.

As a rule, jaguars are not found in Salisbury and are mainly based around Central and South America, but it seemed comfortable and at home, despite the extreme temperature. Its tail curled around it on the ground like a long snake.

The jaguar continued to make the rasping sound. At one point, it tilted its head back to yawn; in profile, its mouth looked like the opening of a giant cave with menacing white stalactites.

The jaguar roared and turned its dazzling, yellow eyes on him. It then lifted itself from a sitting position, rising to its feet. Terrified, Ewan started to back away. The feline started to stalk forward and Ewan could see blood glistening on its fur.

It roared again and bared its sharp teeth; flesh hung from them like vines. It broke into a sprint, and when it was only a few metres away from Ewan, it pounced.

Ewan watched the eyes of the great beast plunge from the sky like two fiery suns.

7

A S THEY ENTERED the hospital ward, currently providing Gillian Arnold medical care, Yorke tried to get as much information out of Topham as possible because he felt grossly unprepared for the interview he was about to conduct. He was still trying to get his head around the fact that someone else had been there. Someone stamping, apparently, in the back of the van.

'Her injuries?' Yorke said.

'The dickhead pressed the knife so hard into her back that they've had to give her a couple of stitches. They are also monitoring her for shock, but have said that she seems to be coping well.'

'And she definitely doesn't know him?' Yorke said, thinking back to their suspicions that Jessica had known her killer.

'Her initial report at the station says not, but I haven't spoken to her directly.'

'And how much have we gathered together already?'

'We have managed to get some excellent CCTV footage of the white Ford Transit on Southampton Road, but his registration remains obscured. I cannot believe he keeps getting away with that? Why have traffic not pulled him over yet?'

'Imagine how many people would be getting pulled over in winter with dirty registration plates?'

Topham nodded. 'We also have a forensic artist on the way. Gillian has said that he looked rather unique.'

Yorke felt a moment of hope and an accompanying burst of adrenaline. 'Anything on the mugger?'

'Nothing yet. We know the direction he ran, and I have some officers down there looking into it. You think he's part of this?'

'It's not a coincidence. And the guy that pulled over for Gillian – what do we know about him?'

'You mean the guy who almost killed her coming off the roundabout?'

Yorke nodded.

'Nigel Wilkes. Local plumber, clean record. We have him at the station, obviously, but I'm not expecting anything from that. He came to her aid. That seemed to be his only role in all of this.'

'Has Gillian contacted any of her family yet?' Yorke said.

'Not that I know of. Her husband died a few years back – suicide.'

Topham tried to get some information out of Yorke regarding Billy Shine and his murder, but Yorke waved it off until later. It was a major incident right now, and Topham may as well wait until the update from Gardner, who'd remained at the scene to coordinate the SOCOs.

A nurse showed them through into a room. Gillian Arnold sat on a hospital bed; she was fully clothed apart from her shoes.

She was an attractive woman; fine-boned with a slim build. *Did you think her delicate?* Yorke thought. *An easy target for your peculiar rituals?*

Your misjudgement is about to be your undoing.

'Mrs Arnold, my name is DCI Yorke and this is DI Topham. I want to say how extremely sorry we are about what happened to you tonight.'

'Don't be,' Gillian said. 'I got away. I'm the lucky one.'

Yorke smiled. 'Well, from what I hear, luck had nothing to do with it. You ran. Quickly.'

Gillian smiled. 'I'm determined to beat last year's time in the Salisbury marathon. I think I will now.'

'I hope you do. And I'd be there cheering you on, if I wasn't running it too.'

Gillian reached over and plucked a glass from her bedside table. She took a long gulp through the straw.

Yorke and Topham sat in the visitors' chairs.

'Now, I know you've been through this already, and I know you're exhausted, but is it possible you could go through it again with me?'

'Of course. Anything to help catch him.'

'Well, I think it will. I think we are getting close.'

Gillian described her initial encounter with the mugger and how the man who called himself Joe had come to her rescue.

'And at that point, did you think there was anything strange about him?'

'I thought he was smartly dressed. He gave me some spiel about a date gone wrong. I thought his hair was too long for my taste, but he looked respectable. And you know, I was all shaken up and he was ... well, he was there for me. It was later when I thought back to this moment, and other moments in the van, that I thought there was something odd about the things he was saying. Everything he said sounded too scripted, rehearsed even. I sensed that he had planned the things he said.'

'What happened after you got into the van?'

The next part of the tale made Yorke flinch. He could only imagine the terror this poor young woman experienced. The crazy man's attempts to potentially drug her; the missing handle on the door and the sudden turn off into the park. He was surprised she'd been able to defend herself so effectively and made such an impressive escape.

When Gillian described the knife carved into the shape of a headdress-wearing man, Yorke started to write faster in his notebook. He could feel a cold tingle running down the back of his neck. She then moved onto describing his damaged ear. From the way it repulsed her, it sounded as if his ear had been through a blender and then stitched back on again. Yorke's mind wandered back to a conversation he'd had with Utter regarding auto-sacrifice and the pushing of thorns through various parts of the body to offer blood to the gods.

The Aztec link was starting to rear its ugly head again.

At this point, Gillian had to pause. 'Sorry ... wow, I thought I was holding it together.'

'Believe me, you are,' Yorke said. 'Have a drink of water.'

After she'd taken another drink, she said, 'I remember something. He said he was a Tenman ... no, sorry, a Tlenamac? At least I think there was an *ac* sound at the end ... sorry.'

Yorke tried his best to write down the word she was saying. 'No, you're doing great Mrs Arnold. I'm just going to ask my colleague something – is that okay?'

Gillian nodded.

'Thanks. DI Topham, I would like you to contact Gary

Utter. I know it is late, but we need him here to interpret this information.'

'Okay, sir.' Topham left the room.

'He also said I was a slave to sadness.'

'A slave to sadness? You have any idea why he might say that?'

'Well, I already mentioned in my last report that he said he knew about my late husband, Geoff. That's when it all became clear that this was planned and that Joe was specifically there for me. He said he was offering me release from the pills and despair.'

'And was he right? Do you take pills?'

'Yes.' Gillian nodded. 'An anti-depressant.'

'So, you are depressed?'

'No, not really. I mean, I've had a tough couple of years, but things have definitely improved ... are improving.'

'I know it's extremely personal, and I'm sorry for asking, but do you mind telling me what happened to your late husband?'

Gillian took a deep breath. 'Geoff had an anxiety disorder, and they gave him pills too – not the same ones I'm on – and he committed suicide. Hung himself.'

'I'm so sorry Mrs Arnold.'

She took another deep breath and closed her eyes. 'His brother thought it was to do with the medication. The doctors, and obviously the drug company, disagreed. Still, it all came to nothing. Everyone was protected by the warnings on the medicine's leaflet.'

'What do you think?'

'I just think that he could no longer cope with the anxiety and crippling panic attacks.' She wiped tears from her eyes. 'Sorry.'

'No need. I'm sorry about your loss,' Yorke said.

Gillian then told him about the journey around the side of the van; a journey which must have felt like her final moments on earth. The threats he'd made to paralyse her were horrifying.

Eventually, they got to the most intriguing parts – the icebox and the person sitting in the back.

'It was too dark, I'm sorry. The plywood blocked off the light from the front of the vehicle and he'd obviously taken the bulb out in the back. The person was a silhouette. They were stamping their feet – it is about all I could tell. Sorry.'

'Please, stop apologising.'

'It is the same with whatever was in that icebox. I felt something, and it was terrifying, but I couldn't *see* it.'

Was it the blue-ringed octopus? And, if it was, how is Billy Shine connected? He cannot be the murderer because he'd been bled dry on a chair in Tidworth, but this is not just a coincidence. The chemical from that little creature had poisoned two people already, and almost poisoned Gillian.

'I genuinely believe he thought I'd been bitten or poisoned by whatever was in that icebox,' Gillian said, 'because he just backed away. He thought I was in trouble.'

And that was your misjudgement, you bastard, and that is the beginning of your end.

'I've just remembered something else,' Gillian said. 'He said he was going to give me a flowery death.'

Yorke chewed his lip. He'd read about this on the internet.

The flowery death – the promise that you would travel in the sky with the sun and be reborn as a butterfly drinking from the flowers.

The flowery death was *a glorious death*. This was why so *many* Mexica had given themselves up for sacrifice.

Jessica's death was anything but glorious.

The only thing glorious right now was that Gillian was sitting here still in one piece.

She took Yorke to the end of the tale when Nigel Wilkes had burst from the roundabout almost killing her, before almost certainly saving her life.

Yorke probed her with questions about her life, desperate to find more connections to the killer. He had *known* her. They had also suspected that he'd *known* Jessica.

Yorke considered the surgical angle and asked about her doctor, and her late husband Geoff's doctor, but there was no connection there. He asked her about her job as a barmaid at *The Rose and Crown*, one of the few pubs in Salisbury he wasn't very familiar with. No disgruntled customers, or fellow workers. Despite the lack of success in the questioning, he was diligent in his note making.

'Do you think he will come back for me?' she said.

Yorke genuinely didn't know, but he did know this: 'If he does come back, he will walk straight into our hands, because we won't be taking our eyes off you until he's caught.'

Outside the ward, Topham approached him. 'Utter is on his way. He's unhappy about the time – he was desperate to get to bed.'

'Fuck, Mark, we all know how that feels.'

JAKE LAY on a mattress by the cot, cradling his son's hand through the bars.

There was a nightlight beaming from the corner, enabling him to look at the tiny fingers as he caressed them.

For the first time in days, he felt a moment of contentment. Until his eyes fell to the mobile phone he'd left on and then it all came flooding back.

Lacey had returned, chasing Billy Shine; he had two police officers sitting outside his house in case she decided to pay him a visit; his wife was irate with him for holding back the truth; and one of his close friends, Iain, was grieving for his murdered ex-wife.

He released Frank's hand; it felt wrong touching him with so many horrible images in his head.

He went out to the landing and looked out through the window. The flurries of snow sparkled in the lamplight like flickers from a fire. He stayed and watched for a while. The car occupied by the two officers, Willows and Tyler, had disappeared under a blanket of snow. He watched, as every now again, the occupants were forced to hit the windscreen wipers, and scatter the snow so they could see again. Only for it to come back again just as quick.

His phone rang; he saw that it was Yorke.

Yorke was on his way to the Wiltshire station to speak to Utter, but he'd found a pocket of time in his journey to update Jake on Billy Shine and Gillian Arnold.

'She sliced through his femoral artery and he bled to death in minutes. The strange thing is she took all of his belongings. His clothes, his bags – assuming he had any, because he'd left none at his mother's house. She even took one of his fucking fingers.'

Jake rubbed his forehead as he listened.

'His friend, Paul Lucas, the owner of the house, is none the wiser as to what happened because he was out at the cinema.'

Jake stared out at the snow, wishing, to some extent, it would just come in and swallow him up.

'Lacey Ray. If it wasn't for her, we may have got what we needed and put a stop to this whole bloody thing.'

'Sorry, sir.'

'What are you apologising for?'

'Well, this Lacey Ray shit just seems to be sticking to me.'

'Are you listening to what I'm saying? She didn't come back for you. We are still up shit creek, but don't flatter yourself into thinking it was your pull that sent her rampaging back up here. Emma is in touch with Brighton now. We will have everything on Billy's crime within the hour. We will scour his records here and, first thing tomorrow, we will be hauling in the fool that sold him the octopus.'

Jake heard Frank murmuring from the spare room. He started to walk downstairs. 'I'm at the station now. Jake, get some rest. This isn't over.'

'When are you getting your rest, sir?'

There was a pause. 'After I've spoken to Gary Utter again, I'll get a few hours before briefing. But don't you leave and come to briefing. Not till I'm sure Lacey has gone. But I suspect she has. She won't last five minutes before we pick her up if she sticks around.'

Yorke rang off and Jake sat at his kitchen table; he reached behind himself to the fridge and plucked out a *Summer Lightning*.

He didn't have any chance of sleeping without one ... or two ...

His phone rang again; it was an unknown number.

'To be honest, Jake, when I sent you the last pigeon, I didn't expect I would be in touch so soon.'

His blood ran cold. Never in a million years had he

expected this phone call, and he'd never rehearsed what he would say if he ever spoke to her again. 'Lacey, I ...'

'Shhh,' Lacey said. 'Take a moment to calm yourself. Remember where your temper got us last time? You were quite lucky with the way that little episode ended.'

'Lucky,' Jake said, 'lucky! You terrorised—'

'You, Sheila and that beautiful boy of yours are only alive because of me. So, a little gratitude would be nice.'

'You are fucking unbelievable!'

'One last time, Jake, I'm warning you. I know you are frustrated. I know life has you all tied up in knots these days. But I have something you want, something you need.'

'I don't know what you're talking about.'

'I know things about Jessica's killer. I know things that you need to know. Listen to me now Jake, and I will tell you things that will mend your wings so you can fly all over again...'

Jake listened.

———

'THANK YOU FOR COMING AGAIN, Mr Utter,' Yorke said.

Utter spooned soup into his mouth from a plastic tub. 'No problem, as long as you don't mind me eating while we talk. I had to leave my dinner at home.'

'Of course not.'

Utter had been made privy to all the details of the case so far and had signed the confidence agreement. It was, therefore, quick and easy to fill him in on the events of the evening regarding Gillian Arnold.

'He called himself a Tlenamac?' Yorke said.

'A Tlenamacac,' Utter said after swallowing. 'That means he considers himself a fire priest for Tezcatlipoca.'

'The deity on the picture that we found at Preston's?'

'Yes. The deity that brings about change through conflict and disharmony. There is also something else that is very interesting in what you just told me. He referred to her as a slave, and himself too. Is that correct?'

'Yes,' Yorke said, checking his notes.

'Well, Tezcatlipoca has an epithet – *He whose slaves we are, we are all slaves.*'

Yorke paused to allow the connections to form in his mind. He wanted it to feel like a jigsaw, coming together with a sense of accomplishment, rather than how it really felt: a spider web being woven and threaded into a whole that would only entangle and trap. 'So, he is choosing his victims based on whether they are slaves or not? What does that mean?'

Utter shrugged. 'You said that he told Gillian that Jessica was also slave to her sadness? What could Jessica have been sad about?'

'Her divorce? Her sick mother, perhaps?'

Utter nodded to show his enthusiasm over the direction of the conversation. 'And Robert Preston could have been sad because of his fetish – one that was destroying his own life?'

'Possibly – although he could have just been murdered because he was a witness?' Yorke sighed. 'Are we not reaching here? I mean, aren't we all sad about one thing or another?'

'True.'

'Could he just be a cold-hearted killer?' Yorke said, sitting back in his chair.

Utter leaned back in his chair too. 'That's where I disagree with you,'

Yorke raised his eyebrows. 'I showed you the pictures; does murder get any more cold-hearted?'

'I'm not saying what he's done is acceptable, but you must understand that he won't see this as killing.'

Yorke leaned forward again.

'Remember, DCI, these gods created the world and mankind through their own sacrifices. Lord Tezcatlipoca, for example, sacrificed his foot to a monster so the world could be made.'

'You see, that's where I start to struggle ... a monster?'

'The Aztecs sacrificed other Mesoamericans to pay this debt. The potent energies contained in the hearts and souls empowered the deities and if you nourish the gods, they would nourish the earth in return. Without divine sacrifice, they believed the earth would end.'

'You sound like you believe this, too.' Yorke said.

Utter didn't respond.

Yorke's eyes widened. 'Really?'

'We discussed this earlier in the investigation. We were clear that my beliefs were irrelevant.'

'Yes, but still ... really? You believe this?'

'Yes, I do. Think about droughts, famine and extreme weather. Lack of sacrifice is destroying us.'

Yorke stood up and walked over to the window. He took a deep breath and stared out at the intensifying snowfall. He had to make this right with himself. He needed Utter; now was not the time for conflict with the man who had some insight into this whole situation.

Behind him, Utter said, 'But let me make myself clear here. I don't believe in human sacrifice. Auto-sacrifice should suffice.'

Yorke turned. 'What he does to his ears? And do you ...?'

135

Utter held up a scarred thumb and nodded.

Yorke bit back his impulse to comment. He took his seat again.

'Don't be shocked, and don't be hostile. I am not who you think I am right now. Pagans, such as myself, are always on the receiving end. It's not all about human sacrifice, and orgies. Unfortunately!'

He smiled at his own sarcasm; Yorke did not smile back.

'You can't argue that modern, more popular, religions don't have chequered histories either. Most people who practise any form of religion are Reconstructionists. We take a pre-Christian religion and we breathe new life into it. This is what I do with a religion that began in Mesoamerica and was developed through the Toltecs and the Aztecs.'

'But still,' Yorke said, unable to hold back any longer. 'The scale of sacrifice. It was worse than Hitler in Auschwitz! Do we really want to be breathing life back into *that* religion?'

'*New* life. And all of my emphasis is on *new*. The religion did not diminish because people stopped believing and the symbols and rituals were invalid; it diminished because it was violently suppressed! So, we *reconstruct* with modern laws and morality in mind. No one I associate with believes that sacrificing life is necessary – human or animal. I'm a vegetarian and proud pet lover. No living thing has anything to fear from me.'

'So, just cactus thorns?'

'Yes, auto sacrifice only.'

'One thing I've learned then about this murderer is that he is not a Reconstructionist.'

'Yes, he definitely wants to keep things *exactly* how they were.'

YORKE JOINED Topham in the incident room where he was poised over a printed sketch of Joe Shaw.

With the forensic artist, Gillian had provided a portrait of a pale and long-haired man with a gaunt aquiline face. His eyes were brown and sunken.

'I suppose that if I was to imagine a blood-thirsty Aztec Priest, this wouldn't be far off the mark?' Topham said.

Yorke said, 'Distinctive, to say the least. Let's get this out to the press first thing; we could easily get a hit.'

'Let me contact Price. It's past midnight and you need some sleep, sir.'

'I'm fine.'

'No, sir, you're not. And unless you want me to shock you with my compact mirror – which you know, due to my pretty boy nature, I do carry around in my top pocket – you should heed my advice. Besides, you'll do nobody any favours if you deprive yourself much longer and start to look like this man in the picture.'

'Oh, I don't know, Mark, it might give me the edge in interrogations.'

'Yes, if you don't scare them to death first.'

'Where's Emma?'

'She had to rush home. Annabelle is sick apparently.'

Yorke's goddaughter. 'She okay?'

'Just a heavy cold, I think. She told me to tell you not to worry. She knows you well. I'll tidy up here, ready for tomorrow's briefing. I'll contact Price to ensure that this is in the press first thing. Gillian has opted for the hospital overnight, so I'll confirm an officer will be there throughout the night; I'll also send some officers to relieve Tyler and Willows for a few hours outside Jake's.'

'We are going to get stretched thin at this rate.'

'Precisely why we all need some beauty sleep; I got mine last night - so please, sir?'

'Okay, okay ... but if you stumble on anything tonight, and I mean *anything*, you call me. We got lucky tonight with Gillian. He'll be back, and we might not be so lucky again.'

'You have my word, sir.'

'I know I do, Mark. You've always been one of the best.'

8

THE TYRES ON Jake's car crunched over ice and snow until he was buried deep in the industrial estate. It was a cheap assortment of small garages, most of them either derelict or vacant. There were only two occupied; a tyre place and another hired by someone who sold motorcycle parts. Both of them were closed. Why wouldn't they be? It was past midnight.

He killed his engine and lights and chewed hard on peppermint gum. The flavour was gone. He reached for the door handle and noticed that his hands were shaking - *the pro-plus he'd downed before leaving, perhaps?*

Or the realisation that what he was doing right now, coming to meet Lacey Ray, was sheer madness.

Outside, he pulled his ski jacket tight. It did little to fend off the cold.

The choice she had presented was simple.

She had Billy Shine's belongings, including a laptop; and she had a recording of his confession linking him to Jessica's murder. She had answers.

'All wrapped up like a gift with a nice red bow,' she had said.

But the cost? He had to meet her. Alone. At this address. At the garage painted blue with the door ajar. If he didn't come, she would burn everything. If he told anyone else, she would burn everything.

She'd made a compelling case. 'With this, you'll catch Jessica's killer, which I'm in full support of. Without it, you'll carry on chasing your tails in the wind, and then the next dead body is on you Jake. *All on you.*'

Compelling.

However, this didn't make his actions any less stupid.

'You want me to meet a killer, in a deserted garage, at one in the morning?' he'd said.

'Yes, I do. Exciting, isn't it?'

'For a crazy person.'

'Agreed, but remember this. If I wanted you dead, Jakey, do you not think I would have achieved that goal already?'

'So, if you don't want me dead, then why not just deliver the evidence to the station?'

'Come on now, where would be the fun in that?'

He stood at the open door to the garage and slipped his hand inside his jacket. The kitchen knife was still there. Yes, he knew this could cost him everything. His job, his freedom, even his life. But evidence that could put a stop to Jessica's murderer? And not just any murderer, but the most brutal, vicious individual that he'd ever come across?

The irony that he would be confronting the *second* most brutal, vicious individual that he'd ever come across in his career wasn't lost on him. Hence, the knife. He would bring Lacey down tonight – one way or another. Two birds with one stone.

Several steps into the deserted garage, he took a deep,

heavy breath of air, scented with oil. It was dark, so he reached around the walls beside the entrance until he was able to locate a switch that threw the old garage into life.

But life was not the appropriate word. The place was deserted. Completely. The floor was littered with debris from old vehicles, and the old plaster walls were decaying and crumbling.

In the centre of the empty garage was a chair.

Jake approached the chair, keeping his hand inside his jacket, ready to pull the only weapon available to him when he eventually sighted her. As he neared the chair, he heard a mobile phone ring. It certainly wasn't his. The ringing was coming from the chair.

He picked up an old phone from the chair and answered. 'Hello.'

'Take your hand out of your jacket, Jake.'

Jake turned full circle, looking for her. Nothing. 'Where are you?'

'Maybe I'm here *watching*? Maybe I just know you all too well? Whatever you have in your pocket, it lands on the floor now or I disappear.'

'You can't seriously expect—'

'*Or I am going to disappear.*'

Jake threw the kitchen knife on the floor. 'Happy?'

'Always. Now sit on the chair.'

Jake obeyed with gritted teeth. 'Can we just get on—'

'*Reach* under the chair.'

Jake reached under the chair and pulled out two sets of handcuffs. He cursed under his breath.

'Sorry Jake?'

'Lacey, this is ridiculous—'

'No, it's security. For me. First, you will handcuff your

ankles together; then, you will handcuff your hands behind your back.'

'So you can cut my fucking fingers off, like you do with all of your other stupid victims?'

'Yes, you're right, they were *stupid*. You, Jake, claim to be anything but. So, if that is indeed the case, the sensible move would be to follow the instructions.'

Shit, thought Jake, *what do I do?*

There was only one option if he wanted the information. He put the phone on the floor and put the handcuffs on his ankles first but left one latch loose. He picked up the phone. 'Done.'

'Fasten the handcuffs Jake.'

'I have done.'

'Goodbye Jake, I hope you manage to live with how close you came to putting your hand on the evidence.'

'For fuck's sake!' He put the phone down and snapped the handcuffs shut.

'Now, put your hands behind your back, and I want you to wrap the cuffs around the spindles.'

'That sounds awkward.'

'Very, but we have time, and I won't be coming out until I can *see* it is done.'

Jake put the phone down on the floor and clamped his left wrist. Then, behind his back, he weaved the second cuff around the spindle and, with his cuffed left hand, managed to slam the cuff home on his right wrist.

He was fucked now.

He knew it *and* she most certainly knew it.

He had to trust her.

God, for my son, for my wife, Sheila, for whoever this killer had targeted next, please let this work. Please make this psycho do the right thing.

He sensed Lacey behind him, felt her hands on his shoulders and then felt her fingers running down his chest.

She withdrew her hands, circled the chair and stood in front of him. 'I've missed you.'

She lifted her skirt slightly, so she was able to lift her left leg over him, and straddled him.

'Get off me!'

Lacey stroked his face. 'I've missed you.'

'I will stand up and throw you to the ground.'

'Shhh ... you won't because then you won't get what you came for.'

'What do you want from me Lacey?'

'What I came for.' She leaned in for a kiss.

Topham put his head down on the table, and was on the verge of sleep, when his phone rang. It was DS Ryan Simmonds. Simmonds had been tasked with online forums and potential cults.

'Ryan?'

'Sir, I think I have something important.'

'Go on then.' Topham rubbed his weary eyes.

'*WindScapes*, a portal for the pagan community of Wiltshire.'

Topham leaned over and turned his computer on. He summoned the Google bar and then he found the appropriate page.

The home page for *WindScapes* showed a woman standing in front of a leafy tree, wearing a black cape and holding out her palms. Topham was pleased that the photographer had opted for daylight; it made the image look far less satanic.

'Okay,' Topham said. 'A dating agency for religious nuts?'

Simmonds laughed. 'It's one of many we've been looking at. Many Pagan religions are covered here *including* Mesoamerican ones.'

'I'm listening,' Topham said.

'Well, we contacted them earlier today. Unsurprisingly, the lady who answered, Sandra Ross, was abrasive and defensive. I told her, without providing too much detail, that we suspected some kind of connection to Aztec theology in the recent murders in Wiltshire. I asked her if there had been any peculiar behaviour in the forum in the last couple of years.'

Topham snorted. 'Peculiar behaviour? Looking at this forum, I'm sure that request would keep her very busy.'

'Firstly, she said she would speak to forum moderators, but then launched into a tirade about how their forums are safe and comply with modern day laws and morality, issuing bans when necessary.'

'So, you asked for the list of banned users?'

'Yes.'

'Good work, and?'

'It gets better. She phoned me back fifteen minutes ago—'

'*What?* At one in the morning! You've certainly got them rattled!'

'Sir, you need a pen.'

'Got one.'

'Someone by the name of Tezcacoatl was kicked off the forum earlier this year.' Simmonds spelled the strange name. 'In these email exchanges with another user, he describes how he wishes to initiate another Aztec empire and call it the Second Age.'

Topham snorted again. 'Realism is not one of his strong points then?'

'It gets better. He thinks of himself as a priest, but he wants to gain some kind of promotion to a ...' he paused, obviously to look at his notes, 'a *High Priest*. And then, from that, another ascension to something called a Tlatoani.' Again, Simmonds had to spell that out. 'Which means – ruler of the Second Age.'

'A little ambition never hurt anyone, but the world's had enough of tyrants.'

'You should see the stuff they've sent through on email, sir. They have all of his posts and emails. He has plans for temples, new schools, *wars*. Wow, this guy could write an interesting book.'

'Hmmm, wouldn't be my cup of tea, but do we think that this is our guy? There are a lot of crackpots out there. We need more. Does he mention human sacrifice?'

'No. Just hints at practising the *old ways*. The implications in these words were used by the moderators to finally cut him loose. They've emailed me a list of people that he was in regular communication with.'

'Who?'

'One moment, sir, I'll just open it ... ah, shit ...'

'Yes?' Topham rose to his feet.

'It's *him*.'

'Who?'

'Billy Shine. He's one of the three individuals he was in regular communication with.'

'Listen. We need to get the IP address that he was communicating from. Unless he was canny and used a proxy server or VPN – which I suspect will be the case. Also, I want this Sandra Ross, and the monitor who flagged all this up from the site, in the station tomorrow morning for statements. Finally, find out all you can about the other two that he was in contact with – we will investigate them first thing.'

After Topham rang off, he stared at his phone and remembered Yorke's request to contact him. If he did, Yorke would be back within the hour, and that man needed sleep.

They had a name. Tezcacoatl. They had a clear link between Tezcacoatl via this forum and the blue-ringed octopus which Billy Shine had purchased for him. The IP address would be run in the morning. Potentially, they may be speaking to these other contacts of Tezcacoatl before the night was through, but he'd let Simmonds get back to him on the findings from that first.

Topham knew that Yorke would be unhappy with him, but he opted to let him sleep.

Then, he phoned his partner.

'Hi Neil,' Topham said.

'Alright, Mark.'

'You said to ring me no matter the time.'

'I did; I like your voice, remember?'

Topham sighed. 'And I like the sound of yours more than ever.'

JAKE LET HER KISS HIM, but he did not kiss her back. At least, he *tried* not to kiss her back. There had to be some movement, or she would accuse him of not giving her what she wanted. However, when she started to gyrate her hips, and move against him, he pulled his head back. 'Enough.'

She was an attractive woman Lacey Ray. After all, he had dated her many years ago. But what she'd *become* since then truly repulsed him.

'I agree. We don't want to rush; whatever will you think of me?'

'You know that all this is pointless, Lacey? You have to be caught. This *has* to end.'

She climbed off Jake's lap and smirked. 'And who will end this, Jake, you? You are in a bit of a predicament right now, aren't you?'

'It's not just about me though, Lacey. So, I disappear. I die. They'll still get you.'

'Stop it with the drama, Jake! *Please.*'

'Why me? What did I ever do to you? We dated, we split? We had good times, but we weren't suited.'

'Weren't suited? That's an understatement. You're a policeman and I'm a criminal. We really couldn't be any more different. But you see, that's what I really like about the whole situation. You know what they say about opposites, don't you?'

'Lacey, just give me the evidence and let me go.'

'Patience, Jake.'

'Patience for what, exactly?'

'Patience for me to make my decision.'

Jake felt sweat crawl out of his palms. 'About?'

'I'll admit, when I arranged this meeting, I had no intention of killing you. This Tezcacoatl, yes, that's his name, Billy told me, has done something particularly grotesque. Even by my standards. And time with him would be … well … what's the word … sensational? But needs must, and we both know, I have to run, and run quick. So, I figured that if I gave you the means to catch him, then at least the evil bastard wouldn't get away … completely. And, like I said before, I let you live once before? Why? Because I touched your wife's stomach and felt that you were going to be a father. And you are a good dad, Jake, I'll give you that. I've watched you a number of times with him. And, all of this would be well and good, if I could just get over one little thing that is nagging me.' She tapped her forehead. 'Nagging me ... nagging me ...'

Jake shivered. 'What? Tell me?'

She pulled the secateurs out of her pocket. Jake took a deep breath.

'But it just sounds so petty. Maybe I should just *show* you how I feel rather than just *tell* you.'

Despite the cold, Jake was starting to sweat. 'Please, Lacey ... just tell me.'

'Okay,' she said, opening and closing the secateurs. 'It was when you called me *emotionally stunted* all those years ago. I really can't move on from it. I'm sorry.' She edged forward.

YORKE CLIMBED CAREFULLY into bed so as not to wake Patricia.

There was no need; she was already awake. She rolled over and pressed her naked body against his. It felt good. *Very good*. But it was late, he was exhausted, as she would be, and he knew they should take the sensible option and sleep.

She stroked his chest; it was enough. It brought some calmness and some reassurance that had been missing from the previous few days.

'You're doing your best, as always,' she said.

'Thanks,' Yorke said, not believing it.

'It feels personal, Mike, because of how close it is, but remember, you have to do your job with clarity.'

'And without emotion.' Yorke stroked her hair, thinking, *easier said than done.* But at least she was trying to help.

He moved his hand down over her back and traced the long scars there. 'One day you will tell me how this happened, won't you?'

'I've already told you. Skiing.'

'No, but you will tell me the real reason?'

'Go to sleep, Mike. They need you early and you need rest.'

Yorke went to sleep and dreamed about all the people he'd loved in his life that were gone: Danielle, Charlotte, his mother. Lined up, they took it in turns to talk to him, but they didn't say anything he could understand. Maybe they were telling him how much they missed him? Maybe they were admonishing him for failing them?

After they left, he dreamed about the goggle-eyed man, splitting his victim's chest open with a huge knife. He looked down at the victim's face, expecting to see Jessica, but instead, seeing Patricia. A river of blood ran from her open chest.

WITH HIS INDEX finger lodged between the blades of the secateurs, Jake Pettman pleaded with Lacey. Over and over again, he said he was sorry.

'But, Jake, how sorry are you, *genuinely?*'

'Truly ... honestly ... *deeply.*'

'I need more sincerity.'

'Listen, when I said those things, I was angry. So, so angry. Defensive. I meant none of them. Honestly, I have a child. A child! Frank.'

When he finally heard the secateurs snap shut, he

breathed a sigh of relief at the absence of pain. He let his head loll forward and took several, long deep breaths.

'Now, isn't that nice.' Lacey came back around to the front. 'You have a child.'

Jake forced back the tears; and the vomit rising up his throat.

'I can't have a child,' she said.

A fucking good thing, thought Jake.

'Now, listen carefully, Jake. This isn't over. I believe you. You have bought yourself some time. No doubt about that. But I have to go away and think about how much time that is and, of course, how you can serve me in the future. I think this whole scenario would have played out a lot better if you'd just fucked me while I was on your lap, but I get your ... difficulties? I mean, you are no spring chicken anymore.'

She pulled a finger from her pocket. 'This is Billy Shine's finger. I only had to take one to get everything out of him. Arguably, he was stronger than you, Jakey, as you bottled it before I even took one of yours.'

She reached into her side pocket and pulled out a USB stick. 'This is his confession. Everything he got up to with his three sweet girls down in Brighton. Compulsive listening. Finally, sitting behind you, in a rucksack, is his laptop, along with some rather peculiar fashion accessories that the grotesque pig used to dance in. And I think that is about everything.'

She put the finger and the USB into his lap.

'What about the keys?' Jake said. 'To the handcuffs.'

'Don't be silly, Jake. I didn't bring those with me. The garage next door opens about eight, they might have some tools to cut you loose. Now, can I get one more kiss before I go?'

Jake almost said, '*Fuck you.*' He forced it back. She wanted to be in complete control. If he broke that, he would be back at square one and, he doubted very much that he would get to square two this time. Instead, he nodded.

She leaned over and kissed him on the forehead. 'You've had more than enough for a first date, Jake. You know, if you play your cards right, next time might end a whole lot better...'

9

L AST NIGHT IN his back garden, Tezcacoatl had heard an owl hoot. Wrapped in a fleece and a black ski jacket, he had searched the skies for almost an hour for shooting stars because they carried the same message as the owls. He had not seen any, but the owl's hooting had been enough. *More than enough.*

Owls were the messengers of the gods of death, calling for those destined to inhabit *Mictlan*, a dark region known as the Underworld. Tezcacoatl was not ready to go to this place of death, he had so much left to achieve. Fortunately, the owl had called just once; it required a second hoot to make his death a certainty.

So for now, he faced only great peril.

He had underestimated the slave, Gillian Arnold, and had relied too heavily on the strength of her sadness. The beginning of the plan had gone well. The homeless man had earned his twenty pounds admirably, but later she had fought hard and *Huitzilopochtli*, the deity of war and the sun, had not been nourished. Was the owl, the omen of death, a warning of danger from his beloved Lord

Tezcatlipoca, or was He, in fact, threatening him with *Mictlan* should he fail again?

For many years, he had striven so hard to resist emotion, but he could not deny now a peculiar feeling inside, numb like a cancerous lump that didn't hurt to touch, but was daunting by its mere presence.

It was morning and he sat in front of a mirror applying foundation. His skin was whiter than usual and, unexpectedly, his thoughts turned to a snowman he had built with his mother as a child. He took a small tub of iron tablets from his dressing table, opened the lid and filled his mouth with tablets. He dry swallowed, wincing at the acrid taste. It wouldn't be long before the burst of iron melted through his pallid complexion like the sun had melted through their snowman.

He had been stunned by the snowman's disappearance and had asked his mother how it could melt away to nothing. *Things do,* she had told him, *but you will escape the same fate, because you're far too important to melt away to nothing.*

Tonight must be a success, he thought, *there could be no room for failure, not now an owl had started calling.*

As he put his foundation back into the drawer, he caught a small splinter on his thumb and his mind was cast back to his childhood again, and a memory that offered little but torture …

… He could smell old wood, splinters were buried deep under his fingernails, and his eyes were raw from crying. He peered through a crack in the wood that had materialised after the cellar door had been repeatedly slammed.

His hands darted out so he could claw at the crack, but eventually, as he always did, he gave up. He groaned. Over time, he had enlarged the gap, but splintered hands were all he had to show for it; the gap would never be big enough for him to get out and save her.

With a hand curled around his mother's throat like an eagle's claw, his father formed a fist and slammed it into her face twice. Blood spewed from the corners of her mouth as she pleaded. 'Our son ... our son is *watching.*'

When her head slumped to one side, she stared at her boy through the crack in the door as her eyes filled with blood. Hot tears streamed down his face when he realised that he *should* be breaking down that door. But just like on all those other horrible nights, the rage inside turned him completely to stone.

His father turned to look into his eyes and a smile crept out of his drunken face like a blade from the sleeve of a thief. Sweat was running down his nose and he was dribbling from the corner of his mouth. His eyes bulged. 'You like to watch, don't you?'

He was unable to move or answer; he could only *think.* So he thought about cutting the cold bastard's throat.

His father's eyes swelled and bloated like those of a dead animal, and eventually swallowed everything ...

... Tezcacoatl's eyes flicked open and he was back in his bedroom.

He thought about the peculiar numb feeling inside him that had caused this recollection. He hoped it would go away. He didn't want to disappoint the gods again tonight. He didn't want the hooting owls to return. And he certainly did not want the owls to start shooting.

He looked at his pale and sunken eyes in the mirror. *One day mother*, he thought, *you will look into these eyes again and be filled with great pride.*

Someone rang his front doorbell. He tried to ignore it, but the visitor was insistent and rang three more times.

After wrapping a yellowing dressing gown around him, he marched down the stairs. It was only at the bottom of the stairs that Tezcacoatl acknowledged a peculiar quickening of his pace.

After checking his hair was concealing his ears, Tezcacoatl opened the door, and peered out. It was the young lady from next door, standing in the rain. She was wrapped in a ski jacket and her blonde hair was plastered to her head. He didn't know her name. Hadn't ever needed to.

'Yes?' Tezcacoatl said.

'I'm sorry ... I'm Rachel from next door.'

'I know who you are. How can I help?'

'Well, it's raining,' she held up her outstretched palms, 'quite heavily.' She tried to offer a cute smile. 'I wondered if I could just shelter for five minutes until my taxi arrives to collect me.'

Tezcacoatl reached up to check that his long hair was still covering his ears; then, he peered over her shoulder onto the empty rainy street. Could anyone see her standing at his door?

'I don't understand,' Tezcacoatl said. 'Why don't you go into your own home?'

'Well, it's embarrassing. I've locked the key inside and my boyfriend is out.'

Was this a set-up? Was someone watching him? He peered over her shoulder again. Nothing. An empty street and many people still had their curtains drawn.

'I'm afraid, I'm not dressed, and I'm rather busy.'

'Just for a moment.' She edged herself into the doorway. 'Wow, what is that?'

She was now standing alongside Tezcacoatl, pointing down his hallway to his fish tank, admiring his precious blue-green feather, Matlalihuitl.

Too late now, he thought. He glanced outside again. No one watching as far as he could tell.

He closed the door and turned to watch Rachel, the girl from next door, march down the corridor towards his prize possession. 'Is something burning in here?'

'I just burned my toast,' Tezcacoatl said.

'I always do that.'

He followed her down the corridor, barely a metre behind her. He was considerably taller that her, and was aware that if he got too close, he would loom, and possibly frighten her.

He had no need, or wish, to frighten her. But he did have a problem to solve now. A very big problem.

She touched the side of the tank; inside, Matlalihuitl hovered, its eight legs hanging free, still bright blue from its morning feed.

'A little octopus,' she said. 'Wow, I don't think I have ever seen anything like this before.'

Tezcacoatl could see his reflection in the tank; no doubt, she could see it too. Eventually, after a few more moments of admiration, she turned to face him and looked up at him. He noticed darkening around her right eye.

'What happened to your eye?' Tezcacoatl said.

She flinched. 'An accident.'

Tezcacoatl felt like reaching out and stroking her bruise just like he had done so many times to his own mother. He held back. 'I hear your arguments – did he do this to you?'

'Who?' She widened her eyes to suggest his question was ridiculous. 'Brandon? No ...'

'Did he?'

A tear ran down her face; quickly, she reached up to wipe it away.

'Why do you let him?' Tezcacoatl asked, but he knew

the answer to that question already, because he had asked it so many times of his mother. *He doesn't mean to*, she had always said.

'I don't. I've left.'

Tezcacoatl was surprised by the response, almost flinched slightly himself. How he wished his own mother had uttered those words.

'Wrote a note.' She wiped tears away. 'Told him I was gone for good.'

'And then locked yourself out?'

'Stupid. I left him the key and came outside to get my taxi. Except it wasn't my taxi was it? It was Tom's over the road. Fortunately, you have offered me five minutes of shelter.'

'I never offered, Rachel, and I'm really sorry you came in.'

She looked confused by his apology.

'Where did you tell Brandon that you were going?'

'I didn't. I'm going to a friend's house. He'll struggle to find me.'

Rachel's phone started ringing in her pocket. 'That'll be my taxi, now. I really should go out and grab it ...'

'I'm sorry Rachel. I can't let you leave now.'

He watched the colour drain from her face. He took no pleasure in her fear. She tried to step around him, but he took a quick step to his right and blocked her. The sudden movement must have exposed his ears, momentarily, because she gasped.

'Your ears?' she said.

'I'm really sorry you came in, Rachel.'

She started to scream. He put his hand over her mouth.

'So very sorry.'

IT HADN'T BEEN hard for Ewan to convince his grandfather that he was sick. When he'd brought him tea this morning, Ewan had looked like death warmed up and his bed sheets were damp. Cue ten minutes over the toilet vomiting what little fluid he had left in his body. He then agreed to spend the day in bed; an agreement he'd no intention of honouring for it was in his bed that he had dreamed of the jaguar.

Except it had felt more real than a dream.

When the jaguar had opened its jaws to swallow him whole, Ewan had not woken up. Instead, he'd entered a kind of black limbo where he could think and feel, but could not move or sense anything. Such consciousness in death had been the worst part. He prayed never to dream in such a way again.

Since his grandfather had already left to open his store, and wouldn't return until early evening, Ewan perched on the end of his Grandfather's king-sized bed with his stomach turning.

He was now convinced that the dream had been trying to tell him something.

On the bedside table, he noticed a tub of Valerian, a herb that his grandfather used for sleep, but which stank of old socks. He tightened the lid on the pot, for fear of being sick again, but the repugnant smell lingered, so he left the room.

Downstairs, he threw caution to the wind and consumed an entire bowl of cornflakes. The gamble paid off and the nausea finally let him be.

In the living room, he reached into the aspen shavings and let Freddy tangle his body around his wrist. The cold made him think of his dead mother again, and then the jaguar returned to his thoughts, remorseless as it prowled and feasted—

Of course! It was so obvious! The Jaguar was a symbol for his mother's murderer, and it was going to strike again, possibly from those trees opposite his father's motorhome.

And here he was, in exile, hours from Salisbury as helpful as ever.

His heart drummed in his chest; he felt like crying. He considered phoning his father and telling him about the dream, but his father was too cynical and would dismiss the warning. The more he thought about it, the more obvious his only course of action became: *he had to return home to protect his father.*

And for that, he needed the train fare.

As he searched the room with gritted teeth, he considered his grandfather and father's belief that it was too dangerous for him in Salisbury, as if you are suddenly immune to danger when you become an adult. After what this person did to his mother, why should he hide away? If he's going to come back, let him come back and get a surprise.

He managed to find over a hundred pounds in a cash box in one of his grandfather's drawers.

That would be enough to get him home to his father.

———

Yorke looked at the floor as Topham briefed the crowd on *WindScapes.*

It was the only thing he could do to stop himself exploding. Topham had waited over four hours to tell Yorke about what he'd found out. Granted, there would have been nothing he could have done in the middle of the night and, yes, Topham was looking after Yorke's best interests, but he still felt it was time wasted, and he still felt somewhat betrayed.

'Sir, you'll thank me later today, when—'

'I will never thank you for not following orders, Detective Inspector Topham.'

Topham had looked away at this point, clearly biting his lip.

'It's not professional.'

'Friendship trumps professionalism.'

Fortunately, the argument had been cut short when Wendy came to inform them that Gardner would be missing from the briefing. 'She went to the hospital last night with Annabelle.'

Yorke had rounded on Wendy with wide eyes. 'What?'

'She said that you'd respond like this. She told me to reassure you that she is fine. She has a dose of croup.'

'What's that?'

'Croup – an infection in the throat that gives you a barking cough. Sounds scarier than it is. Nothing a dose of steroids can't cure.'

Before the briefing began, he had looked around the multitude of faces; some eager, some tired. There was no Jake. *Unusual for him,* he had thought, *he's usually first through the door.*

Yorke had started the briefing by describing, in detail, the murder of Billy Shine. A new incident team and room would have to be set up to manage this one. Despite being pissed off at Topham, he would be putting him in charge of that incident room. The team assigned to that case, which Yorke would provide details of at the end of this briefing, would have to work closely with Brighton police, because the murder of Loretta Marks was obviously linked, and

Lacey Ray was wanted by them also. The problem would be finding Lacey. Always a nightmare.

Then, he moved through the incident with Gillian Arnold the night before. Everyone in the room expressed relief over her escape either by taking a deep breath at the end of the story, or smiling. There were also several satisfied nods when Yorke announced that the sketch of the man who called himself Tezcacoatl, which they all had a copy of, was now in the press. It would be in the papers, and on the news. As Yorke talked them through the Aztec angle – Tezcacoatl's claim that they were all slaves to the deity, Tezcatlipoca, and that Gillian would have achieved a flowery death if he'd seen the plan through, he felt vindicated. The previous day when he had been discussing this link, there had been sceptical looks. Today, there weren't.

That was when Topham had started to inform everybody about *WindScapes*.

Yorke watched Gary Utter out of the corner of his eye feverishly taking notes. It was highly irregular to have him in the incident room, but he wanted the expert's thoughts as soon as the meeting finished, not half-an-hour later after he was forced to go through everything again with him. He could also chip in when it was necessary.

Via the projector, Topham was displaying the homepage of the Wiltshire pagan site while relaying Tezcacoatl's desire to bring back the Aztec religion under the jazzy title – *The Second Age*.

When Topham said that Tezcacoatl wanted to become the Tlatoani – the ruler of the Second Age – Yorke noticed Utter shaking his head and raising his eyebrows.

Yorke jumped in. 'Unfortunately, as predicted, the IP address is a no go. Tezcacoatl wasn't stupid enough to wire himself straight into the forum. Apart from Billy Shine, there were two other people he was in touch with. One is deceased. Lucas Hazard, lung cancer, but DC Simmonds, I would still appreciate interviews with the next-of-kin. The other individual he was in contact with was Ethan Rowe, a chap of eighty years of age. He is bed-ridden, but according to his carer, is still active online. DC Ross, if you could take that interview?'

'We have this correspondence between Billy Shine and Tezcacoatl, but it is very vague in content. There is certainly no mention of the blue-ringed octopus, and Billy's own role in all of this. They were obviously canny enough to continue their dialogue either by email, or offline in some form. Still, Mr Utter and I will trawl through the information we do have, together, after this meeting.'

It was at that point that Jake burst into the incident room.

Yorke was about to pass the remark, 'Better late than never,' when he noticed how pale and visibly shaken his friend and colleague looked. Instead, he chose to say, 'Are you okay DS Pettman?'

'Not really. Can I speak to you outside, please?'

Outside, Jake told Yorke what had happened. Mechanic Lawrence Higgins had freed him from his handcuffs less than thirty minutes ago with some heavy-duty tools.

'You *fucking* idiot,' Yorke rose his voice. Topham's behaviour had now dwindled into insignificance compared to Jake's.

'What choice did I have?' Jake said.

Yorke shook his head. 'You're worse than Mark. With your goddamn justifications.'

'What's Mark done?'

'Irrelevant now. What's relevant is that you could have got yourself killed.'

Jake nodded. 'I know. But, it worked, and I got it.'

'And, if it hadn't worked, and you hadn't got this evidence, do you think anyone here would give a shit about a USB stick if you were dead? Would Sheila give a shit? Would Frank give a shit?'

'I know, Mike ... sir ... I made a judgement call. She's so persuasive; she made me feel like I had no choice.'

Yorke rubbed his head. 'Not to mention the fact that the evidence is ridiculously tainted. Are you looking forward to standing up in court and explaining how you came by it?'

'I know—'

'And let's not forget that a murderer made contact with you and it wasn't immediately reported. And that if you had, we may have actually caught this psychotic woman.'

'Alright, sir. I know, I'm done.'

'You're not fucking done, Jake. You're just a big fucking oaf.'

'So what now, then?'

'Well, we listen to what's on that USB stick, of course.'

Yorke spoke to Topham and asked him to set up the Billy Shine incident room and hand out the day's assignments. Then, he went into an office with Jake.

They plugged the USB into the computer and opened the sound file.

Lacey spoke first. 'So, first, you admit what you've done. Now, I'm assuming you got angry because you're impotent?'

Yorke could hear Billy writhing in the chair. From the corner of his eye, he saw Jake flinch; it was only a few hours since he'd been in a similar predicament.

Lacey spoke again, 'So the impotency?'

'Yes, the bitch laughed at me!'

'Aha, now we're getting somewhere. And what happened when she laughed? The jade ashtray?'

'God, it hurts so much! You cut my fucking finger off!'

Jake reached over to pause the conversation. 'I meant to say, his finger is in that bag too.'

Yorke widened his eyes. 'Is it? Good to know.'

Jake resumed the recording.

'Get to the point or it may not be the only one I take,' Lacey said.

'I saw red when she said it. Probably the drugs, you know. She was always taking the piss. You *all* were. So, I hit her with an ashtray.'

'Hit? That is what I just did to you. You, Billy, you didn't hit her. You *caved* her face in.'

There was a moment of silence. Lacey had been happy to let Billy reflect at this point.

'You know, that really wasn't me.'

'Who was it then?'

'Well ... yes, it was me, but it was *unlike* me. I've never harmed anyone like that before. You know me, I was always nice to you, gentle ...'

'Whatever. You've now told me what you've done. You do not seem repentant in any way, but that is irrelevant, as judgement can come now. I promised it quickly. And it will be quick, but first, I need to know what it has all been for? Why dress up? Why three prostitutes? I'm not complaining mind, it paid well, but why have you ruined your shitty little life?'

'God, my finger ...'

'Is gone. *Why have you ruined your shitty little life?*'

'I've not ruined it. Tezcacoatl has ruined it.'

There was a pause while Lacey clearly digested this peculiar name. '*Who?*'

'Tezcacoatl.'

'I got that – I meant who is he?'

'Someone I met online?'

'Online? Tinder? You were dating someone with that name?'

'No. I'm not gay. Did I not prove that to you enough times?'

'You didn't prove a great deal to me Billy, to be honest, but that is a whole separate conversation. So how did you meet him online?'

There was a long pause. Yorke was sure he could hear some clicking; he looked at Jake. Jake mouthed, 'Secateurs.'

'Okay,' Billy said. 'Look, when I was younger I used to be into different kinds of shit.'

'Different kinds of shit?'

'The devil, Satan, that kind of thing.'

Lacey laughed. 'You were a *fucking* devil worshipper?'

'Are you always such a fucking bitch?'

She laughed again. 'This is fantastic. You worship Satan and I've got you tied to a chair with your fucking finger in my pocket. Is He coming to help?'

'Fuck off. I don't worship Satan anymore. I worship Tezcatlipoca.'

'This gets better! So, so glad I'm recording this.'

'A friend of mine told me about a forum. *WindScapes*. For pagans. That's where I met Tezcacoatl.'

'Who got you into worshipping someone with a name as funny as his?'

Billy did not reply.

'So, what did he make you do?'

'He didn't make me do anything, I did it myself. He claims to be directly in touch with Tezcatlipoca, which is kind of cool. So, I did him a few favours.'

'Like what?'

He sighed.

'Like what?'

'I got him a blue-ringed octopus. Also, some surgical equipment. He paid a lot.'

'Rich is he?'

'I guess so.'

'Where did you meet him?'

'We've only met three times. Near where I live.'

'What did he want a blue-ringed octopus for?'

'He said it was necessary to bring back some of the old ways. They're very poisonous. I think he was going to use it for sacrifices.'

'But I thought you were kind and gentle, Billy?'

'You don't understand. He warned me that no one would understand. It's not murder. The gods sacrificed themselves for us.'

'Wow – fancy that?'

'The Aztecs built a glorious empire. Their beliefs gave them meaning, and their world meaning. I wanted to be part of the Second Age. Life had always seemed so empty—'

'Ever heard of indoctrination, fuckwit? So, Loretta. Sweet Loretta. I was kind of fond of her in my own way. Was she a sacrifice?'

'No. She wasn't supposed to be. Look, I think I'm bleeding to death, from my finger. I'm feeling dizzy.'

'Bleeding to death, eh? Sounds like a good idea.'

Yorke winced, recalling the first time he'd set eyes on Billy, sitting in a pool of his own blood with his femoral artery severed.

'What's with your alter ego as a transvestite anyway?' Lacey said.

Jake paused it again and leaned over into the rucksack at his feet. He pulled out jewellery and a headdress.

'What the ...?' Yorke said, really wondering now how weird this whole situation could get.

Jake hit play.

'I'm an *Ixiptlactli*, an impersonator. I'm impersonating Tezcatlipoca, the deity that Tezcacoatl is in contact with. I get to impersonate him for the whole year. A whole year of unbelievable pleasure.'

'Prostitutes and drugs?'

'Among other things.'

'That's why we were contracted to you for a whole year then, and Tezcacoatl was paying for this?'

'Yes.'

'And that's why you made us sit around and watch you wearing this shit and attempting to play the flute?'

'You weren't watching, you were worshipping.'

Lacey laughed again. 'I really wasn't aware that was happening.'

'Tezcacoatl also promised that we would all marry in March.'

'Billy, did you go to school? Do you not remember the lesson on not speaking to strange men?'

'You don't understand, but you would have done, by the end.'

'When Tezcacoatl came and sacrificed us all?'

'Yes. The flowery death. It would have been glorious.'

'Okay, so I have knowledge now. I *know*. Almost wish I didn't. So, it is time for judgement. I—'

'*No,* I'm not ready.'

'Yes, I get that, but I'm getting bored now; if you want to keep me from entertaining myself, give me something more interesting.'

'Like what?'

'That's not my problem.'

'Wait ... when I took him his octopus, he brought his mother.'

'Say that again?'

'His mother.'

'Bullshit.'

'No, he did. He also told me that she was proud of him and what he was achieving.'

'This is getting too twisted even by my standards.'

Yorke paused it. 'The person Gillian saw stamping in the back of the bastard's van, was that his mother?'

Jake looked at him to say something. Even opened his mouth to speak. But no words emerged.

Yorke played it.

'Do you know what, Billy, if I had time, I would really like to catch up with this Tez ... what's his name?'

'Tezcacoatl.'

'Yes, and I would love to chat to him about his flowery death, even offer him my own version of that.'

'What's that in your hands?'

'It's a scalpel. You should know! Haven't you been acquiring surgical equipment?'

'Yes, but why—'

There was a hiss; it was Billy sucking in air. 'What have you done?'

'Judgement. Severed your femoral artery. Made it quick as I promised.'

'There's blood ... everywhere.'

'Relax, Billy. In my blue room, a place of judgement and knowledge, we also need to attain harmony.'

'Shit, I feel cold!'

'Harmony, Billy, welcome it, feel it. I crave it, you should too.'

'I can't see properly ... please ... I never ...'

'Shhhh,' Lacey said. 'Let me turn this recording off now, and let us relax together, just for a moment longer.'

The recording ended and Yorke and Jake sat in silence for almost a minute; then, Jake pulled out the laptop from Billy's backpack.

10

THE CLUNKING OF a radiator pipe woke Rachel Lister.

At first, she tried to reach out to pat Brandon to wake him for work too, but she was unable to move her arms; and, when she opened her eyes, she realised that she was lying in complete darkness.

But she couldn't sit up because her wrists were above her head and strapped to the radiator pipe which had woken her.

She started to scream, but her cry brought nothing but breathlessness and tears which streamed down her face. She waited, desperately hoping that her eyes would adjust to the dark. They weren't doing so.

No windows? No friendly squeeze of light under the door of this room?

The dark continued. The clunking of the radiator continued. Her tears continued.

Tezcacoatl could hear Rachel's screams from the cellar. His house was semi-detached, so he knew that it would be heard next door. Fortunately, Brandon was out at the moment; Rachel had told him that. However, he would have to shut her up before he arrived home.

He stared at his image, or at least a likeness of him, on the television screen. Gillian Arnold's escape could now expose him. But he had no choice, he must continue; he was too close to stop now.

He channel-hopped to a soap opera and paused to watch the *macehualtin* – the commoners – engage in some frivolous behaviours. Then, he turned to a channel on which a young Asian boy was being pulled from the rubble of an earthquake. Seeing this image reminded him of the rain that fell on the small African village during the night he offered Jessica Brookes. He knew of this because he kept careful track of the world and its changing weather patterns on the internet.

Nourishing the deities *did* nourish the earth.

His eyes found the television screen again. The camera had settled onto a limp Asian hand; this reminded him of the hoot of the owl that morning.

He paused for a moment, wondering if the unsatisfied deity, Huitzilopochtli, would accept his nourishment today? After all, the girl below, Rachel, was also a slave to sadness – just like Gillian had been. She was beholden to a man who treated her like dirt.

Yes, it was unconventional, but when he checked his watch, he realised he still had time before work. He also had all his equipment ready from the previous night. Down there, on the cold stone floor, he could do what needed to be done and leave the mess for later when he returned from work.

He turned the television off. He would consult Tezcatlipoca, the Lord of the Smoking Mirror, and let him command.

RACHEL WORKED HARD against the strap. It hurt, but she'd seen a movie once, in which someone made their wrists bleed, and then slipped free.

How she craved light and how desperately she craved Brandon. Her partner for five long years. Usually protective and warm. Last night a mere blip on their long union.

He didn't mean it. He couldn't have meant it. He doesn't have it in him to hurt me.

The evidence – her bruised face – was to the contrary. Still, it was a blip. She would forgive him and they would reunite and the strange man next door, with the monstrous ears, who had locked her in his basement for looking at his sea-creature, would be nothing but a memory.

A bad memory.

A door opened and the barren cellar was flooded with light.

Brandon, come to rescue her?

She watched the tall man with the long black hair come slowly down the steps towards her. He held a large black duffel bag in one hand.

She strained against the straps around her wrists and started to scream again.

He turned and slammed the cellar door shut.

THE LAPTOP HUMMED INTO LIFE.

Yorke looked at Jake whose tired eyes were fixed on the glowing white screen.

When Yorke looked at the screen himself, he was surprised to see that there was no login request; they'd been sent straight through to the *welcome* screen.

'No, password?' Yorke said. '*Really?*'

'Let's pause to appreciate this moment,' Jake said. 'We caught a break.'

'It's a break we need to be keeping quiet about, Jake, we should be logging this in as evidence, right now.'

'We should be, sir.'

'But that might get you in trouble and slow everything down further. What if he plans to come back again tonight? Make up for last night's fuck-up?'

Once the laptop had booted, he clicked the email symbol on the Google homepage.

Another break. Billy had instructed the computer to save his username and his password, which was represented by nine thick dots.

Billy, like most people, had an inbox full of junk and subscriptions. Yorke looked down the e-mail folders on the left-hand side of the screen. There was a folder named *Tezcacoatl*.

'Shit,' Yorke said. 'There are ten emails here! Get your phone out Jake and take photos as I look through them. We're getting so close to the killer, I can feel him breathing on me.'

They started to read the e-mails. Tezcacoatl was clearly well-educated; he wrote passionately with accuracy and flair. His arguments were thoughtful and engaging, and his justifications for the Second Age were well-constructed.

'Great,' Yorke said. 'We really do have a highly intelligent maniac here.'

Billy, on the other hand, had been anything but intelligent. His replies were brief, badly worded and spoke of an individual with low self-worth and confidence.

'He was an easy target,' Jake said. 'If you had to convince anyone that a year with three prostitutes was worth dying for, you'd definitely start here.'

Yorke hit an email that described the process of worshipping a Mesoamerican deity. All you needed was a makeshift altar, a picture or model of your deity, some incense and a sharp object to let your own blood.

'Shit, and they do that through the ears?' Jake said.

'Utter said you could use a variety of body parts – even the penis.'

'What? You didn't just say that!'

'Unfortunately, I did.'

'And you said Utter does all this too?'

'He worships a different deity to Tezcacoatl, but yes, he does. He told me about his pride and joy – a sacred space in his spare room.'

'And you trust this man?'

'I trust him more than Wikipedia. Utter *lives* this weird shit. I still believe he will get us where we need to be.'

They continued to read the emails. The exchanges regarding the purchase of specialist medical equipment were present, as were the exchanges regarding the Blue-Ringed Octopus.

One email mentioned the other name used by Tezcatlipoca – Tezcacoatl's beloved deity.

The Lord of the Smoking Mirror.

Yorke had heard this mentioned before by Utter, but it hadn't sent a bullet of curiosity through his brain like it did now. Mirror?

Where had he heard a mirror mentioned before?

He chewed his lip, rubbed his forehead, but the curiosity remained just that, curiosity. He couldn't find the answer.

They then moved onto another email that was particularly interesting. In this email, Tezcacoatl refers to one of his defining moments:

'And in this dream, I beheld a beautiful creature with a yellow, spotted body which could move quickly and preyed with great stealth. A jaguar. And when I awoke, I knew, immediately, that the jaguar was my lord, Tezcatlipoca's companion spirit.'

Then, it hit Yorke.

The jaguar ... the mirror ... he *remembered* where he'd heard about these before.

RACHEL LOOKED at the lightbulb swinging from the ceiling. At least, it was no longer dark. This peculiar creature had spared her that much.

But, *he* had not spared her his attention. He sat in front of her on a wooden chair, watching her.

'Who are you? Why are you doing this?' she said.

'My name is Tezcacoatl.'

His voice sounded gentle but it didn't soften the impact of his peculiar name.

'I don't understand that name,' she said.

'In your language, it means the Repenting Serpent.'

She gulped and felt a sudden flurry of tears. 'Please let me go.'

'I can't do that I'm afraid, Rachel.' Again, a gentle voice, but the words carried such impact.

'Brandon will come, he knows ...'

'Knows what, Rachel? You already told me that he thinks you've gone away. Left him. And why would you want to go back to him? Look what he did to you.'

'At least he didn't tie me to a *fucking* radiator.' Only after finishing, did she realise that she'd shouted these words. She cried hard for several minutes while he sat and observed her.

'My work is so important, Rachel. *So important.*'

He reached into the large black duffel bag and pulled out a huge manuscript. He flicked through it until he found the page he was looking for and then showed her a mass of handwritten notes and images of buildings. 'I drew these earlier. These are *schools* Rachel. Schools necessary for all of our macehualtin children to learn to function in the age that is coming. These ones here, attached to the temples, are for the lower classes. Girls will be taught to serve deities and cults here; whereas, the boys will be given military training. And... ' He continued to flick through the manuscript and turned it to show her again. 'These are the schools for the higher classes – or those commoners with exceptional minds, like myself. These will be leaders in the military, religion and politics. They will finish the work that I have started. They will ensure that the calendars are adhered to; the festivals are celebrated and the deities are repaid with Uemmana.'

'I don't know what that means—'

'Sacrifice,' Tezcacoatl said.

She took a deep breath.

'You are shocked?' he said.

She paused to try and get control of her fear, and after another deep breath, said, 'It sounds ... wonderful. It really does, but I don't know how I can help you with that.'

'You can't. It's just good to show someone. You're the

first person to see these, Rachel. One day, everybody will see them.'

'Thanks for showing me. Please, I won't tell anyone what happened, no one will ever know—'

'But they would,' he said. 'You would tell them. And they wouldn't take the time to look as you have looked. They would judge and condemn me before all of this is finished. They see only death; they do not see nourishment and the healing of the world. They do not see the wonders that have already come from Jessica's offering.'

'Jessica? The woman in the newspaper?'

Tezcacoatl nodded.

Rachel vomited.

Yorke explained to Jake everything that he had overheard at Mary Chapman on the day he'd accompanied Brookes to see his dying mother-in-law. How she had behaved in an extraordinary way the night before and emerged from a near catatonic state to issue warnings.

'So, Jessica's mother, the night of her daughter's death, starts to talk about mirrors and jaguars?'

'Yes,' Yorke said. 'I didn't write it down, obviously, how was it relevant? Now, I wonder, is this just a coincidence?'

'Can you remember more?'

'No, but don't worry, I'll be getting in touch shortly with someone who took detailed notes. Dr Reiner. He's full-time at the facility.' Yorke paused to think. 'She said something about the jaguar waiting in the trees and having blood all over it. And flesh on its teeth.'

'Well, didn't Utter suggest that Tezcacoatl may have eaten the flesh he took from her thighs?'

'Yes, but come on, Jake? Dreams? We are here, in reality!'

'And the mirror?'

'It was something about a mirror seeing inside you.'

'And Tezcatlipoca is *Lord of the Smoking Mirror.*'

'Apparently,' Yorke said, 'whatever that means. Look, we'll get Utter in here to discuss it shortly, let's just check this last email, which was sent this morning. It's unopened. Billy never read it.'

Yorke clicked the email.

They both read it with their mouths open.

'Get Utter in here right now, Jake.'

TEZCACOATL, the Repenting Serpent, dressed for work and then sat for a moment. He closed his eyes and turned his attention to the Second Age and his coronation.

He saw himself as the *Tlatoani*, seated on a throne decorated with eagle feathers and jaguar-hides. He wore a crown of green stones; emeralds in the septum of his nose; and anklets decorated with large golden bells. His sandals were made of jaguar skins and he wore a shiny cloak, gilded with intricate pictures.

He then saw himself using a jaguar's claw to offer blood from his ears and legs to the huge round stone that recorded the four ages and suns that existed before this one.

He ran through the other rituals in his coronation, before sitting on his throne once again for the conclusion of the investiture. He ran through the *Ceremony of Speeches* in his head; he knew the speeches off by heart. He particularly enjoyed the one given by the high priest who honoured him:

Now thou art deified. Although thou art human, as are we, although thou art our son, our younger brother, no more art thou human, as we are; we do not look upon thee as human. Already thou repentest, thou replacest one. Thou callest out to, thou speakest in a strange tongue to the god, the lord of the near, of the high. And within thee he calleth out to thee; he is within thee; he speaketh forth from thy mouth. Thou art his lips, thou art his jaw, thou art his tongue, thou art his eyes, thou art his ears. He hast provided thee thy fangs, thy claws.

A tear ran down the serpent's cheek.

UTTER SAT in front of the laptop. Yorke and Jake hovered behind him.

'And this email came to Billy Shine this morning.'

'Yes,' Yorke said, 'It sounds like Billy Shine's christening or something?'

'Let me read it,' Utter said.

Tepiltzin,

I hope you like your new name. It was not a difficult choice, especially after your last message, when you graciously referred to me as 'father'. To act as I must gives me no time for reflection and feeling. However, your attempts to compliment and touch me in such a way, honour me. I repay you with a name that has been a long time coming:

Tepiltzin.

It means 'my privileged son'.

It has been only two weeks since you delivered

Matlalihuitl, my precious blue-green feather, to me, but he has served our Lord well, as have you. The festival of Panquetzaliztli was not as successful as it should have been. Huitzilopochtli was nourished once, rather than the two times demanded of me by Lord Tezcatlipoca. This was through no fault of yours, Tepiltzin, or Matlalihuitl's. It was my fault alone. Last night, in my back garden, I heard an owl hoot and realise that I cannot fail again. I do not worry, because Tezcatlipoca has already looked inside me with his smoking mirror and he knows that I exist only to serve him. This failure will become a thing of the past when he sees the greatness of our successes.

My deeds, and your deeds, Tepiltzin, will echo throughout history. The changes we bring about will ignite the Second Age and our gods will be brought out of obscurity. The macehualtin, know not what they ignore, but He has looked inside all of them, and He knows the capacity for change is there. He has told me so in my dreams.

Today, we enter the festival of Atemoztli. We must decapitate the mountains and let the water gush forth! I can feel the festivities of our ancestors shaking the very ground we walk on! One day, the people will dance again. Tonight, I offer nourishment to Tlaloc, god of the mountain of sustenance, and the rebuilding will continue. I will use Tezcatlipoca's new temple this time - the temple from which the Second Age will begin and will grow.

The money you will need has been deposited in your account. Revel in the pleasure it brings! To hold back on pleasure, is to hold back on what is owed to Tezcatlipoca.

I fear that Matlalihuitl does not have long left. I may have to call on you again very soon.

Tepiltzin, my privileged son, we will be in contact again soon.

Your father,
Tezcacoatl

Jake looked at Utter. 'My first question is: *what the fuck?'*

'It's actually quite clear,' Utter said. '*Unfortunately.'*

'Okay, now why don't I like the sound of that?' Yorke said.

'He's following an Aztec calendar. In the Xiuhpohualli, there were eighteen months, so eighteen festivals. Each festival would celebrate a different deity. So, he chose Jessica and Gillian for the last festival – *Panquetzaliztli* which translates as *The Raising of the flags.* This festival honoured the god *Huitzilopochtli*; the deity that originally led the Mexica through dreams to the eagle on the cactus.'

'Where they built the city of Tenochtitlan – now known as Mexico City?' Yorke said.

Jake looked at Yorke in disbelief.

'Wikipedia,' Yorke said.

'There would be sacrifices on a large scale during this month; literally, football fields full of prisoners. Fortunately, Tezcacoatl is working on a much smaller scale at the moment.'

Not fortunate for Jessica Brookes though, thought Yorke.

Utter checked the calendar on his phone. 'Yes, the new festival begins today. Atemoztli, which means *the Descending of the Water.'*

'So a new festival means new sacrifices?' Jake said.

Utter nodded. 'And in this instance, most definitely on the first day.'

'*Today?'* Yorke straightened up. '*Tonight?'*

181

Utter grimaced. 'But that's not the worst of it.'

'Go on.'

'He will sacrifice to honour *Tlaloc*, god of the mountain of sustenance, who represents the rain, water and sky. He's the one on that image you told me you didn't like, DCI. The goggle-eyed one with the huge knife. He's one of the most fearful deities. He strikes villages with disease if neglected. He really must be appeased.'

'Okay, so where do we look?' Panic crept into Yorke's voice.

'Do you have children?' Utter said, the colour draining from his face.

'*No, why?*'

'I do,' Jake said. 'He's two.'

'Might be too young.'

'What are you talking about Mr Utter?' Yorke said.

Utter trembled and then looked up. 'The Aztecs chose children for the festival and made them wet the earth with their tears on the way to sacrifice.'

A stunned silence fell over the room.

Utter stood up. 'Please excuse me, I really want to phone home. Check in. You see, I have children.'

Yorke nodded.

WITH HOURS of this train ride ahead of him, Ewan still felt frustrated. Every hour was another hour he was not there to support his father in the event that the jaguar did come.

He slid the old mobile phone with the broken screen back into his pocket after deciding not to phone his father. Besides, he was in the *quiet zone*, so he would surely pick up a few dirty looks if he did.

He wasn't stupid, and he knew his dad would be extremely pissed off when he appeared back at the motorhome door, but he'd just have to get over it. He'd already lost his mother; he wasn't going to lose his father too. No chance.

After arguing with his father, he'd probably have to get on the phone to his grandad and argue with him too about the sickeningly high IOU left on top of his broken savings box.

From the backpack containing Freddy, he pulled out a ham and cheese sandwich. His lunch had never been in danger as Freddy only ate mice. He tore off the cellophane and the sudden smell confirmed that he'd overdone it with the salad cream.

He hoped Freddy was alright in his backpack, but there he would have to stay. Freddy had a tendency to scare the shit out of people. This wouldn't be a *quiet* zone if Freddy got loose.

Ewan wondered how the killer would come, if he did, indeed, come again; he'd no idea how accurate the warning in the dream had been. The important thing was to be prepared though, and the great thing about the motorhome was Riley.

Reliable and kind, next door neighbour, Riley, would be there to help.

He thought of Ms. Taylor, his favourite teacher. Not only was she very pretty, but she always said good things about his writing and even cheered him on during his runs on sports day. He hoped she would be proud of him over his decision to come back and support his dad. He really enjoyed the praise; his mum was always so good at giving him that too.

He knew he was young, far too young to be some kind

of hero, but he wouldn't be a spare part that's for sure. He did pause to wonder which hero he would prefer to be; he began with Spiderman, but after cycling through them, he settled on Wolverine. Not that he was too fussy. He would probably settle for Luke Skywalker if he really had to, although these days being waif-like didn't get you very far; you really needed a good set of muscles.

He decided not to try and phone his father again; it no longer seemed important. He was going to be very surprised by his return, but ultimately, it would pay off, and he would be pleased.

After this, his father may even give him that long-awaited blessing to join the police.

11

THE STUNNED SILENCE continued in Yorke's office until Utter returned.

'What's with that fucking name anyway?' Jake said.

'The language is Nahuatl,' Utter said.

'And you understand it?' Yorke said.

'Some of it,' Utter said. 'I have studied it. Did you know that Nahuatl is still spoken by over one million people in Mexico and Central America?'

'No, I didn't. So, what is the translation of Tezcacoatl?'

'It means *King*, but it also means *Repenting Serpent*.'

'Well, he is a snake, no question,' Jake said, 'but what's with the *Repenting*? Did he choose this name?'

'Absolutely. Definitely. The Aztecs were metaphorical. Beautifully so. The *King* translation is obvious – he wants to be the Tlatoni of the Second Age, but the *Repenting Serpent*, I'm not so sure ...'

'Wait,' Yorke said. 'Billy Shine said that Tezcacoatl brought his mother in the van with him when they met, didn't he? Also, Gillian Arnold said that there was someone in the back of the van when he tried to abduct her. Billy claimed that Tezcacoatl said his mother was proud of what he was achieving and that she was close to forgiving him.'

Utter looked confused.

'Listen to this.' Yorke played Utter the entire recording between Lacey and Billy.

By the end, Utter looked repulsed. 'She sounds as bad, if not worse, than he does.'

'Tell us about it,' Jake said. 'It's been an ongoing problem.'

'Well, this Billy Shine was an impersonator. He explained that to this woman, Lacey, yes?' Utter said.

Yorke nodded.

'Well, that means he was being lined up for the *Toxcatl* festival next May. At the climax of those festivities, he would have had his heart removed, his head cut off, and his body flayed. His flesh would have been eaten by Tezcacoatl and the other nobles of the city – if there was any at that point.'

'Well, someone has saved him the trouble,' Jake said.

'Which is a real shame because this man could have led you directly to him.'

'We know,' Jake said.

Unless, Yorke thought. *Unless ...* 'Okay, I've had an idea.' He pointed at the screen. 'You email him back and we trap him.'

'Is that even legal?' Utter said.

'When will this child die?' Yorke said.

'Today, if I'm right,' Utter said. 'But I may not be.'

'But if you are, then what?'

Utter sighed.

'This is about me. *All about me,*' Yorke said. 'I am sending the email. I just want you both to check it is okay.'

'But will it work?' Jake said. 'He may already know that Billy Shine is dead.'

'How?' Yorke said. 'Billy's name is not in the press yet and we will keep it out of the press until our bastard reads the reply.'

Yorke, with Utter's support, drafted an email.

Tezcacoatl,

Thank you for my new name, I'll treasure it.

Don't worry, I've followed your rules perfectly and had an excellent time, you'll definitely be proud. Another reason for my quick reply is that this festival sounds too good to miss. I want to see Tezcatlipoca's great temple.

So I have done something which may upset you. I have come to Wiltshire to see the waters gush forth! Don't be angry, I only want to share this with you. It would be really cool if I could join you tonight. You told me how the Aztecs often sacrificed with four priests and had an audience too, so I figured you'd be okay with it.

'How do we end it?' Utter said.

'He knew how to bring a smile to that cold maniac's face,' Yorke said. 'Let's play on that.'

I also want you to know that I meant what I said - you have been like a father to me. Do you remember our earlier discussions about how I felt as if I never belonged? Now, because of you, I really do.

You will be a great leader,

Your privileged son, forever,

Tepiltzin

Together they hunted through the older emails again.

Checking Billy's mistakes and colloquialisms. They noticed that he'd spelled discussions, *disscussions* – so they edited this in the email. They then found five other spelling mistakes to use. They also took the capital letter off Aztecs and took away the paragraph breaks. After twenty minutes of careful editing and checking to see if Billy actually used expressions like 'cool', which he did, the email looked acceptable.

After Yorke had sent the email, he asked for a moment alone.

He stared out of the window at the whitening world and realised he had crossed a new line.

But the killer was coming again, and he needed stopping.

RILEY BANGED EVEN HARDER on the motorhome door.

'You up yet, for God's sake?'

He turned around and looked out across the white emptiness. It was desolation. And the snow drove hard into it. The trees were covered, and the branches looked like a network of black veins, bursting through white skin.

'An old man could freeze to death out here ...'

The door opened behind him and he turned to look at Brookes, hunched over in the doorway, wearing only a dressing gown.

'Is that how you dress for all of your guests?' Riley said.

'Come in,' Brookes said.

Inside, Riley noted the quarter-full bottle of whisky on the table and gave his friend a knowing look.

Brookes shrugged.

'Did it help?'

'Helped me stop thinking for a while.'

'And now?'

'I'm thinking again. Coffee?'

'Yes.'

Riley limped into the room and took his place on the sofa. He tried not to groan as he sat, but it was difficult; his leg really played up in the cold weather.

Brookes came over with two cups of coffee and sat down beside his neighbour.

'Ewan?' Riley asked.

'I was just about to ring him; he'll be helping out at Dad's store.'

They both drank some coffee.

'That helps,' Riley said. 'So, what you been thinking about? If you want to talk about it, that is?'

'A few things. What I'll do when they finally catch the bastard for starters.'

'Which is?'

He shrugged. 'Well, I've got the gun you gave me in the back if needs be.'

'Hey, that's for emergencies. Don't you go off hunting and stitch me up.'

Brookes laughed. 'Don't worry. If Mike and company can't even catch him, what chance do I have?'

'Behave,' Riley said. 'A man that leaves that amount of devastation behind him is *always* living on borrowed time.'

'Well, we can only dream he'll pay me a visit.'

'Be careful what you wish for.'

'Don't worry, Riley, I wouldn't fucking miss.'

Riley sighed and then finished his coffee. 'Thanks for that, starting to feel human again.'

Brookes nodded and forced a smile. 'Also, I've been thinking about what me and Ewan are going to do.'

'How so?'

'Well, I can't bring him up in a motorhome.'

'Suits some people,' Riley said.

Brookes looked at him.

Riley smirked. 'But that wouldn't be right for Ewan, would it?'

'Nope. Shit, Riley, I know you are the most obvious person in the world to ask this question to, but do you ever wish you'd done things differently? I mean *so, so* differently?'

Riley patted his Jacket pocket. 'You know what I have in here?'

'Go on.'

'A letter from my daughter.'

'And what does it say?'

'Don't know, haven't opened it.'

'Why not?'

'Disappointment, Iain. I've got far too old to cope with it.'

Brookes finished his coffee. 'How do you know it's going to be disappointing?'

'I let my daughter down. I went to jail for a long, long time due to my impulsive actions. She'll never forgive me for leaving her. And I don't want her to forgive me because I don't deserve it.'

'You've paid your debt. What are you supposed to do? Never talk to her again, and die? What good is that going to do anybody?'

'I did talk to her, years ago. We met up a few times, didn't we? But I couldn't help myself. Always the judgemental old prick; always wanting to get involved. I told her that the husband she was with was a cheating snake, which he was, and she didn't want to hear it from someone who'd not seen out her childhood. I totally get it.'

'So, how do you know that letter isn't going to ask you to come back so you can try again?'

'Well, it probably is, but like I said, do I really want more disappointment? I'll go back and make the same mistake all over again. I have no right to care after what I did, so if I start to care, it backfires.'

'Sounds to me like you're overthinking it.'

'The point of my story is this, Iain.' He put his coffee cup on the table and turned himself on the sofa to look directly at Brookes. 'What happened to you, and Ewan, is heinous and unbelievable. It really is. But you are both still alive, and Jessica has gone. It must be the most painful thing to hear, it really must ...' He paused because Brookes' eyes were filling with tears. 'But you still have each other. That gun is for protection? Fight the desire to do anything impulsive. You're looking at one man who has been there and has worn the T-Shirt. Listen to me, Iain, you have one priority left, that son of yours. That bold, handsome and *cocky* little tyke. Promise me right now that that's it. That is all you focus on. That is all Jessica would want you to focus on.'

'It's hard, Riley, it really is.' Brookes used his thumb and forefinger to brush tears from his eyes.

'Well, make that promise and I'll promise to open that envelope right now.'

'I promise.' Brookes looked at Riley and forced a smile. 'Now *fucking* open it.'

Riley pulled the envelope out of his pocket and opened it. A passport-sized photograph fluttered out. He leaned over to pick it up, groaning over the stiffness in his leg.

They both looked at the picture of a young boy, no more than two, with cropped black hair.

'Who is that?' Brookes said.

But Riley didn't answer; it was his turn to cry now because the little boy in the photograph was clearly his grandson.

YORKE CONTACTED Dr Reiner at Mary Chapman and asked him to read the exact words that Karen Firth had said to him the night of her explosion.

He then read them out to Jake and Utter.

'You're right,' Utter said. 'She seems to be referring to Tezcatlipoca's mirror seeing inside of us, and she is also probably referring to his familiar, the jaguar.'

Jake shook his head. 'That's too much of a coincidence.'

'It may seem like a coincidence, but some of these deities work in powerful ways,' Utter said.

'No, Utter, I'm not having that. We're not bringing that into the equation. We work on fact only around here,' Yorke said.

Utter's face reddened.

'I am not admonishing you for your beliefs, Utter,' Yorke continued. 'I'm incredibly grateful for how far you have clearly taken us, but discussing dreams and influential gods is not going to help us out here. Now, let's think, let's reason this out. Jessica Brookes has been murdered and her mother, Karen Firth, has spoken of a dream *possibly* involving Tezcatlipoca. What put Tezcatlipoca on her mind?'

Utter looked down; he still clearly believed *Tezcatlipoca* had put Himself on her mind! Yorke left him to sulk and said, 'Had Jessica herself ever discussed these matters with Karen Firth?'

'We have found nothing to suggest that Jessica had any involvement with these Aztec beliefs,' Jake said.

'Also, she has been in no state, for a long time, to have any discussion. Yet, she knows, somehow. Has our killer, Tezcacoatl himself, being in contact with Karen Firth?'

'But why, for what end?' Utter said, raising himself from his sulk.

'Which is a good question,' Yorke said. 'Let's look at this from another angle. Our first victim's mother has demonstrated knowledge of Tezcatlipoca despite being practically catatonic; our second victim, Robert Preston, was probably murdered because he was a witness and, besides, his mother died years ago. Which takes us to the third victim. The victim that never was. Gillian Arnold.'

Gillian Arnold was currently with them in the Wiltshire station being interviewed in another room.

Yorke was already on his feet, heading there. Jake followed while telling Utter over his shoulder to remain there.

Yorke burst into the interview room and the interviewing officer looked up surprised, 'Sir?'

'A minute, please.' Yorke bypassed the leaving officer, and took a seat opposite Gillian. He heard Jake take a seat alongside him. 'Strange question coming, Mrs Arnold.'

'I wouldn't expect anything less under these circumstances and call me Gillian.'

'Your mother, Gillian, and I'm sorry if this offends you, but is she still alive?'

Gillian sighed. 'Barely. She has Alzheimer's– why do you ask?'

But Yorke was too stunned to answer, so the next question fell for Jake. 'Where is she, Gillian?'

'The Mary Chapman Assisted Living Facility,' Yorke said, answering for her.

It was Gillian's turn to look stunned. 'Yes ...'

'What's her name?' Yorke said.

'Michelle Miller. Why?'

But Yorke didn't answer because he was already up and out of the room.

IN A VAN that smelled of old age, Tezcacoatl checked through his equipment one more time. Content that everything was in order, he reached up to switch off the van light, but when his eyes fell to his mother, and he saw how beautiful she looked this afternoon, he paused. There was still time until he had to make a move, and the plywood board that walled off the front, ensured that no one could see in from the car park, so why not allow himself a moment?

He had changed her into her favourite outfit. A sunflower-yellow silk dress with a low-cut bodice and, despite her age, she looked as fresh as she had done all those years ago on that bench in the garden, when he had nestled in her arms and felt the smooth silk against his skin.

Again, he checked the belt that kept her secure in the wheelchair and he checked her head was supported by its mount. You couldn't conduct enough checks, especially considering the driving he was forced to do yesterday when he took a sharp turn off the road into the park where he eventually lost Gillian.

He wiped dribble from the corner of her mouth and

kissed her on the forehead. Her head was warm, and, while he gazed at the cherry colour flourishing in her cheeks, he reached up to touch his own cold face. He wished she could kiss him there again like she had done all those times when the sun awakened the day.

He saw her hospital wristband. It was rather sloppy of him not to have noticed it last night. He reached into his pocket for the penknife on his key ring, and as he started to cut the band, he read her name—

His hands started to shake and the penknife fell. He staggered back and felt every muscle in his body twitch. This was an unusual situation, certainly not one he was used to. His legs weakened and he slumped down to the floor. He managed to drag himself to the side of the van, so that his quivering back rested against the metal bar. After closing his eyes, he willed his entire body to be still, but it felt like he was melting just like that snowman they'd built all those years ago ...

... The air stank of sweat.

His eyes flicked open and he saw that the ends of his fingers bled from scratching. The gap in the wooden door was now the size of a letterbox. He heard his father shouting and peered out the gap.

Tears immediately filled his eyes; it was getting worse.

His mother's yellow silk dress was ripped and blood stained. The bastard gnashed his teeth and sucked air in through his nostrils like a hound scenting blood. His mother's face turned to the door under the stairs. Her nose was crooked and one of her cheeks seemed to reach further up her face than the other one. He couldn't help but think of that snowman and how its face looked peculiar as it melted away.

Tomorrow, while his father, or Douglas — because he

no longer wished to think of him as his father — slept with an empty bottle of whisky, he would sketch a line across his throat with a kitchen knife, which would open and bloom like a glorious new rose.

He stared into his mother's eyes; they looked like dead animals buried and fossilized in the mud. Emotions flooded him: anger, love, guilt, sympathy. Too many to count. His father kept him locked inside, forced him to submit, *to watch*. He cursed these emotions. Every single one of them. He would one day be rid of them.

After taking a deep breath, his mother smiled. It was the most beautiful smile he had ever seen. If he hadn't been frozen, he would have smiled back.

When she breathed out, she smiled and her expression solidified. He could tell that she was no longer looking out through those eyes. All he had left was that smile. She had left it for him. Everything else could go to hell, including Douglas. He *took* hold of this feeling, let it liberate and *unleash him*. He dug his fingernails into the wood and scraped; he bashed the door with his fists; and he pounced to his feet to bury his shoulder into the door until his body could take no more. Then he lay back on the floor with his fingernails hanging lose ...

... Tezcacoatl rubbed his eyes and glanced around the van. He held his hand up to his face. It was still again. 'What is happening to me?'

He stood up, grateful that his legs were strong again.

So much preparation and training! Why, now, was he experiencing these debilitating flashbacks?

He walked over to his mother and picked the penknife up off the floor. He cut the wristband off and read her name again:

Michelle Miller.

12

FOR ALMOST THREE sleepless days, DCI Michael Yorke had been watching a blender that was loaded with death, violence and hideous motive; and, for the first time, he genuinely felt that he had a finger on the stop button. Yet, even as he charged, alone, through the ice rink that was the car park of Mary Chapman to the entrance, he knew that the end mixture would be vile.

Gardner met him at the entrance; she looked worn out.

'Tomorrow, when this is finished,' Yorke said, 'because it *will* be finished, my first stop is your place. Actually, first stop is the town centre to buy that little princess a mountain of toys.'

'Tomorrow, when this is over, we'll all be sleeping, but the day after should be fine.'

'I'm so glad you came back, Emma.'

She looked at him for a few moments, clearly seeing someone as worn out as herself. 'I am too.'

On the journey down here, he'd briefed her by phone on everything that had happened in her absence, and she had briefed him on some equally important information – Anabelle, his goddaughter, was on the mend.

'We go in here, and we throw Dr Reiner off guard,' Yorke said.

At the reception, they asked for Dr Reiner, and within seconds he was there; his suntanned face looked completely out of place in the dead of winter.

'Are you okay DCI? I wasn't expecting anyone—'

'I wasn't expecting to be here until several minutes ago.'

He looked taken aback. 'So how can I help you?'

'Let's go through to your office.'

They sat in an office decorated with pictures of Reiner, shaking hands with a variety of famous and influential people.

'Lots of recognisable faces up here,' Yorke said.

'We've served the local community for a long time.'

And charged them an incredible amount of money for it, Yorke thought. 'Let's start with Karen Firth, how long was she in your care, Dr Reiner?'

'Off the top of my head, I can only give you a rough estimation. Three years perhaps? I can head to the files now if that would be of use?'

'No, that's fine,' Yorke said.

'And how would you describe the relationship you had with her?' Gardner said.

Reiner leaned back in his chair with raised eyebrows. 'Sorry ... what?'

'The question was clear, Dr Reiner, how would you describe the relationship?' Gardner said.

'The same as any other relationship with a patient. I care for them and treat them with respect and I try to make what little time they have left as rewarding as possible.'

'And when one has died,' Yorke said, 'do you eat a sandwich and leave the plastic container on the body?'

Reiner's eyes widened. 'That was an unfortunate incident, which I've already spoken to DS Brookes about. It was completely accidental, and I was mortified by my actions.'

Yorke didn't respond, just stared long and hard at him, trying to figure him out. 'Did you ever take Karen Firth out of this home?'

'That's ridiculous. Why would I do that? Where would I take her? The suggestion is absurd.'

Yorke made notes. He gave Reiner the date and time Jessica Brookes was murdered. 'And where were you, Dr Reiner?'

'At that time? At home, of course!'

'Who with?'

'My wife and my eighteen-year-old daughter.'

'Asleep?'

'Yes, of course, but they would know if I'd left the house. My wife, in particular, is a very light sleeper. Both of them would be willing to give you a statement to that effect.'

'And where was Mrs Firth?'

'I don't know without checking with admin. It is possible she could have gone to the hospital? This happens regularly, of course. Testing and emergencies. You met Dr Page the day you were in here with DS Brookes. You know that he also takes certain patients away for testing.'

Yorke looked at Gardner who was already looking at him. *Were they thinking the same thing?* He thought. 'Michelle Miller?'

Reiner raised his eyebrows. 'Yes, I know the resident, why?'

Gillian Arnold's experience was not common knowledge at this point.

'Was she here yesterday?' Yorke said.

Reiner considered. 'Well, I know she was out yesterday evening, because she was absent on my final rounds.'

'Where did she go?' Yorke said.

'Let me contact admin,' Reiner said.

Yorke and Gardner watched Reiner ring through to his admin department and ask the relevant questions; he also asked about Karen Firth's whereabouts several days before.

He hung up. 'Both of them were at the hospital with Dr Raymond Page undergoing tests. Michelle was also part of his research project.'

Yorke could see the blender he'd been staring into for almost three days churning and churning ... *Was this it? Was this where it stopped?*

Was Dr Raymond Page, Tezcacoatl, the Repenting Serpent?

'Excuse me, Dr Reiner.' He looked at Gardner. 'DI Gardner, could you stay here a moment please?'

'Yes, sir.'

Outside the room, he phoned Jake.

'Listen, get me the location of Dr Raymond Page now and then phone me straight back.'

Less than three minutes later, Jake rang back. 'He left the hospital thirty minutes ago and we have his home address. He lives fifteen minutes from the hospital and should be home by now. Are you sure it's him?'

'No, but he was with Karen Firth on the evening of Jessica's murder; he was also with Michelle Miller last night when Gillian was almost abducted.'

'So, he is taking them to watch? As he kills? That's crazy,' Jake said.

'Maybe Utter was right. Maybe this is how he repents; and how he gets his mother to forgive him. Except if his mother is dead, then what? Maybe he is sick enough that a stand-in will offer some form of satisfaction.'

'I'm struggling with this—'

'Well, consider the facts again. Karen Firth issued a warning about things she couldn't have known about. Either there's something supernatural happening here, or she was there, watching and listening when Jessica died; the murderer somehow communicated all this mumbo-jumbo about smoking mirrors and having a jaguar as a familiar. Did he maybe get into Jessica's house easier because he had her mother with him? There was no forced entry after all. And do you remember the urine on the sofa? Could that have been Karen as she watched her daughter ...' He couldn't even finish the sentence. 'And then Gillian? If that was her mother, no wonder she was stamping. The poor woman was trying to *warn* her.'

Yorke waited a moment for the stunned silence to pass.

'I'll get whoever I can, sir, and we'll go and get him,' Jake said.

'Yes. I'm minutes away, so I'll be there before you. I'm going to leave Gardner to continue interviewing Reiner.'

ON THE WAY out of the station, Gillian Arnold stepped in front of Jake. 'You can't just do that to me! The way DCI Yorke walked out like that. What is going on? Why the interest in my mother?'

Jake looked down at her. 'I'm sorry, Mrs Arnold, you're going to have to trust us. We don't know anything for sure yet anyway—'

'Oh God.' She stumbled backwards, away from Jake. She supported herself against the wall. 'She was there, wasn't she?'

Jake didn't respond.

'That was my mother in the back of the van. She was stamping her feet. She was trying to warn me.'

'I'm sorry, Mrs Arnold, but I'm really going to have to go now.'

'Is she dead? Has he killed my mother?'

'There is no evidence of that. We really don't know anything—'

'This is my *fucking* mother!' Tears rolled down her face.

Jake took her by her shoulders. 'She is probably fine.'

'But she isn't, is she? Whatever happens, she's still sick. And the worst thing is I've betrayed her. I didn't even think she knew me anymore, and she was warning me ... communicating with me ...'

'I'm sorry, Mrs Arnold, we've really got to go. I'll try my best. I promise.'

NOT EVEN A HANDFUL of crabs could tease Matlalihuitl, his precious blue-green feather, from the rock it was slumped on. It had wandered far, performed its tasks admirably, but its three hearts were slowing. Tezcacoatl knew that there could be no sadness in its death though; it had lived well and shone brightly. Now, he needed to send Billy, or Tepiltzin as he would now be referred to, an email request for another octopus. He would name its successor Matlalihuitl also, in honour of this one.

Naked, he rose from the chair stationed at Matlalihuitl's tank and slipped into his living room by the front door. The cold clawed him as he moved from the hearth, but still, he felt much better after his steam bath; cleansed both spiritually and physically, his failings from last night and the events with Rachel, from next door, were already fading memories.

His living room was as sterile as the rest of the modern world. White sofas, curtains and a black 50-inch television. This room disguised him as an ordinary person with an ordinary life; if Rachel had not been so impetuous and charged all the way down to see Matlalihuitl, he could have taken her in here and their encounter may have ended very differently.

He sat down on the sofa and opened his laptop and connected straight to his email account. He was surprised to see an email reply from Tepiltzin because it usually took him days to get back to him. He opened it and read it.

And then read it again.

Afterwards, he deleted the five spam emails in his inbox, because clutter had a nasty habit of interfering with his thoughts.

This email is not from the man I have taken under my wing, he thought.

Tepiltzin was a man attracted to hedonism and had been using Mesoamerican beliefs for his own gain. Tezcacoatl had been certain that he would pose a problem when the festival finally arrived and he would be offered as a sacrifice. No, this email definitely was not from the boy he had been keeping a close eye on.

So Tezcacoatl was content. The email clearly demonstrated that Tepiltzin was finally changing for the better and adapting to his new responsibilities. He shouldn't have come to Wiltshire without Tezcacoatl's permission, but the fact that he wished to join the worship this evening, demonstrated an attractive burst of enthusiasm.

He composed a reply, providing the location of Tezcatlipoca's new temple. Tepiltzin may struggle to find it, but it would be good for him to use his brain. He decided not to request Matlalihuitl's replacement just yet; he could now leave that until later when he saw him.

The mouse cursor hovered over SEND, but then something bothered Tezcacoatl and he took his hand away from the mouse. Did Tepiltzin think that by acting more interested, he would be rewarded financially?

Undoubtedly.

But was this really such a problem? After all, Tezcacoatl was financially secure, and maybe it was best to keep rewarding Tepiltzin in order to strengthen his hold over him.

So, if this was his only concern, why could he still not press SEND?

It had spelling mistakes, punctuation mistakes and no paragraphs. But it felt structured somehow. His letters had never possessed structure before. This one seemed to offer an argument.

Had someone helped him?

He dismissed the idea. Tepiltzin wasn't intelligent, but he certainly wasn't an idiot; he would not have told anyone about this and risked losing what he had gained.

There was a knock at the door. Abandoning the email before it was sent, he jumped to his feet and ran upstairs. His ankles throbbed from a night of relentless auto sacrifice. He threw on his dressing gown and tied it tight; then, he grabbed his knife from his bedside table and slipped it under the dressing gown belt at the back. As he came down the stairs, the impatient person at the door started to knock harder.

———

YORKE KNOCKED AT THE DOOR.

He felt as if his brain was actually drowning in the vile poison the blender had coughed up.

Karen Firth and Jessica Brookes had both been incapacitated, but *aware*. Together they had watched death rushing onto them like a tsunami, and neither of them had been able to do a thing about it.

He knocked harder now.

Jake and his team were minutes away; he'd just got off the phone to Topham, who'd provided another burst of information: *Page has no record ... 43 years old ... unmarried, no kids ... well-educated ... countless publications concerning Alzheimer's and several awards.*

There had been nothing about him being a violent, murdering bastard.

The door opened. The tall, pale doctor stood there in his dressing gown. His long, damp hair hung loosely down to his shoulders.

'DCI Yorke?' Page said. 'I remember you from the hospital.'

Yorke glanced around the wide hallway. Art lined the walls. The curtains were drawn, and the light was dim. The scent of incense was strong in the air and an illuminated fish tank stood at the end of the hallway.

'What are you doing this evening, Dr Page?'

'That is rather a peculiar question,' he said, linking his arms behind his back.

'Still ... could you answer it please?'

'Well, I finished work less than an hour ago and I've just had a shower ... look ... why don't you just come in?'

'One moment, Dr Page. I will wait for my colleagues to arrive.'

'There's going to be more of you, now why is that DCI?'

'Because of Michelle Miller.' Yorke said and paused for a reaction.

He did look surprised. 'Why? What is wrong with Michelle? I saw her yesterday, at the hospital, I haven't heard anything ...'

'Did you check her out from Mary Chapman?'

'Yes, that's correct, and we took her to the hospital for some tests, and then we returned her.'

'And what time was that, Dr Page?'

The time he provided did not fit with the time that Gillian Arnold was abducted, and almost killed.

'The problem is that she was not returned at that time.'

'Well, that's ridiculous, because she was taken from the hospital at that time and returned to Mary Chapman.'

His phone rang. He saw that it was Gardner. 'Excuse me.' He took a few steps back and turned around to take the call. 'Yes, Emma?'

'Sir, Dr Reiner has just told me that Michelle Miller was checked out from here again *today*.'

'Why didn't he say anything when I was there?'

'He didn't know while you were here; admin just informed him ...'

'Jesus! When was she checked out?'

'Quarter past four.'

'By Page?'

'Yes?'

He turned, Page was no longer standing in the doorway. He walked towards the house. *Was Michelle Miller here?*

206

He couldn't wait. He hung up and went through the front door and marched several metres down the corridor towards the illuminated fish tank. There was a closed door on his right.

'Excuse me, but what are you doing?' Page said from behind him.

Yorke spun around to see Page standing by the front door again. 'Where did you go?'

'Nowhere. I was sheltering from the wind behind the open door. It's freezing.'

'Where's Michelle Miller?'

'I really don't know what you're talking about.'

'I'm going to ask you once more and then I'm going to arrest you.'

'Honestly, DCI, I really don't.'

He heard a cough coming from the room behind him. It sounded feminine. He looked at Page's face.

The doctor suddenly looked very anxious. 'No, not that room ...'

Yorke turned and opened the door.

TEZCACOATL KNEW he had no option but to strike now that the fool had opened the door to the cellar and was standing at the top of steps. So that's what he did. As hard as he could, he jammed the same knife he'd used on Jessica between his shoulder blades.

His victim tried to take in several deep breaths but was clearly struggling. It was likely the knife had found its way into one of his lungs.

Tezcacoatl slid his knife free and watched the blood spread and bloom over the back of the ruptured shirt. His victim started to say something, but it was incoherent. Merely splutters and gurgles at this stage.

Then Tezcacoatl pushed, gently, and his victim went headfirst down the steps into the darkness. He could hear the body breaking and smashing against every step.

As it was so dark down there, he was unable to see the fall. The only indication that the fool had reached the bottom were Rachel's screams, muffled to a moan by the gag he had used.

LACEY WASN'T FEELING her usual self.

The train surprised her by being on time; unusual, especially in these weather conditions. Yet, here it was, burrowing out of the white wilderness into the relatively dry station.

She wondered what was making her feel this way.

As she boarded the train, she ran a hand over her expensive and pristine fur coat, and glanced down at her Louis Vuitton shoes. She could rule out her clothing as the reason for her feeling of malaise; she looked good.

She headed to her seat in first class and considered her recent achievements. Although Billy Shine had been an imbecile, she had successfully tracked him down and executed him. She had restored some sort of balance to the world following his vile treatment of Loretta Marks. So, she could rule out a lack of achievement as the cause for this lingering unease.

She had reserved two adjacent seats in first class. This wasn't out of any selfish reason, she concluded; if anything, it was kind. I mean, was it really that safe to sit next to her?

As the train rumbled away into an afternoon that was

starved of light, but overwhelmed with snow, she thought of Jake. Was he the source of her restlessness?

While the train clawed its way through surely impossible weather conditions, she ran through the entire encounter with Jake again. *Every single word.* It had gone perfectly. He had been terrified, which had been a wonderful piece of revenge following his obnoxious behaviour on her last visit to town. She had provided the key to unlock the puzzle of Tezcacoatl, and potentially, bring someone who had viciously murdered a young woman to judgement (not her preferred method of judgement, but a form of judgement nonetheless). She had even indulged in a moment of passion with Jake, which she could have sworn he enjoyed. She smiled over the *stirring* she felt beneath her while she had been on top of him.

However, there was a single moment in that entire interaction that she kept returning to and she was struggling not to become fixated on it.

The train pulled in at a station and a young mother and her son boarded. He must have only been about six, and she was barely out of her twenties.

They held hands. In fact, they *clutched* each other's hands.

She followed the pair with her eyes as they passed her in the aisle. The young boy was letting himself swing from his mother's hand now. His mother looked down at him, 'Jordan, stop that.' She wasn't shouting, or in any way angry, she just wanted him to be careful.

Not to fall. Not to hurt himself.

Lacey watched them through the space between the two headrests. Jordan, the little boy, was climbing all over his mother now. Burrowing his head into her neck, making her giggle.

She now had his cheeks between the palms of her hands and was talking about the 'cuddle monster' and how he was coming to eat her son. The result? A huge hug. After which, they both descended into hysterics.

And then she remembered again that single moment.

The moment she told Jake that she couldn't have children.

The train screeched to a halt at the next stop. Lacey grabbed her bags. She'd had an idea. She would head back to Brighton immediately. Put this right. End this feeling inside her. She disembarked.

THROUGH THE THICKENING SNOW, Jake approached the front door with his heart pounding in his chest. Alongside him, marched Topham, who looked purposeful and confident. It was bravado; Topham would be feeling the same dread he would be feeling.

Was this really it? he thought. *Are we at the house of one of the most vicious individuals the South-West had ever come across? And, if we are, what was Yorke doing in there alone?*

There were three police cars on the road behind them; and the armed response officers who had accompanied them were preparing themselves. A further two police cars had already gone around to the back of the house.

Jake approached the door, noticing it was ajar. He rang the doorbell and then knocked.

The door was opened by someone he did not expect to see.

13

TEZCACOATL SWITCHED ON the light as he descended into the cellar. He negotiated the steps carefully to avoid the splashes of blood which could, quite easily, take his footing. He still held the knife in his right hand.

At the bottom of the stairs, he stepped over the body. The lower half of his victim's body had twisted to an impossible angle to the upper half of the body and would be unlikely to return to its previous position without some force.

Her moans were dying down now, but the tears were coming more freely. He pulled her gag out and she started to murmur his name repeatedly. 'Brandon ... Brandon ...'

'I had no choice.' Tezcacoatl slid over his chair. 'He was becoming aggressive at the door. Said a neighbour had seen you come into the house. I think he genuinely thought you and I were ... well ... ridiculous, I know. But he just marched straight in, went into the lounge, then the kitchen and then, unfortunately for him, he decided to try the cellar door. I guess he has always been the impulsive type. That's probably why he hit you, Rachel. I'm not proud of what I've had to do, it serves no purpose, but I hope it can offer you some sort of relief from the burden you have had to endure—'

'How ... could ... you?' She'd been crying and screaming so hard that she was now hyperventilating.

'Relax, Rachel.'

Still lying on the floor with her arms tied to the radiator, she rocked her head from side-to-side with her eyes closed.

Tezcacoatl waited for her to tire, and then said, 'I have to go, but before I do, I want to tell you a story. Help you understand.'

She continued to rock her head.

'I was fourteen when Lord Tezcatlipoca started to come to me, Rachel. And it wasn't long after this that the dreaming began,' Tezcacoatl said. 'But they were more than dreams, much more. I took the position in the body of a boy who shares my soul. It felt so strange to enter the body of this past life, because I immediately knew everything about him. How his father worked himself to exhaustion as a farmer; how they were training him and his older brothers to fight in the youth-houses; how one of his elder brothers had been sacrificed during the Flower Wars – and how proud his whole family were of that.

'In one dream, I watched the 500-strong Spanish army come to Tenochtitlan. Led by Hernàn Cortès – a leader clothed in black upon a white horse, wearing a soft hat with a protruding feather. Our city contained 300,000 people, yet still they came! Thousands of our people swarmed over the lakes in canoes to meet them; thousands more over the roads.

'Our Tlatoani, Motecuhzoma II, was carried out the city and along the causeway to meet Cortès. He wore a turquoise crown and golden jewellery, which whet the appetites of the Spanish, who came in the name of a false god, and cared only for gold. I had to strain against the crowd to see Motecuhzoma II conduct his ceremonial walk and was almost up on the shoulders of the person before me to see the gifts they exchanged.

'I saw Motecuhzoma II lead Cortès inside the city. The Spanish had proven themselves efficient, ruthless fighters in the open field, so Motecuhzoma believed that keeping the Spanish, and their allies, within the city walls was the best way of maintaining control. But he was wrong. So, so wrong. It was the beginning of the end.

'The dreams continued, Rachel, for years and years. In one dream, I had to contend with losing my father to smallpox – a good man. I watched my mother succumb to despair as the owls and the shooting stars came to signal that the end was near. I would have had no problem dying there with them, Rachel, you must understand that, but our link was only in the dreamworld. Physically, I would always return here, to now. To this sterile wasteland.

'After the Spanish troops took control and erected a place for Christian worship on the Great Pyramid, and one of our lords was murdered, Motecuhzoma II was condemned by us, his own people. He had welcomed the Spanish in and broken his warrior code; he was stoned to death pleading for reason.

'I want to tell you about the last dream I had because it was by far the most visceral and vicious, Rachel. It will show you that I am not a stranger to sadness, as you may think, and that I do understand your current emotions.

'It started with one of my elder brothers marching on the Great Pyramid; I remember his face emerging from the open mouth of a jaguar head while he proudly displayed his shield and maquahuitl. I followed him, and admired the Great Pyramid, the centre of our great universe, rising 35 metres in the air via four superimposed platforms, each one stepping back to form its pyramid shape.

'I stood back and watched with pride as my brother and his squadron climbed the steps and then, at the top, launch missiles into the palace courtyard where the Spanish were quartered.

'Cortès led the charge on the pyramid and I retreated far back, behind the walls, to watch. The Spanish and their Tlaxcalan allies in feathered headdresses and skirts began to ascend. Arrows rose into the air like a sheet of rain, distorting shapes. The firing of enemy muskets shook the air around me.

'I watched my brother's squadron with a pride that cannot be described, Rachel. They sent burning logs crashing down the stairs, lifting the enemy off their feet, sending them bouncing, smouldering, from step to step. The Spanish fought back hard. The muskets and crossbows would send many of our warriors plummeting 30 metres from the side of the pyramid. It was sad, but ever so glorious.

'People swarmed in around me, desperate to see, and before I knew it, I was drowning in the crowd. I couldn't breathe. The boy, whose soul I share, died under a thousand raining feet.

'And then my lord, Tezcatlipoca came for me, as he so often does. He raised my soul to the summit of the temple, so I could look down upon the great battle, and at the brother of my now-dead spiritual twin. The Spanish and their allies had breached the top, and my brother, charged into the fray, bringing the maquahuitl crashing down on the helmeted head of a Spaniard; the bronze metal split like an egg shell, and the contents of his skull spilled out like yolk. Several of my brother's companions, and men I knew, were impaled on spikes and pushed to the edges gripping the shaft of the weapon that had speared them. Once the pikes were torn out, the warriors plunged to their deaths.

'Despite being vastly outnumbered, the Spanish quickly took control of the battle by marching in tight columns. They either speared into the warriors en masse, or sometimes formed small defensive squares which my people found hard to penetrate. The Spanish also operated on a principle of protecting each other and working together. When my brother fell to the floor and a Spaniard stamped on his windpipe, I begged Lord Tezcatlipoca to wake me up, so I didn't have to watch him writhe, gargling blood and gasping for air.

'When the Spanish noticed their Christian shrine had disappeared, they began to ransack the temples. Tlaloc-masked pots and other ceramic vessels were among the many objects smashed and thrown over the side of the pyramid. Idols and shrines were set alight and many were cast down the steps of the pyramid. I watched the skeletons of a jaguar and a crocodile being torn apart by a snarling Spaniard, while masks, seashells and jewellery were all crushed under the feet of his companions.

'Plumes of smoke spiralled up from the Great Pyramid. The victorious Spanish and their allies started to march down the steps away from the carnage. Few Aztec warriors remained alive. The eyes of all of Tenochtitlan were unwavering as they watched the beginning of the end.

'At that point, everything started to fade away: the colours of Tenochtitlan; the smoke of its burning heart; the people in despair; the victorious strangers; the bodies of my family, until there was only me and I was floating in emptiness.

'And it took me years to realise, Rachel, that no matter how hard I beg Him, no matter how hard I work for Him, I am never to return. I am never to see my people and my family again.

'So, whenever I think about the crumpled body of my spiritual ancestor thrown onto the smoking pile of death and destruction back in Tenochtitlan, 1519, I always feel a part of myself turn to ash with them.'

Rachel looked at him and widened her eyes. 'Please let me go.'

Tezcacoatl took a deep breath. He had never told anyone that story before and paused to consider the significance of its sudden emergence now.

'Please,' she continued. 'I won't tell anybody, you can carry on doing what you're doing and no one will ever know.'

'But I want people to know, Rachel, do you not see that? Everyone needs to know. It *all* has to change.'

He glanced at his watch. He had no time to clean up this mess now and reflect.

'We will talk more later,' he said as he stepped over the body of Brandon and climbed the steps.

'You can't leave me here!' She shouted. 'In here with Brandon. He's dead ...'

He closed the cellar door, went back into the living room, went upstairs, changed into his uniform, gathered his equipment and left to continue his life's work. He only realised, when he'd locked the front door behind him, that he'd forgotten to send the email to Tepiltzin. He looked at his watch again; he didn't have enough time to go back in and send it now.

SARAH GAVIN, wearing a silk dressing gown, had led Jake and Topham into the living room, where Yorke was interviewing Dr Page.

The room was dimmed. A black futon lay in the middle of the room, red petals were strewn around it and there was a strong smell of incense.

Sarah said, 'I'll be in the kitchen. Tea?'

Everyone nodded.

Sarah was at least half Page's age and had already explained her presence at the front door.

'Raymond is my partner of two months,' she had told them, before explaining that they worked at the hospital together. 'Your boss just walked in ... on me.' Her face had flushed at this point.

Jake noticed that Yorke was clearly not bothered about having invaded her privacy. He was simply concerned with finding the truth. And why wouldn't he be? Especially with the ugly threat to a child's life on the horizon.

'So,' continued Yorke, 'Sarah has confirmed that you were with her all night on the two dates in question. So, the question is, if you weren't with Karen Firth and Michelle Miller at those times, who was? Because they weren't at Mary Chapman.'

'But the answer is surely obvious?' Page said.

'How so?'

'Well, it must be the nurse that transported them to and from the hospital.'

Jake watched Yorke flinch, and then observed as his eyes wandered over to him. His look said everything. It was obvious. So perfectly obvious. Why had they not thought to check out the person taking these elderly patients to and from the hospital?

Yorke stood up and turned to Jake and Topham. 'Contact Mary Chapman, find out who is transporting these patients.'

'I can tell you that already.' Page rose to his feet also. 'His name is Terrence Lock. He works as a nurse for Mary Chapman and is also their registered driver; he takes the patients to and from the hospital when an ambulance is not required.'

'Describe him to me,' Yorke turned back to Page.

'You would know him if you saw him. He has a bad case of Plummer-Vinson syndrome, and suffers badly from iron-deficiency anaemia. He's as white as a ghost and has very long hair.'

'Like your own?' Topham said.

'Yes, except he doesn't tie it back.' Page reached up to stroke his ponytail.

Yorke looked back at Jake. They were clearly thinking the same thing. *The bastard can't tie his hair back because then you would see his ears.*

Yorke pulled the sketch of Tezcacoatl from his pocket.

'Yes,' Page said, 'That does look like him.'

'Have you not been watching the news? His picture is all over it!' Yorke said.

'Been very busy, I'm afraid.'

'Is there a possibility that Jessica would have known Terrence Lock?' Yorke said, replacing the sketch into his pocket.

'Every possibility I imagine. Jessica visited her mother a lot, and Lock and some of his colleagues would have been in and out of that room attending to her.'

Jake knew what Yorke was getting at. There had been

no forced entry into Jessica's house. If Jessica had known him well enough, he would have found it easier to slither into her house. What excuses he must have given for turning up at her house at that time with her sick mother was anybody's guess. The tragic thing was though: it had worked.

'Anything else you can tell us about Terrence Lock?'

'Not much. I doubt anyone would be able to really. He is very quiet. Keeps himself to himself. Most people would consider him peculiar enough no doubt.'

'Why didn't any of you notice?' Volume crept into his voice. 'Did Reiner not wonder where his patients were when they didn't come back? I mean, they weren't with you and they weren't at Mary Chapman. Whose alarms bells were supposed to be ringing?'

'I can only assume that Lock is altering the paperwork,' Page said. 'I have a few patients participating in these drug trials, but I very *rarely* request them overnight. A few hours will usually suffice. He must be altering my signed requests when he collects them, possibly changing the return date and time. Reiner should have questioned it, I guess, due to its irregular nature. But you've met Dr Reiner, haven't you? To be perfectly frank, his incompetence doesn't surprise me.'

'When I saw you at the hospital that morning on the day Karen died, did no one think to ask you why you'd kept her overnight, that she'd only recently returned?'

'Sorry, DCI Yorke.' Page shook his head; he genuinely looked quite sad about this.

'And Michelle Miller, you requested her yesterday?'

'Yes, for a couple of hours again.'

'And she was returned this morning?'

'Like I said, not per my instructions.'

'And how long did you request Michelle for today?'

'I didn't.'

'So, he's gone one step further, he must have forged the entire form? Because he's taken her again.'

Page looked concerned about this. 'I hope she's okay. You know Michelle has been a wonderful addition to the study; I hope to learn more ...'

'Stop right there,' Yorke said, 'If you are really about to deliver a speech about the importance of your studies over the lives of these people, you will see another side of me.'

Jake looked down at the floor. Topham too. It was rare to see a display of such emotion from their boss towards people he was interviewing.

'I'm sorry ... I genuinely hope she's fine.'

'DI Topham,' Yorke said. 'Go and pull everything on Lock now.'

'Will do, boss.'

'DS Pettman, contact DI Gardner at Mary Chapman. Get the details of the vehicle Lock is using to transport the patients.'

'Yes sir.'

Jake joined Topham in the hallway to make the phone call.

Yorke said his farewells to Page and followed the two men outside.

Jake came off the phone first. 'Guess what? A white Ford Transit. I have the licence plate – let's just hope he's cleaned it, so we can see it. I'll get an APW out now.'

'Thanks Jake.'

As Yorke waited for Topham to finish his call, his mind raced over the following: how did Lock communicate so efficiently with women suffering from late-stage dementia? Unless, he'd been working at this for years and so began his communication with Michelle and Karen, when they were still high functioning? Had these mothers, and God knows how many other mothers, revealed information about their children? It had probably been confusing, broken information, but would have been information nonetheless. He could have learned about Jessica's broken marriage and Gillian's depression over her husband's suicide.

Learned that they were *slaves to sadness*. Learned that they were suitable for the *flowery death*.

And the bigger question still: why did Lock want these mothers with him so badly? And why did he refer to them as his own when they weren't? He was repenting for something, but *what?* What had he done so wrong to his mother to justify all of this?

Topham approached, but Yorke already had his first question. 'What happened to his mother?'

Topham raised his eyebrows. 'Yes, interesting that. Horrible really. His father beat his mother to death.'

'And where was Lock?'

'Trying to claw his way out of a cupboard under the stairs. And when they eventually found him; it seems he had witnessed everything.'

'I need Lock's address *now.*'

14

BENJAMIN RILEY FOUGHT back the quiver in his voice. He did not want his daughter to know he was emotional, not under any circumstance.

'Thank you,' Riley said again into the phone.

'You don't have to keep saying thank you. It's right and proper,' Cynthia said. 'He's your grandson and everyone deserves to know their grandparents.'

'Thank ... sorry. Great, when can this happen?'

'Whenever you want, Dad.'

'In that case, I would like it to be sooner rather than later.' His phone beeped and he looked at it. 'Sorry, I'm down to one percent battery – apologies if it cuts out. How does next week sound?'

'Fantastic. I'll make up the spare room.'

Riley's sensor light came on outside his static caravan. He knew it wouldn't be Brookes, because he'd gone out over an hour ago – probably to drink again. This bothered him, but what more could he do? He'd warned Brookes about making his life any more of a mess than it already was.

He went to the window, hoping Ewan had not made a

surprise appearance. It was more than likely that DCI Yorke had come to check on Brookes, or it could be an animal trying to shelter from the cold. He edged back the curtain and peered outside.

'Dad,' Cynthia said, 'where did you go?'

Standing two metres in front of Brookes' motorhome was a tall man in a long black cloak.

'I'm going to have to go, Cynthia. I'm sorry and thank you.'

The man stood there, ankle deep in the snow, looking at the motorhome. He seemed ambivalent to the flurries swirling around him. Content to simply stand there, and stare.

'Is everything alright Dad?'

'Yes, I love you, darling.'

He hung up and limped over to his kitchen. Trying to ignore the sudden tremble picking up force in his hands, he laid his mobile phone down, and opened the cupboard beneath the kitchen sink. He reached to the back and pulled out his shotgun; another illegal purchase, and one that he was now very grateful he'd taken the time to make. Turning, he kept the shotgun facing down, flat against his good leg and edged his way back over to the window. He peered out again.

The white face stared back in at him.

Riley gasped, stumbled back and let the curtain flutter closed.

He'd been in jail for a large part of his life and he'd seen thousands of tortured souls before, but never one like that. At this point, Riley was under no illusion. The man who had murdered Jessica was here.

Trembling all over, he peered out again, just in time to see Brookes' motorhome door shut.

Instinctively, he reached for his mobile again, and phoned Brookes, but he was sent straight to voicemail. He tried again but got the same result.

Then his battery gave out and his phone screen went blank.

Riley wasn't a fighter, never had been. Even in jail, when such behaviours were necessary to keep you alive, he'd only used it as a last resort. It would be easy to lock his caravan door and hunker down. Riley stared down at the shotgun; he cracked it to check that both barrels were loaded. He knew it was, but a simple check never hurt anybody. His best option was to get his phone plugged in, and phone the police.

And then Riley realised something. It might take five minutes for his old phone to burst back into life. If Brookes came back now, he would go into his motorhome and he would either be killed or kill this murderer and destine himself to the life that Riley had led. A dark life caged in behind thick walls. He looked down at his shotgun again. If he himself went, he could rid the world of this tortured entity and then, if they banged him up again, so what? His life was surely nearing its conclusion, and the opportunity for Brookes and Ewan to live together in peace was worth far more.

Decision made.

He scooped up the photograph of his two-year-old grandchild; a young boy with the same smile as him and slid it into his jeans pocket. He also buried a handful of shotgun shells into his other pocket. He limped to his door, opened it, took his cane with his left hand while he held the shotgun with the other and stepped out into the cold.

Eddies of snow circled, and the icy wind pounded him. His old body struggled. He knew all about nature from his younger years working on his father's farm. It issued warnings and demanded respect; if you ignored it, you left it no choice, and it would take you inside itself. There you would stay.

His leg creaked and the red lamb's wool jumper failed him. He'd only gone four metres when he started to wobble on his cane and his strength melted like the snow on his forehead. He glanced back at his own caravan; it glowed like a burning star. It felt as if he'd been away from the warmth, light and his daughter's soothing voice for an eternity rather than a matter of seconds. He turned back to Brookes' motorhome.

After seeing that face, Riley had realised that there was nothing in that man that could be salvaged; there was no similarity with that poor boy that had tried to take his leg off in jail. That kid had been bloated on hate, and anger. This man was different. He did not have the capacity to hate - he simply brought death with him, wherever he went, like a plague.

Here we have the true definition of evil, thought Riley.

The lights went on in the motorhome.

Riley realised he was close now, only five metres away. He thought of the photograph in his pocket. He thought about Ewan. He felt ready to protect the world from this man.

A shadow passed across the curtained window at the back of the motorhome; the bastard was in the master bedroom. Riley stopped. If the psycho opened the curtain, he would see Riley coming towards the motorhome. He knew he didn't have the strength left to fire his shotgun standing; the recoil would put him flat on his back, so he dropped his cane and crouched to his knees. The pain in his bad leg was excruciating and was soothed only momentarily by the cold snow soaking into his jeans. In a two-handed grip, he lifted his shotgun high and supported it against his shoulder. As the curtain fluttered, he cocked his head to the right, squeezed shut his left eye and put the window in the sight.

Nothing happened. Riley feared that the killer had seen him and was now hidden and waiting. If he lost his advantage, he was doomed—

The icy face appeared. Riley only paused long enough to confirm it wasn't Brookes or Ewan before squeezing the trigger on his double-barrelled shotgun. The window exploded and the shot echoed like a thunderclap. Riley slid back but managed to stay on his knees, although he bobbed back and forth like a pendulum. It took him a moment to regain his composure and then he stared at the shattered window and the curtain flapping in the wind.

Possessing limbs that had mostly failed him in recent years, he was proud to see he was able to shoot straight. After catching his breath, he took some shells from his pocket and reloaded. He doubted anyone could have survived that from five metres away, but if the murderer had made it out of the way, he would need to be ready.

He grabbed his cane and, fighting the burning pain in his leg, forced himself back to his feet. The snow spiralled down even harder now, so he moved quickly.

Even though he was confident that he'd shot him, the sight of the door of the motorhome banging open and closed in the wind caused him to hesitate. He dropped his cane, took his shotgun into a two-handed grip again and used both barrels to wedge the door open. He crept inside and surveyed the interior of the motorhome. He couldn't see anyone. He took another step inside and the door slammed behind him.

Despite being out of the vicious weather, Riley had never felt so cold. The monster in this motorhome, alive or dead, had presence. With his finger curled around the trigger, he limped as quietly as he could with his mouth closed tightly, so that his rapid breaths did not whistle as they slipped past his lips.

Leading with his shotgun, he entered Brookes' bedroom. The curtains billowed next to the shattered window. His eyes darted around the room and he stared down at the floor. Nothing but smashed glass.

The lights went off.

He took a deep breath as his blood ran cold, then turned and limped out of the room; his heart thrashing in his chest so hard it hurt. He could hardly see, but swung the shot gun back and forth, determined to fire at the first sign of movement. His hands were sweating so much that he feared the shotgun may slip. He looked at the front door, weighing up whether he stood a better chance out there—

The toilet door to his right burst open. Riley snapped his head around and saw a cavernous mouth bearing down on him. He tried to swing the shotgun, but it now felt as heavy as a cannon and Riley wasn't the quickest.

The jaws of the creature closed.

Two QUICK PINTS of *Summer Lightning* managed to kill the hangover Brookes had worked up the previous evening with a bottle of whisky.

He moved his eyes from the hearth, where the fire sizzled, popped and threw up hypnotic spiralling embers, and looked at the bar.

Decision time.

Riley's words from earlier moved around his mind: *you have one priority left, that son of yours. That bold, handsome and cocky little tyke. Promise me right now that that's it. That is all you focus on. That is all Jessica would want you to focus on.*

He watched Kenny turn from the bar, clutching a fresh pint of *Lightning*. He was almost seventy-five; his hand trembled slightly as he lifted the ale to his mouth and, despite looking frail, he proved there was nothing wrong with his drinking skills and took a huge mouthful.

He sat down beside Brookes.

'The thing I like more about *the Haunch*, more than any other pub,' said Kenny in his thick, Wiltshire slur, 'is that this pub is older than me.'

'Every pub around here is older than you, Kenny,' Brookes said, suddenly feeling empty-handed without a pint.

'True, but this one is even older. The shit that used to go on under these old oak beams; the fighting, the gambling, *the prostitution*. Ah, to have been born in the fourteenth century!'

'Kenny, you wouldn't have made it to seventy-five if you'd been born in the fourteenth century.'

He held up his pint. 'You can survive anything when *fuelled by the lightning.*'

'There wasn't any Summer Lightning then!'

'I would have invented it.' Kenny tilted his head back and journeyed to the half-way point in his pint. He wiped his mouth with the back of his hand. 'You not having another one?'

'Don't know, haven't decided yet.'

'Well, what's the dilemma?'

'The usual one. If I have another one, I'll have to go all in.'

'Sounds like a familiar dilemma.'

'Okay, so if it hasn't harmed you ...'

'I'm a seventy-five-year-old man sitting in a pub on his own.'

'There's worse ways to spend old age.'

'Yes, but not nearly every day of the week.'

'So, your advice is to go home?'

'I don't give advice.' Kenny smiled. 'Look at me. However, if you ask me, I never found what I was looking for in a glass, and I've been looking for it a long time. By the way, how is that son of yours? Ewan?'

Brookes stood up. 'Safe.'

'Good.'

'And that's the way I plan to keep it. Bye, Kenny.'

Kenny smiled. 'Be seeing you, Iain.'

On the way out of the *Haunch of Venison*, he took his phone from his pocket to see if he had any missed calls, and noticed his battery was dead.

It was only on the journey back to the caravan park, with his phone plugged into the charger, that he able to receive his message from Riley about the man in his motorhome that could have been Jessica's murderer.

When his phone rang again, his voice shook. 'Yes?'

'Iain, it's your dad.'

'Dad, I've got to go, something has come up ...'

'Listen! I just got home from the shop. I'm so sorry, son ...'

'What?'

'I'm sorry ...'

'Now, you're really scaring me.'

'Ewan's gone.'

'Where?'

'Back to you. He left a note. He found some money in the house and used it to get a train. The note says that you needed him.'

'When?' The word crackled; his throat was dry now.

'I don't know; it doesn't say. I'm sorry, I had no idea—'

He hung up. The road ahead of him seemed to pulse and he couldn't swallow. He took a deep breath and slammed his foot down on the accelerator.

———

YORKE and his colleagues hung back and let armed response do their work. As soon as the location was secure – and Terrence Lock's absence confirmed, the place was taped off as a crime scene. There was a dead body in there and a young lady who was, quite remarkably, still alive.

Yorke lit a cigarette and Gardner narrowed her eyes.

'Not now, Emma,' Yorke said.

'When I chose a godfather for Annabelle, I chose a non-smoker.'

'That's quite dramatic, Emma,' Topham said.

'True though,' she said.

Yorke threw the cigarette on the floor. Gardner held her hand out and Yorke, with a sigh, pulled the cigarette packet from his pocket and placed it in her hand.

In one pocket, she slid the cigarettes; from the other, she pulled some tic tacs. 'Try these. They work for me.'

'No thanks,' Yorke said. He heard Jake chuckle to the left of him.

One of the officers was leading the kidnapped woman out through the front door. She was trembling and leaned against the officer's shoulder. 'Jake and Mark,' Yorke said, 'interview the young lady. Emma, we'll go in.'

Yorke and Gardner crunched through the snow and through the front door, pausing briefly to access the bagged-up white suits, and ensure they were logged in.

Lance Reynolds, who was managing the SOCOs, came down the corridor with his camera dangling from his neck. 'It's cramped in the cellar where we found the body and the girl tied to a radiator.'

Reynolds explained that the woman was called Rachel Lister and provided the details of how she'd ended up in the cellar, and how her partner had been murdered.

Yorke pointed down the corridor at the fish tank. 'The octopus?'

'Gone,' Reynolds said. 'What we've found upstairs is particularly shocking, sir. I suggest I take you both up there first?'

Yorke nodded and they followed Reynolds up the stairs. It seemed to grow colder with every step, and he wondered if a window had been left open upstairs.

Reynolds led them down the corridor and, despite knowing he wasn't going to be seeing a body up here, Yorke still reached up to check the top button of his shirt was fastened underneath the white suit; he could already feel the cold beginning to prickle him there. At the door of the last room, they all froze and stared at the two clubs laced with blades; they looked primitive, but deadly nonetheless.

Reynolds opened the door and ushered them in. Two SOCOs nodded in greeting and then continued their own explorations.

The filament of a red bulb flickered and the room beneath it twitched. Yorke and Gardner moved inside and although the walls weren't stone, the place had a cold damp feel you would expect from a temple, and their footsteps seemed to echo. Incense was heavy in the air. Walls were buried beneath tapestries Yorke recognized from his hours of gruelling research on the internet; their colours blunted by the crimson light. His eyes fell to an image of a sacrificed man with his chest open; he was surrounded by a gaggle of priests watching his heart begin its ascent to the sun.

This was the diseased and pulsating heart of Lock's world.

Yorke glanced at Gardner, the colour had drained from her face. 'This place feels like a fucking tomb,' she said.

Yorke didn't reply, he was staring into a stone basin filled with ash. Lock certainly had an old-fashioned approach to heating. He headed towards the altar, on which a statue was poised to attack from a pyramid of slabs. He touched Lock's venerated deity, Tezcatlipoca; it was ice cold. The statue was carved from obsidian, with all the attention to detail Lock probably took over dissecting his victims. Tezcatlipoca danced as if to mock them in their belief that they could stop his faithful servant and wore his smoking mirror on his foot. *The mirror that could see inside all of them.*

Yorke then leaned over a small frying pan with a handle shaped like a serpent. It was half-filled with sand to provide insulation from the heat; while copal, the aromatic tree resin Utter told him about, was burned on a heated charcoal tablet. This close, the smell stung his nostrils. Beside the incense burner was a small, flint knife and next to that a jade bowl, which Yorke recoiled from when he caught the scent of blood. It was surely the bowl with which he offered his sacrifices. He also noticed two plastic tubes; one tube contained a clump of black hair and the other had longer, blonde hair inside. *Preston and Jessica's hair perhaps? Was he keeping souvenirs?*

'Prepare yourself for this,' Reynolds said, and guided them over to the altar. He pointed into the shadows beside the statue. Above them, the filament of the bulb flickered and buzzed again; it wouldn't hold out for too much longer.

The SOCO backed away from a glass jar they were dusting for prints. What Yorke saw made his blood run cold; beside him, he heard Gardner gasp. He prayed for it all to be a hallucination and closed his eyes, but when he opened them again, the jar was still there.

The bloodless heart took on the yellow glow of the sallow liquid it floated in. Severed veins and arteries rose from the organ and swayed in the liquid, like seaweed.

'Do you think ...?' Yorke said, but he couldn't finish his question.

'That it's Jessica Brookes' heart?' Reynolds said. 'I don't know.'

'Does it matter?' Gardener said, unable to keep the fact that she was nearly in tears from her voice. 'It was someone's ... and he took it.'

The filament fizzled one more time and then they were in darkness.

15

BENJAMIN RILEY WANTED to look this man in the eyes just once before he died; and while doing so, wanted to ask him why he had murdered Jessica Brookes.

He had experienced darkness many times in his life before. The time his wife was raped; the time he murdered the wanker who did it; his years behind bars; and the kid who tried to hack off his leg – to mention just a few. Riley certainly was no stranger to it. He'd actually thought, or believed, for quite some time he *understood* it. But now he realised how wrong he'd been.

This was new.

Quite different.

The wound on his left cheek stung, and the blood showed no sign of slowing. He could taste it in his mouth. He spat on the floor, and then looked up at the source of the darkness pacing back and forth in front of him.

The peculiar-looking psychopath, who looked as if he had been dipped in bleach, had come at him like a savage animal. If he had bitten as deeply into his neck as he had done his cheek, he would be dead already. After he'd been overcome, Riley had been lashed tightly to a wooden dining chair.

The situation had worsened when the killer had discovered the gun Riley had given Brookes on the bedside table. How Riley wished that his hands were free, and that his own shotgun, which the fucker had kicked under the sofa, was still in his possession.

The killer paced back and forth, staring at the floor, holding the gun, thinking about what, God only knows. *What do psychos think about?*

The snowstorm outside was now raging and the persistent winds rocked the motorhome back and forth. Under different circumstances, Riley would find the motion soothing, but now, he was sure that only the demon child was the one being soothed. He half-expected the branch of a tree to break through a window like the hand of a great maternal demon and stroke its child's head, to encourage its malevolent mind. Encourage it to mature and become a prince.

At that point, Riley would, most certainly, die.

But Ewan wasn't here and so was safe. Also, Brookes would get the warning by voicemail and would evade this ambush. Riley's family were now happy; true, he not had chance to meet his wonderful little grandson, but you couldn't have everything. All in all, it was as good a time as any to die. He was old and he had seen more than enough senselessness. He reckoned he could handle it; besides, it would give him a break from this damned leg ...

So, fuck the weather and fuck you killer, tonight, I'm ready to die. Just so long as I get to look you in your eyes, just once, before I do, and ask you why.

As a child, Terrence Lock had loved knots. As a scout, he'd been fascinated by the sense of finality that a tied knot brought. He had mastered them all; the figure-eight knot, the reef knot, the bowline, the timber hitch and his beloved sheep shank. There was logic in a knot that wasn't in life. It always felt finished and complete; and more importantly, incorruptible. Climbers, sailors and skydivers all entrusted their lives to a knot. Since becoming Tezcacoatl, he was certain his plan had been a well-tied knot.

Yet, since Gillian, nothing seemed to be going right. *Could knots defy their certainty and unravel?*

Tezcacoatl walked over to the old man, forced a rag into his mouth, pinned the gun to his leg and blew a hole in it.

Riley's scream would have emerged like a homeless banshee, braved the winds and snow to seek out help, and torn the skin from the murderer's face on route.

But the rag forced into his mouth held the scream and the pain inside. So, instead, he let out a long guttural moan and rocked back and forth in the chair.

When the killer pulled the rag out of his mouth, it seemed to help, and the agony subsided, momentarily. More than likely it was the sudden onset of hyperventilation and blood loss working together to kill the pain.

'Where is the boy, Ewan Brookes?' The killer asked.

'The least you could have done …' Riley paused for another breath. 'Was shoot me in the other leg. The one which is already fucked.' He closed his eyes.

'Well, if I shoot you again, you will die. You will bleed to death and you will not have achieved anything, because I will stay here and wait for Ewan all night if I have to.'

Riley opened his eyes and, for a moment, was quite surprised that he was still alive. He groaned when his leg started to feel like it was going through an incinerator again. If he survived this, he would be spending the rest of his days in a wheelchair. He remembered the old idiom – *you won't have a leg to stand on*, and a smile crept across his face.

'Why are you smiling? Do you not believe me?'

'It's not that,' Riley said. 'But you can wait, if you want. All night. He isn't coming back.'

'This is where he lives.'

'For a bigshot serial killer, you do not seem so intelligent or well-organized.'

Gritting his teeth in agony, Riley considered the monster. How this waif had managed to wrestle him to the ground, he had no idea; his face was gaunt, and he looked like he hadn't eaten in months. His black hair fell past his shoulders and combined with his long black cape, accentuated his albino skin. The bastard looked and sounded like he had just climbed out of a coffin.

The killer turned away.

'Hey! You turn back around. Show some respect to your elders! That's what we do in this country. We respect one another, and we don't take mothers away from their children – *you murderous animal.*'

The monster turned around. His face looked as if it had been frozen in ice. He said, 'First of all, this is not my country; and secondly, you talk of murder.' He cocked his head to the left. 'I do not murder, because that implies I act from hate or anger; I do not act from either, no matter what you and others choose to believe.'

Riley sucked in a deep breath. 'No, I don't believe you.' Unflinching, he stared into the killer's eyes. 'Your face doesn't move, but I can still see that fucking look in your eyes. I've seen it in people's eyes before. Never quite this bad before, admittedly, but I've seen it.'

The killer averted his gaze.

The old man could hear the steady drip of his own blood on the motorhome floor; he was also starting to feel light-headed. He didn't look down at the wound; he didn't want to know how much damage had been done to his good leg. He took some deep breaths to try and ward off the pain, so he could continue talking. 'Let me tell you about someone I knew once. Okay?'

'Why is that relevant?'

'Trust me, it is.'

The murderer nodded.

'When I was in jail, I knew a man called Darren Crawford. A fool who was sentenced to ten years when he ran over a young girl while drunk and high on cocaine. Crawford was only thirty and was, despite his behaviour, a happily married man with a high-flying job. It all disappeared that night in one reckless moment. Eventually, Crawford became a *Creeper.*'

The tall man narrowed his eyes, clearly confused.

'A *Creeper* is someone who cannot cope with what they've done, or what they've lost. They change. Become hollowed out almost. You can see it in their eyes. We called them *Creepers,* while we were inside, for obvious reasons. They'd linger in the shadows, often silently. They'd lie awake at night, muttering to themselves; sometimes masturbate. You get the picture.' Riley paused to cough; he turned to his side and spat blood on the floor. 'So, there they were, these *Creepers,* skulking, thinking, often plotting and generally freaking many people out in the vicinity. But remaining passive. Or at least that's what we thought.'

'I am not seeing the point of all this.'

'You will, or maybe you won't. I don't care much either way.' He took a deep breath, and continued, desperately trying to hide the tremble in his voice. 'One day, he smashed another inmate's head so hard into the tap on the shower, the poor bastard was literally left hanging there. Then, Crawford himself charged into the wall, again and again, bouncing his own head off the tiles, until he was no more. The other inmates stood back and allowed him to do it while the guards attempted to get through to him. They were happy to see Crawford smashing in his own skull. It was the least he deserved for his savage behaviour.' Riley paused again, feeling incredibly light-headed now; he wondered if fear and blood-loss had turned his own face as pale as this cold-hearted monster in front of him.

Riley looked up at him; the killer was staring at him intently. Riley continued, 'The inmate hanging off the tap? It was his first day. Crawford never even knew him. Maybe he looked at him funny? Maybe Crawford just felt like it? *Creepers*, you see. Hollowed out, empty. They lose their humanity and their souls.'

'What is your point?'

Riley spat out more blood; this time, on the maniac's shoes. Then, he stared deep into his eyes. 'I'm saying that you can stand there and tell me that you kill for a reason, and I will look you right back in the eyes and call you a *Creeper*. A hollowed-out *Creeper*.'

Movement flickered over the monster's face like the tiniest ripple on a lake.

'An empty, soulless creeper.'

The killer turned away. Riley stared down at the floor. He closed his eyes and took a deep breath. 'An evil fucking *Creeper*,' he said and then thought of the picture of his grandson in his pocket and the smile that would one day break hearts. 'Why don't you just leave us all alo—'

———

AFTER HE'D SHOT the old man twice in the chest and watched his last breath trail out, Tezcacoatl put the gun to his own head and it felt right.

Brandon, and now, this old man.

These deaths today had not been willing sacrifices; they had been pointless. He had always known that people would die in battle during the building of the Second Age, but he'd always believed death in battle should be honourable. There was nothing honourable about these deaths today. They were merely victims, not warriors.

He should have put the gun to his head this morning after the owl had sung. He should have realised why Lord Tezcatlipoca had not spoken to him in so long - he had failed and he had been abandoned.

His finger settled on the trigger.

He closed his eyes and thought again of the gentle touch of his mother's silk dress against his skin as he lay on her lap; their hands brushing against each other as they smoothed out the body of the snowman; and the sunrises that seemed to promise a glorious future despite the pain she was enduring.

I am sorry, he thought, *I tried, I really did.*

And now what was it they called him. A serial killer? A psychopath? A monster? *A Creeper?*

Alone, never to be accepted, he had failed in his bid for the Second Age. He would have to leave them all alone now to wallow in their self-obsession and destructive natures.

He felt tears in the corners of his eyes. He almost didn't

recognize the sensation; it had been so long. He tensed his finger on the trigger. This time he would—

The motorhome glowed. His eyes flicked open. 'My Lord!'

And the light was everywhere. It moved around him, and then it seemed to move inside him. It was like sunrise with his mother. He felt his soul warm and he knew he wasn't a cold killer - he had a purpose!

And for the first time, since he was a child, he felt what the commoners would describe as joy; and he realised that emotions were not all bad, and he would happily welcome this one again.

He ran to the broken window in the back bedroom. The raging wind smashed into his face and his long hair rose in the air around him. He watched the young slave climb out of the taxi beside the caravan the old man had come from.

'Lord Tezcatlipoca, I hear and I understand!'

Despite the fact that Riley's caravan had looked like a burning meteorite buried amongst the trees on his approach in the taxi, the place had never felt so cold and desolate to Ewan. The snow drove fiercely into his face as he ran the five metres from the taxi to the door. He knocked hard on the caravan door and, when no one answered, he looked back, with regret, to see the rear-view lights of the taxi disappear into the emptiness.

He was suddenly gladder than ever for Freddy, who was buried in the backpack slung over his shoulder. He waited another ten seconds or so for Riley to open the door, but it was too snowy and cold to remain outside, so he opened it himself and entered.

Inside, he dodged past the leaves and vines hanging from the many planter baskets on the ceiling, coiling forth like tentacles reaching out from a hostile world. 'Riley?'

Wondering why the old man had not announced himself yet caused a faint tremble in his legs and he moved quickly around the caravan, calling his friend's name, holding onto the expectation that he would eventually emerge from behind one of his two huge, potted bonsais.

He noticed a letter from Riley's daughter by the sink and read it. It was a plea for Riley to let their relationship heal; that her husband was a changed man who desperately wanted to get to know the grandfather of his son. His eyes lingered over the words that were darker than the others; here, she must have pressed her pen down hard.

And Sam, your Grandson will adore you, and when you meet him you will see that none of what has gone before really matters. It is the future that matters. It is him that matters.

For a moment, Ewan wondered if Riley had gone to see his family, but he threw that idea out when he remembered that the front door had been unlocked. But where could he be? The lights in his father's motorhome were out, leading him to conclude that his father was away ...

Unless, maybe Riley and his father were in there watching television with all the lights off?

Back outside, he struggled to keep upright in the deepening snow. He was glad he had put a ski jacket over his fleece but cursed himself for leaving behind his hat. The cold was really biting deep now.

He spotted the smashed window and stopped dead. His eyes swung to the trees, drowning in snow, and he heard himself swallow even above the howling wind.

The jaguar.

He broke into a run and flung himself through the door of the motorhome. Inside, he saw Riley collapsed forward, straining the ropes holding him to the chair, his open eyes fixed on the growing pool of blood at his feet.

'*Riley?*'

The motorhome rattled around him under a sudden gust of wind.

'*Please Riley ...*' He took another step forward.

A long line of drool extended from Riley's mouth. Ewan knew that he was dead. He also knew that he needed to run. But first, where was his father?

'Dad?'

He stepped around the pool of blood, shuddering when he glanced at Riley's wide-open eyes. He switched on the first bedroom light and saw that his father was not there; he then tried his bedroom. He wasn't there either.

Then he felt something press into the back of his head and knew that the jaguar had come.

'Ewan, I have a gun to your head. I want you to kneel on the floor and put your hands behind your back,' the beast said into his ear. The voice was clear to understand but felt very wrong. 'I have your father, if you want to see him again, do as I say.'

Ewan knelt. He felt Riley's blood soak into his jeans and experienced a wave of nausea. Seeing Riley dead, and now hearing his father's life was in danger, made him feel like he was in a plane spiralling out of control. He felt his wrists being lashed together, grimacing as the killer tightened the coarse rope.

'Stand up.'

'Where's my dad?'

'Stand up now, or I will do to you what I did to your friend here, and to your mother.'

Ewan felt the world tilt underneath him.

Your mother. They used to be words of tenderness, but in the aftermath of her execution, they closed around his throat like a noose.

'I want to speak to my father before I do anything.'

The killer scooped up Ewan's backpack from the pool of blood. He shook it out and Freddy flopped to the floor. At first, Freddy looked stunned, but then he hissed and flicked his tail in the blood, splashing Ewan's face.

'Freddy ...'

'Your snake doesn't have to die, you know, serpents are wonderful creatures. I would prefer your snake to live.'

From the corner of his eye, Ewan saw the monster raise its boot above Freddy's head.

'No ... don't, I'll do what you say.'

Ewan rose to his feet.

'Now, we need to go outside and Freddy will be fine.' He scooped Freddy up and threw him back into the backpack.

Back outside in the cold, the monster marched Ewan through the trees. He wondered how far they would get, before his mother's killer chose a suitable place of execution. If he died here, it would be days before they found him. Days in which nature would feast. He considered running, but that would condemn Freddy and his dad - if the killer wasn't bluffing - to certain death; besides, he'd seen enough movies to know he'd definitely take a bullet in the back.

He wriggled his hands; they were firmly tied by rope. The wind whistled through the trees and Ewan felt like he was wading deeper into a sanctuary for tortured souls.

Eventually they emerged from the patch of trees onto the country road that turned into the caravan site. He looked around desperately, but no one was coming. He was led by his kidnapper to a threatening white van.

When he stepped around him to open the van door, Ewan got his first glimpse of his mother's killer, and realised how grave the danger was. Riley's blood speckled his pale face and his eyes seemed dead.

The killer waved Ewan into the van with his gun. When he climbed in, he saw an old woman gurgling in the corner. The man untied his wrists but then handcuffed them to the rail running around the van interior. He tried kicking out at the emaciated, white creep, but his feet were brushed away.

Maybe this is just part of the dream that began yesterday, thought Ewan.

'Where's my dad?'

'I need you to cry, Ewan.'

'What are you talking about? I want my dad!'

'I said I need you to cry. The festival of Atemoztli depends on it.' Ewan detected a little excitement in the bastard's voice this time, as if there were actually traces of emotions in him, which glowed occasionally like dying embers. 'Think of your friend, the old man. Or think of your mother if that is easier. But I want you to cry.'

Ewan decided he'd had enough of doing what this vile beast said. 'No – I want to see my dad before I do anything else you tell—'

'Your choice,' the killer said and emptied the rucksack on the floor. Freddy didn't like being disturbed a second time; he tried to slide away from the madman and out the van door. But the monster was too quick. He ground Freddy's head into the floor with his boot and Ewan started to cry.

16

I T WAS LATE, and Yorke's mind raced. He was journeying home from yet another crime scene and he was verging on exhaustion.

He couldn't wait to pull Patricia close against him and feel her skin on his. She would help him forget everything for at least a few hours.

His phone rang. It was Brookes, talking so fast that he was barely comprehensible; however, he got the gist of what he was being told.

As he changed direction, Yorke told Brookes that the man was called Terrence Lock, and that he believed he was an Aztec Priest required to initiate a Second Age. He also told him anything that he thought could help him if he was to bump into the killer before he got there.

He didn't bother attempting to talk Brookes out of going. What was the point? He wouldn't listen. Roles reversed – would Yorke have listened?

After the call ended, he phoned the station and then contacted Gardner.

Iain Brookes wanted his world back.

A world where he had known love, and the sharing, for better or for worse, of a warm embrace in the cold hours of the morning; of the hope in a child's first smile; and of a passionate argument that would burn for days. He wanted the world where he had known life, and its taste, for richer and for poorer, of that jug of iced tea brewed on a summer's day; of the crash of that first wave on an open mouth; and a tear drunk from the eye of another.

Iain Brookes did not want this world. He saw loss as a cadaver with its heart cut out, hanging from a meat hook, spooling in the cold wind. He saw evil as a living corpse with a lifeless brain, dragging its decaying feet along the ground, scraping bloody lines into the bitter snow.

The white Ford Transit van, partially camouflaged by the swirling snow, burst from the night.

Brookes didn't have much time to think, so he had to assume that his son was in the van with Jessica's murderer.

He punched his brakes, let the snow suck him across the path of the van at a ninety-degree angle and braced himself. The passenger door of his car caved inwards, the wind was bashed out of him and the window imploded. His vehicle was dragged sideways down the road with the van lodged in its side like a spear.

The killer forced his van onwards, clearly desperate to plough Brookes' car out of the way. The wind howled through the smashed car window.

Eventually, the killer was forced to concede defeat, and let his van grind to a halt.

Everything was still. Brookes glanced around the interior of his car, illuminated by the van's headlights which were pressed deep into his vehicle's bodywork. His front window was completely cracked, and no piece had been kind enough to break away, to allow him to see outside. He undid his seatbelt and then heard the clunk of the van door opening.

There was a loud gunshot and he felt chunks of glass pepper his face. He threw his hand out, grasped the door handle and pitched himself from the car. He hoped the snow would soften the blow. It didn't. He attempted to climb to his feet, but it was too slippery, and he hit the deck again. Winded, it was even harder to rise the second time, but he did, and even made it into a squat—

Another gunshot. A white flash. He hit the snow *again;* this time, face first.

When the cold ground started to burn his face, he lifted it from the ground and then groaned at the agonising pain in his shoulder. He rolled onto his back, looked down and saw blood seeping through his jacket.

His ex-wife's murderer hovered above him, looking down at him like a predator, instinct-driven and emotionless. The killer stepped nearer, exhaled sharply through his nose, bared his teeth and aimed the gun at his head. With a shudder, Brookes recognised it as the gun from his motorhome. 'Where's my son?'

He didn't respond.

'Is he in the van? Let him go.'

'I cannot.'

Brookes narrowed his eyes. 'You feel at home out here in the wilderness, do you?'

'What do you mean, Iain?' He cocked his head from side-to-side as if to examine his prey.

'Exactly what I said. Does the feral animal feel at home out in the wild?'

The bastard could pull the trigger at any point. It was either taunt him or beg him. And if he begged and then died anyway, he'd never forgive himself if there was an afterlife.

But the killer didn't appear taunted, just inquisitive. A burst of wind raised his long hair up around him and when he took a step forward, he looked like he was stepping out of a black cloud. His ears looked like large, fleshy tumours.

'It's over, Lock.'

Terrence Lock paused and looked confused.

'Sorry, did I pronounce it wrong? *L—o—c—k.*' He paused, stressing the letters had caused him excruciating pain. He glanced down at the bullet wound and saw that he was bleeding a lot. 'Wake up, Lock, we know who you are, it's over!'

Lock shook his head. 'No. It's only just beginning.'

'Are you not listening? We know your identity.'

'We are not born with identities, we are given them, so I have given myself a new one.'

Despite his flimsy black gown, Lock wasn't shivering. Brookes suspected that he thrived off the cold.

'You murdered the mother of my child. It's a shame you are the one with the gun,' Brookes said.

'She gave herself for a reason. One day, people will realise the significance of her sacrifice.'

'Jessica never gave herself,' He attempted to sit up; the pain was unbearable, so he eased himself back down.

'You cry for Jessica, but what I have given to her was preferable to the life of slavery she was living. A life of slavery given to her by you, Iain. You are another perfect example of a slave to his own need. A need that has destroyed lives. First Jessica's, then Ewan's, and finally, yours.'

'You're insane.'

'Where were you when she needed you? When her mother was sick? When your son was being bullied at school? I know all about you, Iain. I know what you denied them.'

'I had a job, *gobshite*, helping people. Doing something about you will also help people. *A lot of people.*'

'You are not in any position to do anything. All you do now is delay me, because what I have to do far exceeds the importance of this dialogue.'

'*Show me my son!*'

'It is over.' He aimed the gun at Brookes' head. 'This is not what I wanted, or envisaged, but ...'

'Is it what your lord wants?' Brookes said, thinking back to his brief conversation with Yorke and what he could remember from it.

'You know a lot. Too much in fact.'

'I know everything. And I'm telling you, Lock, you need to end this right now, before it is ended for you, and not in the way you'd wish.'

'What if I told you I already offered to stop, and that Lord Tezcatlipoca refused? That He wishes me to continue?'

'Come on, Lock, even if this Aztec deity was real why would he communicate with you?'

'He has been communicating with me since I was fourteen years old.'

'They're delusions, Lock. My God—'

'*Your god, Iain?*' It was as if he'd hurled a stone at an approaching snake, causing it to hiss now with bared teeth.

'*Do you even know who He is?*' The hand holding the weapon had started to shake. Accidentally, or intentionally, that gun was going to discharge.

'No,' Iain said.

'So do not speak to me of your false god. He is the delusion. A delusion created for profit. The Conquistadors looted our graves for gold, and what do the slaves do who turn to a Christian god? They hoard, they self-obsess, and they destroy in the name of personal enhancement.'

Brookes could see that Lock was losing control and sensed an opportunity to use this situation to his advantage. Brookes' own hatred for this man was consuming him inside and out, and the pain in his shoulder was excruciating, but he could still act rationally. If he didn't, he would be dead within a matter of seconds and his son would quickly follow. He looked over at the van.

'Okay ... so show me, Lock, take me with you now.'

'What?'

'Make me understand.'

'Why?'

'I can be willing too, just like Jessica was, just like my son is.'

Lock sneered. 'And you expect me to suddenly believe you?'

'Probably not, but would you deny me the opportunity to understand? How would your lord feel about that?'

'Your attempts to trick me are pathetic.'

'Tell me why you do this Lock?'

'It is *not* Lock, *it is* Tezcacoatl!'

'Okay, so tell me, Tezcacoatl – you told me that you want people to understand.'

'Isn't it obvious? Our world heats up and we all melt. Around us, it's brittle and it crumbles. Nature is changeable and angry. I watch the sun rise every day, but sometimes I expect it not to come.'

'And how did you find out that *this* way works?'

'Lord Tezcatlipoca showed me Tenochtitlan in my dreams. It is a glorious place. At that time, the people knew about the cyclical nature of man and the natural world, and they understood the respect that had to be shown to the gods.'

Brookes remembered something else that Yorke had told him. 'And this will happen again, with the Second Age? The one that you will lead?'

'You really do know a great deal.'

'Everything. Like I said to you already. And I'm interested, genuinely. Educate me.'

'It would be quicker to just—'

'Execute me? And how would your lord feel about you executing someone who desires to know? A non-believer looking for truth? It will be difficult for your lord to build a new following if the people cannot trust Him.'

'I think that He would know, at this point, that it was completely necessary.'

'Really? He wouldn't consider it *vindictive*?'

Lock's eyes darted both ways. Colour even crept into his pale face.

'Educate me and then I will offer myself as a willing sacrifice,' Brookes said.

'This is nonsense,' Lock said, but he took a step back, and the gun wavered in his hand.

'Take me with you and Ewan. I am willing too, but not out here, not on the road like a dog. That is cold-blooded, Tezcacoatl. Even as a *slave to need* as you called me before, I deserve a good death.'

'A flowery death?'

'*Yes, that's right*, a flowery death.'

Lock paused to think; meanwhile, Brookes shivered and chewed his bottom lip. The pain in his shoulder was intense, and his head grew lighter by the second.

'Behave like a leader,' Brookes said, 'not someone who is vindictive and untrusting. Show your lord that you are worthy and give me this flowery death.'

Lock looked annoyed. He took a deep breath. 'Get to your feet.'

Brookes used his left hand to push himself into a sitting position; he realised his entire body was drenched now from the falling snow. Lock backed away to allow him room to get to his feet. The killer's eyes remained wide despite the flakes of snow melting on his irises.

'If you make any sudden movements, you will lose any entitlement you have, and I will shoot you. Face the van and walk towards it.'

Brookes did as he was told, and they conducted the journey to the back of the van in silence. Shielding his eyes from the snow, he glanced at his shoulder; it was difficult to see the damage through his blood-soaked jacket.

Once they reached the back of the van, Brookes didn't need to be told to open it. His son was inside, so he had to restrain himself from tearing the door off.

Inside, the air stank of desperation. An elderly woman stared at him from the back of the lit van. Her eyes were wide open and looked empty. A long line of drool swung like a pendulum from her chin. Ewan was curled up on his side, facing the door; he was handcuffed to a metal bar that ran the length of the van, about half a metre from the floor. It must have been uncomfortable. His eyes were that puffy he looked as if he'd been beaten.

'*Dad!*' Ewan said.

'Son!' Brookes forced back tears.

'This man killed Riley and Freddy.'

Riley. Brookes clenched his hands; his nails dug into his palms.

Brookes noticed Freddy's body on the floor in front of Ewan, glistening in the light. The monster had turned his head into a bloody pulp. Brookes longed to turn and face Lock but knew the risks of doing that were too great.

'Get into the van, put your hands behind your back,' Lock said, 'and lie face down.'

Brookes forced his body to obey. The stakes had intensified because the possibility of him now dying in front of his son existed. He climbed into the van and lay face down on the floor, careful not to brush against Freddy's remains.

The turbulent weather outside would, on any other occasion, have made the back of the van a blessed relief, but the despair inside made it as welcoming as a torture chamber.

As Lock knelt on his back, Brookes glanced at an icebox and large black duffel bag to his left and wondered what they contained. Out of the corner of his eye, Brookes watched Lock's left hand disappear into the bag. He sensed an opportunity to buck and throw the bastard off but Lock still held a gun and if he failed, the outcome was unthinkable. Brookes heard Lock pulling tape from a roll, and then felt it being wound tightly around his wrists. He gritted his teeth at the pain in his shoulder.

His son, *here*. With this killer. How the hell had he allowed this to happen?

'Dad, you're bleeding—' Ewan said.

'It's nothing to worry about.'

He saw Lock reach into the bag again and take out a

rope. He felt his legs being lashed together. The killer was quick and clearly skilled with knots.

'Is this how you treat all your willing sacrifices?'

Lock didn't answer; rather, he lifted himself from Brookes' back, slammed the door and left them to the darkness.

The elderly woman moaned, and Brookes said, 'Who are you?'

She moaned again.

'She doesn't talk,' Ewan said, 'I think she's sick.'

What was going on around here?

Brookes rolled onto his back and sat up. He fought the pain in his shoulder while trying, unsuccessfully, to wriggle his wrists free of the tape. He managed to shuffle ninety degrees and then manoeuvre himself to the side of the van, so he was sitting upright beside his son. He sighed when Ewan put his legs across his own and he leaned over to kiss him on the head. His soul warmed.

He looked at the handcuffs fastening his son to the rail. 'They on tight?'

'Yes,' Ewan said.

'Shit.' Brookes kept his voice low in case Lock heard. 'Why did you come back?'

'Because you would've come back.'

The van rumbled into life. At first, it reversed, and Brooke could hear it ripping itself free from his car. Lock then drove, slowly, which was good, because their last hope was that Yorke was close. Yorke would have been fifteen minutes away when Brookes crashed. After delaying Lock out in the snow, he must now only be five minutes out; if Yorke saw the white van, he would jump to the right conclusion and intercept.

While he continued to wriggle his wrists, he stared at

Ewan, desperately wanting, but unable to, throw his arms around him.

'I had a dream about the jaguar you asked me about,' Ewan said.

'And that's why you came back?'

'It ate me and you,' Ewan said.

Brookes kissed his head again. 'It was just a dream.'

'It felt real.'

'Sometimes dreams do.'

'The jaguar that ate us felt *very* real.'

'It wasn't—'

As if someone had grabbed his legs and yanked him, Brookes slid forward and banged the back of his head on the metal bar. Ewan also yelped in pain. Lock was becoming more erratic behind the wheel and had taken a sharp turn.

After the van had stabilized, Brookes worked his way back into the same position next to his son. The back of his head throbbed but that was nothing compared to the pain in his shoulder.

Ewan looked as if he was going to burst into tears. 'I made a mistake, Dad. I should have stayed away.'

'Yes. But I'm still glad to see you.'

'What is he going to do to us?'

'*Nothing.* Uncle Mike is on his way. Is Riley definitely ... you know?'

'Yes.' Ewan looked away.

Brookes stared at Freddy's mashed head for a minute, holding back tears and a need to scream. Once he'd buried the anguish for another day – if there was to be another day – Brookes turned to his son again. He could see him more clearly now because there was some light coming in around the edges of the plywood board; they must have entered a more built-up area. He caught his son looking at the wound in his shoulder.

'It's nothing ...'

'You're bleeding a lot.'

Brookes realised that his constant effort to break free of the tape – an effort that was going nowhere – was causing him to bleed more. 'I've told you, Ewan, it's *nothing*.'

'This man, the one who killed Mum, why is he doing this and why does he look so messed up?'

'His name is Terrence Lock and he suffers from delusions. That's all I know.'

'Delusions?'

'He's imagining things. He thinks someone is telling him what to do.'

'He said he wanted me to cry, said it was necessary for some kind of festival – what does he mean Dad?'

'I don't know, Ewan.' Which was almost the truth. 'He's a sick man. Something inside him is wired all wrong.'

'Is he a monster, Dad?'

'He's evil, yes, but he is not being driven by a supernatural force, no matter what he looks like and what he says. He's just a man, same as you and me, only with faulty chips.'

Lock turned sharply again. Prepared this time, Brookes kept his legs and backside tense to stop the slide. Ewan's legs were draped over his, so he didn't slide either.

'I've let Mum down, and now I've let you down, Dad. I'm so sorry.'

'Pack it in Ewan. You've done nothing wrong. You've come back to help – how does that in anyway make you a let-down? And Ewan, there is absolutely nothing you could have done about your mother. Honestly.'

'What are we going to do, Dad? Uncle Mike? Will he really know where we're going?'

'Yes. And even if he didn't, we're going to stop him.'

'How?'

He paused, unable to provide an answer, simply because there wasn't one yet.

'Because we'll get a chance, and when that chance comes, I'll know.'

The van slowed down and then stopped.

Ewan was crying now. Brookes leaned down and kissed his son on his head once more; the pain in his shoulder irrelevant. 'I love you so much.'

'I love you too, Dad, and Mum still loved you.'

'I know.' And deep down he knew that it was the truth.

'I wish you'd come home.'

'I wish I had too.'

Brookes realised that he, too, was crying now.

The van door opened, and Brookes squinted against the rush of cold air and the blinding moonlight reflected off the snowy ground. Framed by this white wonderland, Lock looked out of place, as if he had just clawed himself to the surface from the dark depths of the earth. His hair billowed around him, and his wide, unflinching eyes darted from one victim's face to another. He let the ramp down and scurried up it.

'Lock!' Brookes' voice rose. '*Listen to me!*'

He wasn't sure if his words could be heard over the wind. Lock freed the elderly woman's chair from the bar and wheeled her down the ramp. He left her outside to the mercy of the furious weather and came back in. This time, he unlocked Ewan's handcuffs and while pointing the gun at his head, said, 'Pick up the icebox and carry it outside.'

'*Lock!*' Brookes was straining against the rope around his legs and the tape around his wrists. '*Untie me!*'

Ewan hoisted the box down the ramp at gunpoint. Lock scooped up the bag on the way out, brushing aside Freddy's remains with the tip of his boot. It rolled down the ramp and disappeared into the snow.

Unblinking, Brookes stared outside at his son; his tearful eyes burning under the onslaught of the wind.

Lock put the large duffel bag on the old woman's legs and pointed ahead with his gun. Ewan looked at Lock one more time, before walking off into the snowstorm.

Lock, whose black cape was speckled with snow, marched back to the van door. He stared right into Brookes, who felt a chill deep inside him; it was as if the demon's hands were clawing around for his soul. He took a deep breath, preparing to have that soul snatched away.

'One at a time.' Lock slammed the van door, leaving Brookes alone, like a caged animal, thrashing around in the darkness.

17

YORKE BURST OUT of his car and charged towards Brookes' abandoned vehicle. Behind him, he heard Gardner screeching to a halt.

'*Fuck!*' Yorke circled the battered vehicle. 'Fuck ... fuck.' He took in the smashed windscreen; the huge indent in the side where a larger vehicle – presumably the Ford Transit – had impaled it; and the empty driver's seat. DS Iain Brookes was gone.

His friend was gone.

'What's happened?' Gardner said, a few metres behind him.

Yorke turned, and watched Gardner close the gap with her head lowered against the winds, rather like a charging bull.

'I don't know,' Yorke said. 'Not exactly.'

Gardner wiped snow from her eyes and surveyed the wreckage. '*Jesus.*'

'He's got them. Both of them.' Yorke kicked the side of the car. 'Fuck!' He put both of his hands to his face.

'Let's carry on. Try Iain's motorhome.'

'What's the point, Emma?' He took his hands away and showed her his tearful eyes. 'We're too late.'

'Oh no.' Gardner pointed at the ground ahead; Yorke swung around to look.

There was a huge patch of blood in the snow. He wanted the winds and snow to swallow him whole. He turned back to Gardner. 'Too *fucking* late.' With tears running down his face, he kicked the side of Brookes' car again.

FOR FIVE MINUTES, Brookes wrestled with the tape binding his wrists and, as he fought, exhaustion descended. Then, he sobbed for his lost soulmate, Jessica, and the son he was on the verge of losing.

When he felt his wrists move against one another, his eyes widened. Either the tape was loosening, or his hands were slippery from the blood running out of his shoulder and down his arm. The reason was irrelevant. What was relevant was the fact that he sensed freedom. He ground his wrists back and forth against one other; the lubricating blood helped with the friction burn, but he still had to grit his teeth against the pain in his shoulder. He almost whooped in delight when the tape loosened still further—

The van door flew open and Lock was standing there holding the icebox.

He stopped grinding his wrists. 'Where's Ewan?'

Lock slid the icebox back into the van. 'Dead.'

Brookes threw everything he had against the tape, desperate to put his hands around the neck of this soulless fucker. He wailed at the top of his lungs.

'Be still, slave, it is not your son who is dead. It is Matlalihuitl who is dead.'

'Who?' Brookes managed to ask, despite hyperventilating

'My blue-green feather.'

'Your *what*?'

'I thought you knew everything about what I was doing? Was that a lie, Iain?'

'No – you're the liar. You said I could come.'

Lock looked down at the ice box containing his dead creature. 'It is a shame. Matlalihuitl was a good servant. However, it was anticipated. I came prepared.'

He disappeared around to the front of the van, and Brookes continued to fight the tape. He wasn't given long enough though before Lock returned, holding a syringe.

'What's that for?'

'It is necessary, in this modern era of trepidation, that the willing slave be made even more willing. But don't worry yourself, Iain. Try to relax for a few minutes—'

'We made an agreement. You said you would show me, educate me. Then, I could be a willing sacrifice too.'

Lock's hair was turning white under the snow and blending in with his skin, making him look like a peculiar creature evolved to function in these uninhabitable conditions.

'*I'm willing!*' Brookes said.

'Be still, slave. I will grant you your wish. You will be next.' He slammed the van door again.

Brookes rolled onto his front and fought the tape as hard as he could. He bit his bottom lip to stop himself screaming out in victory when one hand slipped halfway out. He took a deep breath and tore his hands free. Working hard with the tight knot around his ankles, he prayed he wasn't too late. The rope came loose. He cast it aside and darted for the door, almost slipping on his own blood. Desperately hoping that the door wasn't locked, he grasped the handle. It wasn't. He hurled himself outside, where he immediately felt like he had been swept up by the tongue of a monster.

He shielded his eyes from the growing storm and took in his surroundings. Empty, desolate fields, broken by the occasion patch of snow-covered trees. Ahead of him was an old barn. Yellow light trembled between the slats and smoke rose from the back. Something was burning inside.

Brookes marched towards the barn, which was maybe ten metres away; he bent his head against the winds and moved as fast as he could. He was struggling to breathe, but it did not concern him. Neither did the fact that he was unarmed. His only concern was in the barn ahead—

There was a crunch. Suspecting feet in the snow behind him, Brookes spun, pounced and wrestled his would-be ambusher, Lock, down to the ground. After forcing his hands around the killer's neck, he began to squeeze the life from him. Images of Jessica and Riley, and then his son, filled his head, providing the only motivation he needed to end this demon's life. He tightened his grip and then leaned forward to sink his teeth into his face—

Brookes' stomach exploded.

He gasped, loosened his grip and sat upright. He looked down at the hole in his stomach, swayed and flopped forward. He felt Lock brush him aside as if he was merely an insect.

On his back, taking deep breathes, Brookes could only watch as Lock rose to his feet, holding Riley's gun with one hand, while brushing snow from his black gown with the other.

'I am Tezcacoatl – *The Repenting Serpent!* Do you think I wasn't ready for this? For you?'

Lock certainly was a serpent. The slippery reptile had predicted Brookes' escape and waited behind the van; he probably even set it all up by using tape instead of handcuffs. Now, he had eliminated the threat without being vindictive and annoying his lord. Cunning. Brookes wondered if he'd just seen Lock smile, but it was hard to tell; his face was blurred by snowfall.

'Dying in battle is honourable, *slave.*' He leaned down and hissed, 'She begged for you, you know? Just before she offered herself.'

Brookes spat at him, but Lock had already started to rise, and it only hit him in his chest. The serpent turned and slithered off towards the barn.

Brookes' breaths were ragged, and when he looked down, he saw that the bullet had pierced the left side of his stomach. It had not hit his spine, because he could move his legs, but he doubted his internal organs had been so lucky. Stomach wounds could kill quickly, or slowly. He'd been fortunate with the shoulder wound, but not this time; he was already feeling a peculiar sensation taking hold.

He tried to sit up, but the pain intensified, so he slumped back again. 'No ...' he said between shallow breaths.

He glanced to either side of him where his hot blood melted the snow; then, he looked up at the stars which glimmered and refused to be camouflaged by the swirling eddies.

'No ...'

My son, he thought. *I must ...*

One of the stars moved. It shot across the night sky, sketching a perfect arc. It moved with strength and purpose.

He refused to blink despite the huge snowflakes. He refused to miss the comet.

I won't give up on Ewan ... Jessica ... I promise.

He sat up, moaning from deep inside himself. He could see, ahead, Lock was also looking up, captivated by the shooting star. Brookes was surprised that anything could have halted the creature in its erroneous task.

After Lock had disappeared through the barn door, Brookes forced himself to his feet clasping his stomach; blood washed over his hand and he clenched his eyes against the searing pain, but he managed to start stumbling towards the barn - which felt like it was ten miles away rather than ten metres.

He almost made it, before he fell to his knees, sucking in so much air that he made more noise than the wind. With stinging eyes, he looked up at the barn. Its walls looked thin and he was surprised the storm didn't crush it like a cardboard box.

He looked up at the sky and could still see the line sketched by the star. Again, he struggled back to his feet; the hole in the stomach was making the shoulder wound from earlier seem like a shaving cut. He stumbled the final few metres to where the barn wall stopped him falling. He turned and flattened himself against the slats by the window and looked down; the front of his ski jacket glistened like a writhing fisherman's catch. He didn't have long left.

He turned, peered into the window and swallowed hard.

The interior stretched high enough to accommodate six steps arranged at the centre. They rose to an altar presided over by a metre-high golden statue of a man dancing; before this was another statue of a man with large goggle-eyes.

Brookes gulped and moved his hand from his wounded stomach to his mouth.

Watched by these statues, Lock stood over Ewan, who lay unmoving on a slab.

The place was lit by a hearth at the back of the interior; black smoke billowed out. A hole had been cut out in the roof just above it to allow most of the smoke to escape. Scattered around the room were a mixture of sandstone, jade and gold statues. Lock had an audience of deities. Some watched, snarling, while others reclined with self-indulgent expressions, like gluttonous parasites feeding off despair. The elderly woman was amongst them, next to a tall urn which had a long snake carved into it. The snake curled its entire body around the two-metre-high ornament.

If the hearth didn't do it first, Brookes would burn this abomination to the ground. But first, he needed to get his son—

Lock picked up a piece of electrical equipment, resembling a saw. Brookes watched as it burst into life and the hearth's amorphous flame throbbed.

'Jesus ...' Brookes said, and he stumbled back as if struck by lightning.

He returned to the window and shouted as loud as his failing body would allow. '*No!*'

But his shout was drowned out by the squeal of the saw as it tore open Ewan's chest.

Brooke moved as quick as he was able to the door. His legs didn't appreciate the sudden pressure, so he fell through the open door and landed face down on the wooden floor.

Unable to get back to his feet, he writhed in his own blood; the screaming sound from the saw felt like a heavy weight pinning him to the ground. He started to cry. He had so little left. 'Jessica,' he murmured. 'Give me strength.'

He began to drag himself forwards as the tears and sweat streamed down his face, and the blood spewed out of him. It now felt like something was inside him eating his insides, but he didn't care, he just clawed at the floor. If anything, the blood was helping him slide. The sound of the saw stopped. Brookes forced some words out. '*No – damn you, Lock – no!'*

The bastard didn't reply. So, he tried again, willing, desperately, for the words to come out louder. '*Lock, leave him alone, don't take my son away!'*

He'd now dragged himself as far as the elderly woman's feet, and the tail of the snake entwined around the urn. Then, he saw hope. In the form of Riley's gun lying on the bottom step.

Brookes lifted his heavy head and glanced up. Lock was inserting a steel contraption into his son's chest.

'*Please ...'* His vision was starting to blur, but he still managed to swivel, and lurch forward a few times on his broken stomach. His hand was close to the first of the steps, and the gun, but his eyes were closing now. He wheezed and rested his head on the floor for a moment. *Hold on*, he thought, *you must hold on.*

Lock's voice boomed as he spoke in an unfamiliar language and Brookes' eyes flicked open. He threw his hand out and let it settle on the gun. He tried to clutch it but couldn't. He felt everything turn around him and things stopped feeling real. His eyes closed again ...

... a fissure had opened at the core of this world and something had slithered through it. Something that darted around, hissing, rearing up, baring its teeth. It had many forms. One second a snake, the next a jaguar.

Then; a mosaic of twisted forms and shapes grew in the air above the metamorphosing monstrosity; Jessica's face, Riley's face, Ewan's face. The images gorged on each other, twisting into one disgusting mess, until the Repenting Serpent sprang into the air, coiling its long body around the images and squeezing the life from everything ...

... Brookes forced his eyes open, but he was too late.

Ewan's chest cracked and his head slumped to one side.

His son's frozen eyes met his and then everything disappeared.

YORKE AND GARDNER pulled up alongside the abandoned white van and sprang from the car. As they approached, Yorke answered a call from Jake.

'Is the address right?' Jake said. He was the one, who about ten minutes ago, had phoned Yorke with the news that they'd found an unsent email on Lock's computer at his home. The email had been prepared for Billy Shine and had given the address of Tezcacoatl's new 'temple.'

'Yes, Jake, his van is here.'

'Thank God, thank God,' Jake said. 'Where are they then?'

Yorke and Gardner looked in the front of the van, and in the rear. It was empty. He looked up at the old barn ahead. 'I'm assuming they're in that large barn.'

'Okay ... armed response will be about seven minutes,' Jake said.

'We won't be waiting that long,' Yorke said.

'Be careful, sir.'

'We will.'

He hung up on Jake. He noticed Gardner was looking in the icebox with her torch.

'Anything?' Yorke said.

'His dead sea creature. There's also blood everywhere. Someone has been injured. Iain? God forbid, Ewan? He's only twelve for pity's sake.'

'I've no idea, but let's just hope it's only an injury. Come on, we have to get in there.'

With their torches scraping a tunnel of light in the darkness before them, they charged towards the glowing barn.

The blood snaked towards the barn; they ran on either side of it, leaving it undisturbed. The trail took them directly to the window where they could see inside the barn.

And Yorke struggled to stop himself from gasping.

Lock, surrounded by statues of his deities, was hunched over Ewan. He'd already opened his chest and was reaching into a black duffel bag for something.

To cut with? thought Yorke. *Please, God, don't let it be something to cut with.*

Yorke's eyes swung to Brookes, who lay at the bottom of the steps; there was a pathway of blood behind him where he'd clearly dragged himself as far as he could before losing consciousness. Sitting in a wheelchair beside Brookes was an elderly lady who Yorke concluded was Gillian's mother, Michelle Miller. She *was* conscious but wore a glazed expression.

Gardner grabbed Yorke's hand, tearing him from his observations, and dragging him towards the open door.

Gardner was first through the door, but Yorke was the one who declared their arrival. 'Police! Terrence. It's over. Step away from Ewan.'

Lock plucked something out of the bag. The sharp object glinted as it reflected the fire burning in the hearth in the corner.

A scalpel.

'Armed response is approaching, Terrence. If you do not put the weapon down, and step away, you will be shot.'

Lock leaned closer to Ewan.

Yorke looked into Gardner's widening eyes. She was looking over at Brookes' prone form at the bottom of the steps. Yorke grasped her arm to help her resist the impulse to charge for her colleague. 'No, Emma. Not yet. It'll spook him.'

Yorke looked at Lock again. 'This is your last warning, Terrence. I'm telling you to put that down and step away ...'

Lock had already moved into Ewan's chest with the scalpel. Yorke couldn't charge and stop him. He was too far away, and a sudden movement could easily end Ewan's life.

He released Gardner's arm, gestured Brookes with a nod of his head. 'Slowly, Emma.'

She nodded back.

Yorke took a small step towards the stairs. 'Terrence, listen, I know what you saw, when you were younger. I know why you are doing this.'

Yorke saw Lock hesitate for a moment, considering something, before continuing.

Yorke took another small step. 'I know why you have your mother here, watching.'

Lock paused again, but then shook his head, and tensed his arms to begin cutting.

Stronger then, thought Yorke. *I'll go in stronger.*

'Why didn't you go and help her?'

Lock pulled his hands back. '*I couldn't!*' His voice echoed around the barn.

Yorke took a deep breath and continued shuffling forwards. 'You were fourteen years old, you could have—'

'Be quiet!' Lock lifted his head from his work and stared at Yorke.

Yorke stopped. Their eyes locked. 'You watched your mother die, Terrence. Someone who brought you into this world, loved you, held you and you sat there, and you *watched* her die.'

Lock stood up. His eyes were so wide he could have torn all the muscles in his face. *'Shut up!'*

Yorke showed him the palms of his hands. 'Listen, Terrence, it's not too late. Your mother wouldn't want this. This is not the way to ask for her forgiveness.'

'And how would you know?' Lock's face was twitching. 'You are one of them. None of you understand—'

A hideous loud moan tore through the barn. Ewan's back arched as if he was trying to squeeze the metal retractor from his chest. He smashed his head from side to side as froth spewed from the corners of his mouth and his eyes rolled back.

Lock looked down at his victim. He seemed to be refocusing and his trembling subsided. He started to kneel again.

Ewan stopped convulsing and Lock began to reach inside his chest again with the scalpel.

Yorke had made it to the first step, but he was too far. He was going to be too late. He'd failed …

There was a loud series of thuds from where Brookes was. Lock froze again and looked up in the direction of Michelle and Brookes. Yorke looked and saw that Gardner was almost beside them now. He also saw that Michelle was stamping her foot; in much the same way that she must have done on the night that Lock almost took her daughter,

She opened her mouth. '*Stoooooop*!'

Yorke looked back and saw that Lock's eyes were wide and unflinching as they looked at the woman whom he considered his mother.

'Stop!' This time Michelle's use of the word was short and sharp.

Lock looked down at Ewan and then up at Michelle again. He pulled his hands from Ewan's chest again and said, 'But mother, I'm doing this for you—'

There was a loud bang and Lock seized his throat in both hands; the scalpel slipped from his grip and clattered against the top step. He stood up as blood squirted out from the cracks between his fingers. Still looking confused, and unable to take his eyes from Michelle Miller, he reached out to her with one of his bloody hands. There he lingered on the sixth step, until he couldn't stand any longer, and then he plunged. His bones cracked as he bounced from one unforgiving step to the next before his head finally burst on the bottom one, half a metre from Brookes.

Yorke turned to watch Lock's twitching form grow still underneath the snake-embraced urn, and then looked up at Gardner, who was holding the gun.

EPILOGUE

'**Y**OU'RE THE FOURTH nanny we've interviewed, Zofia,' Jane Young said, 'since Julia just upped and left. No notice given.'

'Well, that is not good,' Zofia said in her strong Polish accent. 'You can see from my references that I won't do that.'

'Yes.' Jane paused to sip her tea. 'Well, as you can imagine, Simon is keen to avoid any more drama. He's a busy man. I need to be available at his every beck and call; social function here, quick holiday with clients there. We need this to be one hundred percent.'

'I will take good care of Tobias,' Zofia said, wondering if gangsters such as Simon Young really used expressions such as *social functions*.

'Good. And the accommodation is to your needs?'

'Yes.'

'And you are satisfied with the package?'

Well the last girl wasn't, thought Zofia, *it cost me next to nothing to pay her to take off!*

'It's very nice,' Zofia said.

'Well,' Jane said. 'Obviously, we have to wait on the final checks to come through, and this other reference, but I've seen enough to be honest. And I think Tobias will love you. I also think Simon will be over the moon.'

You make him sound like a gentleman, Zofia thought, *do you know he's been pimping out girls across Brighton?*

'Can I take you out back to meet him now? He's in the garden with my father. Have you got the time?'

'Yes,' Zofia said.

Outside, in the garden, Zofia was handed the two-year-old boy with chestnut hair. 'Adorable.'

'Most of the time,' Jane said. 'Now, if you'll excuse me, I'd like to contact my husband to tell him we've got someone perfect.'

Zofia smiled. *Would that be the husband who showed no remorse after Loretta Marks, one of his employees, was beaten to death with a jade ashtray?*

'I'll leave you with Derek, my father,' Jane said.

Jane disappeared into the house and Grandad approached. He was a smartly dressed man with a well-oiled side parting. Zofia could tell that his eyes were lingering on her far too long. *Well, let him,* Zofia thought. *After today, he won't get another chance.* Tobias, who clung to her side, reached up and stroked her face. *He likes me already.*

'Poland is a beautiful country,' Grandad said. 'I used to visit regularly with my late wife.'

Zofia noticed him emphasising the word *late. Do you really think you are in with a shot?* Zofia thought. Well, at least she could use this to her advantage. She started to cough.

Grandad stepped forward and put his hand on her shoulder. 'Are you okay, dear?'

'Sorry. I've had this cough for a while.'

'Glass of water?'

'Thank you so much.'

Grandad disappeared into the house. Zofia looked around the huge garden. It wouldn't be a bad place to spend a sunny afternoon if she was going to stay. Which she wasn't.

She walked to the bush at the far side of the garden and then turned back to look at the huge house. Tobias was still stroking her face and had added a delightful little giggle to the process.

Zofia smiled. 'I'm surprised that they've not lost you already in that palace.'

She paused for a moment longer. This all felt too easy. Part of her wondered if it would be more interesting if she just waited a few moments longer for someone to emerge before she ran?

She looked at his handsome little face. *No, you're a mother, now. Time to grow up. Be responsible.*

Zofia wriggled through the bush and found the part of the fence that she'd been loosening from the outside over the previous few nights.

Seconds later, she was running to her car, parked around the corner, clutching Tobias.

As she fastened him into his baby seat, she heard Jane screaming from the garden.

While driving away, Zofia looked in the rear-view mirror at Tobias, who was starting to look a little concerned now.

'Don't worry, sweetheart,' she said, dropping the fake polish accent. 'Mummy will look after you. We are going to be very close, you and I.'

Lacey smiled in the mirror and was happy when Tobias smiled back.

'Ever so close.'

It had been a harsh winter, and not just because of the weather. While the gales and snowfall had ravished Wiltshire, death and loss had paid a visit to Yorke and his colleagues, and now, as they walked through the graveyard, they were all thankful for a warm breeze, and some time for quiet reflection.

'I always liked graveyards,' Gardner said.

Jake looked at her sideways as they walked. 'Why?'

'The colours, mainly.'

And she was right, thought Yorke, as he looked around at the beautiful flowers, each with different shapes, sizes and patterns.

'Well, I don't like graveyards,' Jake said. 'I always put on extra layers when I come. There's a cold here that chills your bones, rather than your flesh.'

'You've always been one of the cheeriest people I know,' Yorke said, smiling.

Yorke kept his reflections to himself. As usual, they included his first real girlfriend, Charlotte – someone who had captured his heart and never really let it go. And his sister, taken so young, and in such an unforgivable fashion. These reflections ensured the world remained unfamiliar to Yorke. But he remained positive. Cast into an ocean of pain you would be left uncertain over which way to swim; if you didn't drown, willingly or unwillingly, you would eventually sight land, step onto it, and hopefully conquer it.

It seems the birds had taken the opportunity to exploit

the quiet of the graveyard, and they embraced a wholesome tune for a moment, before Gardner placed the flowers on DS Iain Brookes' gravestone.

'Miss you, buddy.' Jake laid his hand on the top of the gravestone.

'Likewise.' Gardner released the flowers and stood back up.

They both turned and looked at Yorke.

'What you did for your son, Iain, took courage. And I hope that where you are resting now,' he looked at the adjacent gravestone inscribed *Jessica Brookes*, 'gives you some peace.'

———

EVERY TIME EMMA GARDNER had looked at her husband since the night of the shooting, she'd thanked her lucky stars that she had him. And now, as they sat together, with Annabelle pinned between them, watching the bedtime story on *CBeebies*, she thanked her lucky stars once again.

Later, while Annabelle slept, she said the same thing to her husband that she'd said every night since. 'I just wish we'd got there sooner.'

Then, like every other night since, he'd hugged her, and reassured her that she'd saved a life that night. The life of a little boy.

And that made her the most heroic person that he'd ever known.

———

'COME BACK TO BED,' Sheila said.

Jake turned from the window. 'Sorry, I just, you know, couldn't sleep.'

'I understand.' Sheila lifted the blanket up.

He climbed in and embraced her.

'Wonder if Frank will sleep through tonight?' Jake said.

'Well, if he doesn't, you let me handle it.' Sheila kissed him on his forehead. 'You need some sleep.'

'Thanks.' He kissed her back.

'And try not to worry, it's been months since you heard from her.'

Easier said than done, Jake thought and closed his eyes.

WHEN YORKE WENT into Ewan's room to say goodnight to him, he moved the boy's hand away from his chest.

'But it itches,' Ewan said.

'If you scratch it, then it will take longer to heal.'

Ten inches of scar tissue had recorded the events of that night on Ewan. Yorke often wondered if it was pointless to hope that the scar would be the only long-term damage he suffered.

On the other hand, he thought, *is it not better to keep on hoping even when things are hopeless?*

He kissed the boy he was in the process of adopting. 'Goodnight, Ewan.'

'Goodnight, Uncle Mike.'

He thought again of the ocean he felt lost in and his uncertainty over which way to swim. It was his responsibility to find a way out because other people depended on him.

After climbing into bed, he apologised to Patricia for being late back from work and then held her close.

'I've got some news,' she said.

'What?'

She leaned back, took his hand and placed it gently on her stomach.

That night, Yorke dreamed about a clear day, a warm breeze and the birds singing a wholesome tune. And, in this dream, Yorke and his family ventured forth to conquer new lands together.

WHO IS CHARLOTTE?

Find out in the FREE, EXCLUSIVE DCI Michael Yorke
quick read – ***A Lesson in Crime***
https://dl.bookfunnel.com/77umhbozcf

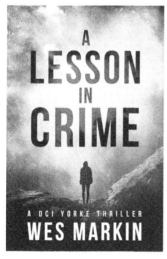

Scan the QR to
READ NOW!

CONTINUE YORKE'S JOURNEY WITH
SILENCE OF SEVERANCE

Your wedding day should be the most unforgettable day of your life.

And this is one wedding that will never be forgotten.

When a police officer's wedding day ends in brutality and chaos, DCI Michael Yorke is pulled away from his own wedding into the bloodiest chain of events Wiltshire has ever seen.

As a heatwave tightens its grip on Salisbury, Yorke and his team face a race against time to find the most sinister and intelligent adversary they have ever faced. Christian Severance.

But as the team chase Severance into the shadows of a dark past, Yorke's own history starts to drag itself into the present ...

Can they stop Christian Severance before he achieves the unthinkable? And will Yorke survive the revelations that claw at him from the darkness?

Scan the QR to
READ NOW!

The Silence of Severance is a true edge-of-the-seat,

nail-biting page turner.

START THE JAKE PETTMAN SERIES
TODAY WITH THE KILLING PIT

A broken ex-detective. A corrupt chief of police. A merciless drug lord.

And a missing child.

Running from a world which wants him dead, ex-detective Sergeant Jake Pettman journeys to the isolated town of Blue Falls, Maine, home of his infamous murderous ancestors.

But Jake struggles to hide from who he is, and when a child disappears, he finds himself drawn into an investigation that shares no parallels to anything he has ever seen before.

Held back by a chief of police plagued and tormented by his own secrets, Jake fights for the truth. All the way to the door of Jotham MacLeoid. An insidious megalomaniac who feeds his victims to a Killing Pit.

And the terrifying secrets that lie within.

Scan the QR to
READ NOW!

JOIN DCI EMMA GARDNER AS SHE RELOCATES TO KNARESBOROUGH, HARROGATE IN THE NORTH YORKSHIRE MURDERS ...

Still grieving from the tragic death of her colleague, DCI Emma Gardner continues to blame herself and is struggling to focus. So, when she is seconded to the wilds of Yorkshire, Emma hopes she'll be able to get her mind back on the job, doing what she does best - putting killers behind bars.

But when she is immediately thrown into another violent murder, Emma has no time to rest. Desperate to get answers and find the killer, Emma needs all the help she can. But her new partner, DI Paul Riddick, has demons and issues of his own.

And when this new murder reveals links to an old case Riddick was involved with, Emma fears that history might be about to repeat itself...

Don't miss the brand-new gripping crime series by bestselling British crime author Wes Markin!

What people are saying about Wes Markin...

'Cracking start to an exciting new series. Twist and turns, thrills and kills. I loved it.'

Bestselling author **Ross Greenwood**

'Markin stuns with his latest offering... Mind-bendingly dark and deep, you know it's not for the faint hearted from page one. Intricate plotting, devious twists and excellent characterisation take this tale to a whole new level. Any serious crime fan will love it!'

Bestselling author **Owen Mullen**

Scan the QR to READ NOW!

ACKNOWLEDGEMENTS

A huge shout-out must first go to Jake Lynn for his relentless encouragement and fantastic understanding of the industry. It is down to him that this sequel came quickly and was not lost for years in the land of procrastination. Thanks again to Cherie Foxley, who knows how to create an unforgettable image!

Thank you to all my Beta Readers who took the time to read early drafts and offer valuable feedback. Huge appreciation goes to Jenny Cook for that much-needed, ruthless final edit. Thank you also to my wonderful wife Jo, and my mother, Janet, who continue to offer support during the most tiring parts of the process. Also, thank you to my lovely little people, B & H, who never fail to make me smile and have earned themselves a book dedication!

Lastly, thank you to every reader, and every wonderful blogger, who has spent their valuable time with my fiction. I hope I have offered you some entertainment, and would love to do so again in the near future...

STAY IN TOUCH

To keep up to date with new publications, tours, and promotions, or if you would like the opportunity to view pre-release novels, please contact me:

Website: www.wesmarkinauthor.com

facebook.com/WesMarkinAuthor

instagram.com/wesmarkinauthor

twitter.com/markinwes

amazon.com/Wes-Markin/e/B07MJP4FXP

REVIEW

If you enjoyed reading ***The Repenting Serpent***, please take a few moments to leave a review on Amazon or Goodreads or BookBub.

Made in the USA
Las Vegas, NV
20 November 2023